SISTE

GENESIS

BY
LISA BETH DARLING
Book #1 in the Sister Christian Series
Moon Mistress Publishing USA

Moon Mistress Publishing
New London, CT 06320

Cover Art Designed by Lisa Beth Darling
Advisers: Donna Ruggieri and Cathy Chester—Thanks ladies!
Text set in Calibri12

Dedicated To:
G.H and H.L.

As Always—To The Big Guy

Books by Lisa Beth Darling

Fiction:

OF WAR Series
The Heart of War
Child of War-A God Is Born
Christmas Eve on Olympus
Child of War-Rising Son
Women of War
Kingdoms of War

Sister Christian Series
Genesis
Sins of the Father
Mysterious Ways
Prodigal Son
The Doc Series

On A Hot Summer Night
Cold November Rain
Regret Me Not

Standalone Novels/Stories
OBSESSION

Non-Fiction:
The Shame of Eminent Domain-Fort Trumbull
A Window to Magickal Herbalism

Visit http://www.lisabethdaring.com

Chapter One

Dr. Richard Mason sat alone in the darkened living room of his one-level one-bedroom ranch with a certified letter in one hand and a double-shot of J&B Scotch in the other, a Royal Jamaican Corona cigar burning nicely in the ashtray next to him. When he found the note asking him to pick up the letter at the Willington, VT Post Office he thought he was going to find that someone filed suit against him...again. Taking a puff off the cigar, he opened the letter in one swift stroke of his deft hand.

Usually, he liked his news the same way he liked his scotch; straight up, bold, and never watered down.

Tonight, was a different story. Tonight, his entire identity changed in just four short paragraphs.

July 2nd
Dear Dr. Mason:

I am writing with regard to the passing Judge James Rice III (your father) who departed this Earth on June 30th. While we realize this news may come as somewhat of a shock to you, we hope you will accept our deepest condolences on your loss.

In accordance with Judge Rice's Last Will and Testament, you have been awarded Temporary Conservatorship of your sister, Johannah Morgan Rice by the Michigan Probate Court. Additionally, the Court temporarily installed you as the Administrator of the Johanna Morgan Rice Trust Fund. As of this writing, said trust fund has a value of 3.5 million dollars. Full copies of these documents, along with an inventory of Miss Rice's current assets, are enclosed with this letter.

Unfortunately, time is of the essence in this matter as the group home where Hannah currently resides is closing its doors on September 1st. This only gives us two scant months in which to find Miss Rice another suitable living arrangement. In accordance with the

5

Trust Fund for the Benefit of Johannah Morgan Rice, (copy enclosed) your sister must be moved to a group home that is close to you. We have researched such homes in your area and have enclosed their pertinent information for your review. Also enclosed you will find a certified copy of the Last Will and Testament of James Rice III along with a copy of the Terms and Conditions of the Trust Fund for the Benefit of Johanna Morgan Rice. After going over said enclosures with your own attorney, please respond to this letter as soon as possible so that we may arrange to have Hannah moved to Vermont.

Please do not hesitate to contact me with any and all questions you may have. I understand this entire process is very new to you and I wish to be of service in any way that I can.

Sincerely yours,
Christopher Lawrence, Esq.

"What the hell? My father was Edwin Mason, the blessedly *late* Edwin Mason," he grumbled reading the letter again and again until all of the words ran together before his confounded eyes.

Tossing the amber liquid down the back of his throat Mason let the letter slip from his fingers to the hard wood floor at his bare feet. The Last Will and Testament of James Rice III came into his view. Sucking down the last few drops in the glass, he took several puffs off the expensive cigar before pouring another glass. Confused and confounded, he thumbed through the will until he got to

Article V: Johannah Morgan Rice

As to the welfare of my daughter, Johannah Morgan Rice, deemed incapable to handle her personal and financial affairs by the Good Court of the State Michigan and residing in a Michigan State run group home. I hereby install my son, born James Rice IV but now known as the Honorable Doctor Richard Mason, and my only capable heir as the sole Guardian of the person and estate of Johannah Morgan Rice. I do hereby designate Doctor Richard Mason to be the

6

sole Trustee of The Trust Fund for the Benefit of Johanna Morgan Rice previously established by my late wife, Adelaide Morgan Rice. Doctor Richard Mason, in his duties as Trustee, shall be bound by all terms, conditions, and adherences of the Trust a full copy of which shall be provided to him with a certified copy of this my Last Will and Testament.

Should James Rice IV a/k/a Doctor Richard Mason refuse these responsibilities I direct that someone from the State of Michigan Department of Developmental Services be appointed Guardian and Trustee to serve under the same terms and conditions as noted within said Trust.

Even as the will fell from his numb fingers he thought it had to be a joke or a mistake. Yet deep in his soul, Mason knew it was not. Still, he had to admit this was one hell of a way to find out he was adopted or the bastard child of The Honorable—or the Not-Quite-So-Honorable—Judge James Rice III a man he barely remembered.

In that instant, Richard Mason's entire world shattered so completely he swore he heard it break like a fine china plate hitting a cement floor.

In a long whirring rush of memories locked deeply away from his brilliant mind, Richard Mason's entire life flashed behind his blurry hazel eyes. He had been born in the early spring of 1963 in Osaka, Japan where his father (or the man who he thought was his father until ten seconds ago) General Edwin Mason, United States Marine Corp, had been stationed. It did not take a genius like himself to count backwards and realize he had been conceived in the summer of 1962.

Summer.

That was when his mother, Claire, made her way to her own mother's old farm in upper Michigan leaving Edwin Mason behind for six to twelve weeks out of every year. It was altogether possible that three years after they were married Claire began an illicit affair with Judge James Rice. Mason himself wouldn't blame her for the deed; in fact, to him it made her a bit more interesting as a human being to think of her as having such a deep dark secret. Although he couldn't quite understand it either.

His father, The General, was an asshole, that was truer than true, but James Rice! As far as Mason could remember, Rice hadn't been much better. He had been gruff—he was always yelling at someone or talking down to them—he was cold, insulting to nearly everyone but especially women every one of which he seemed to consider beneath him. By today's standards, he'd be a misogynist but back then, as he grabbed their asses, made lascivious comments on their breasts and their weight, he was just considered a little rough around the edges. Hell, from what he remembered the guy wasn't even all that good looking.

James Rice got away with being an overbearing bully because he was the County Judge. No one wanted to get on his bad side.

Sitting there in the darkened living room with a million thoughts running wild through his mind as they dredged up long forgotten memories, he just couldn't see his sweet mother getting all hot and bothered over Judge Rice. However, people did all kinds of strange things and he'd know since he'd seen it all from someone getting the handle of a plunger stuck up their ass to someone else having to have their stomach pumped to relieve the pressure of a quart of jizz swirling around in there. Let's not forget the spectacular case of the couple who contracted e. coli from rutting around in a pig pen getting their jollies off.

All that couple had said was that it was summer, it was a beautiful day, they were young and horny, they wanted to have sex outside and the pig sty was the closest private area.

Summer.

Even though he was depressed and confused he still found it to be a beautiful word full of long-ago memories. After he was born Claire made summer her trips to Michigan to visit with her mother dragging little Ricky Mason with her

8

and away from his father for those same six to twelve glorious father-free weeks. Often those trips meant taking him out of whatever school he was attending and transferring him to one in Victorville, the last of which had been St. Mark's High School—a Catholic Hell if there ever was one.

Pouring another glass of scotch, he stared out the rain-soaked window into the night as the amber liquid warmed his throat reminding himself that Vermont was a long way from Michigan and the Late General Mason. Somehow, the years and the miles just melted away as though they never even existed at all. Glancing down at the letter at his feet, he tried to tell himself that his father always knew he was a bastard and the child of a torrid affair. That was why The General always seemed to treat him so poorly and never once told him that he loved him.

The General was a cold, calculating, tough, and demanding man who was never satisfied. He was hot-tempered and quick to rush to judgment and then to deal out punishment for the smallest of childhood infractions. Such punishments normally came in the form of running laps around whatever military complex they were living in at the time, spending twenty minutes in a tub full of ice water and kneeling on grains of rice as he faced the wall for hours at a time. If the supposed crime called for drastic measures, then Ricky might be spending days and nights outside the house in a tent like a dog or find the flesh sliced from his bones with the lashing of his father's belt.

"Imagine what he would have done to his own kid," Mason mused aloud as he took another long sip and laughed at his own little joke. For a moment, the fantasy of being the product of two people so hot for each other they denied all convention and just went for it seemed the better alternative. At least it meant that for one moment in her life his mother knew passion. He doubted The General was capable of doing more than issuing orders in the heat of the moment.

9

If he was adopted and The General had sworn he'd open his arms, heart, hearth, and home to a child he knew wasn't his then the things Edwin Mason had done in his attempts to make a man out of his son amounted to little less than cruel and inhumane treatment. Leaving the physical abuse aside for just a moment, even the intellectual wasn't enough for The General. Throughout his entire academic career, Ricky Mason made straight A's. No matter where they lived, what the native language was, or how many times they moved in the space of a school year Ricky Mason never got anything less than an A on anything. Yet The General would always want to know why Ricky couldn't pull off an A+.

According to The General, joining the Honor Society was good if you wanted to spend your time with 'a bunch of nerds'. The General wanted to know why Ricky didn't join the ROTC instead. That's where the action was. There they could teach him how to be a man and not such an oaf. At the tender age of seventeen, Ricky Mason was certified a genius was invited to join MENSA. The General angrily asserted that they were 'a bunch of pansy-ass liberals' who would only use his intelligence and his naivety for their liberal agenda to pussify the whole world. According to The General the military was a better place for his son's talents, and it would help to toughen him up a bit.

Scoring 2378 on his SATs Ricky pulled off the very highest SAT grade St. Mark's High School had ever seen, and the faculty lauded him. Not The General, to him that was okay but he thought his son could have done better and had been hoping for at least 2390 when the highest one could ever possibly score was 2400.

Richard Mason was St. Mark's High School's Class Valedictorian and gave the class speech for which The General was not present. The General was off playing golf that night with the President and his closest advisors. That was all right with the young Richard Mason who knew in his heart that the

10

speech he worked so long and hard on for two months would not have been good enough for his father even though he received a five-minute standing ovation for his efforts.

Claire Mason saw things differently and while the General was off at the Pentagon putting out some smoldering fire in the Middle East, she threw her son a party to which she invited all of his friends and all of his grandmother's neighbors. Telling him that no mother could ever be prouder of a son than she was of him, she gave him five hundred dollars in crisp one-hundred-dollar bills to use anyway he wanted. It just so happened that four hundred dollars was the exact amount he needed to buy the used Camaro he'd been saving for the last three months. At seventeen Ricky Mason was already 6'3" that made the shiny sports car nearly totally impractical but that didn't stop him from wanting it.

That Monday he went straight to the used car dealer down in Uncasville, cash in hand, and drove home his very first car that night. Claire took a Polaroid of him standing next to the cherry red two-door with a smile a mile wide. That photo was still stuck in the corner of her vanity mirror faded by nearly forty years of sunlight and dust. Six weeks later, Richard would drive that Camaro from his grandmother's farm in Michigan to the halls of the University of Pennsylvania. He wouldn't drive back across the Michigan State Line for another four years returning only when his grandmother died and then just for three days to comfort his grieving mother knowing that the General wasn't capable of the compassion she needed.

Sitting here now, it seemed no wonder to him if his mother should have turned to The Not-So-Honorable Judge Rice for the same comfort and compassion on those long hot Michigan summer nights. Although for the life of him, he couldn't remember Judge Rice being anything other than as cold at The General. The man never smiled, he never laughed, in fact, Mason didn't think the man had ever shown any emotion other than displeasure. Then again, fifty years later,

11

that could just be an impression lingering in his mind and not the truth. Ricky Mason never did know Judge Rice very well.

Hannah was a faded memory. A girl two years his junior with a mop of sunny blonde hair and devilish titter that always made him smile during those hot summers on the farm. She had sparkling blue eyes and an endless supply of energy.

But not anymore.

Times change.

Even before this exact moment, everything had changed for little Hannah Rice.

"Hannah the Banana," he muttered scornfully and gulped greedily from the glass remembering the skinny little girl in the yellow dress. The one who hardly ever smiled past her tenth birthday because, five days after that happy event her mother, Adelaide Rice, sat in a running car with the garage door shut. Hannah wore that frilly yellow dress until it was nothing but a faded rag thus earning her the cruel nickname.

"Uhhh," he muttered taking another drink not wanting to think about Hannah the Banana any longer. Nevertheless, his brilliant mind was insistent on taking its trip down Memory Lane on this rainy night. The best he could muster was to steer it away from James Rice III, his suicidal wife, and their little waif of a daughter.

Instead of that path, his inebriated mind switched tracks and went back to thinking about his younger (his much younger) self. He remembered all the colleges and universities that practically begged him to let them give him a free ride. There was Yale but his father called the prestigious university 'another bunch of liberal bastards' and made such a stink that Richard turned down the scholarship even though Yale had been his dream ever since he was in the eighth grade. There was Harvard but they were 'a bunch of snobs dependent on daddy's money' and The General didn't want his son to be like them. After much yelling and bitching, The General finally capitulated and allowed Richard to accept the full ride to The University of Pennsylvania where he graduated

12

in just under three years at the very pinnacle of his class and the only graduate to achieve the distinction summa cum laude. Again, The General was unable to be present having better things to do than watch his son get Bachelor's Degrees in Anatomy, Chemistry and Physics.

The University of Pennsylvania was very happy to offer Mason a full ride through their very prestigious medical school, but Mason turned them down when Johns Hopkins made the same offer. It wasn't that he didn't like UPENN or think it was a great school, but Maryland was farther away from Michigan where his parents were beginning to settle down. Claire, the only child of Rose and John Montgomery, inherited the old farm. It was tattered and worn but she wouldn't let it go. When The General finally retired the couple moved into the property full-time.

Four years later, and for the last time, Richard Mason graduated at the top of his class and gave his last Class Speech. The General and his mother sat in the audience.

Sitting here in the darkened living room pouring himself another glass of Scotch, Mason remembered the beaming smile on his mother's face and the way that she dabbed tears of pride away from the corners of her blue eyes. The General sat next to her in stark comparison with his arms folded over his aging chest and the stone expression on his face.

Walking up to his parents for the first time as Doctor Richard Mason, he was surprised when his father held out his hand. Diplomas in one hand, Richard shook his father's hand with the other only to hear the General say:

"Now that this is over with when are you going to let the military make a real man out of you?"

Richard stood there trying to hold back his anger for his mother's sake. He already had offers to do his residency in some of the finest and most prestigious hospitals across the country but that meant nothing to The General. Well-respected facilities with the world's leading doctors were

13

chomping at the bit to get the brand-new Doctor Mason on their payrolls and the only thing his father gave a shit about was whether he was going to join up or not.

"I can you get into the War College no problem, son." Edwin held on to his son's tightening grip without flinching and even patted him on the back. "They'll make a man out of you and you can serve your country by working in the medical field, what do you say?" The truth was young Richard Mason caught the brass's eye a long time ago. They'd been after General Mason to turn his son into Major Mason post haste. The military didn't want to let Richard slip through their fingers and into civilian life when he could obviously be of much better use in a military uniform.

Putting one hand on each man's shoulder Claire tried to intervene, "Richard has an offer from the Mayo Clinic and another from Mount Sinai, isn't that spectacular? Let's go celebrate."

Edwin sloughed off his wife's hand with a roll of his old but still meaty shoulder, "The United States military has some of the finest medical facilities,"

"Bullshit," Mason snapped before thinking, "VA hospitals suck. Your precious soldiers aren't treated they're warehoused. I'm not going to spend my time in some research lab coming up with new and improved ways of wiping out entire countries. I became a doctor to save lives not take them."

Before they could get into a heated argument in the emptying auditorium, someone behind them cleared their throat and drew their attention to her. In her cap and gown stood a rather beautiful young woman with long black hair and big hazel eyes stared at them. Richard let of his father's hand and held his arm out to her when she came to his side his mother gasped with joy. "Mom, Dad, this is Barbra McKinney."

"Your girlfriend?" Claire asked with unabashed hope in her slightly trembling voice.

14

"Actually," Richard looked own at his feet for a moment as he felt guilt settle on his shoulders before he met his mother's gaze again, "she's my wife, we got married last month."

The joy breaking on Claire's face turned to disappointed and then to hurt, "Oh," she whispered politely reaching for the woman's hand on instinct, "nice to meet you," she stammered and tried to hold back the tears but she couldn't make it. "Oh Richard! How could you do this?"

"She pregnant?" The General gruffly asked as he pointed to Barbara's stomach.

Claire ran off up the ramp to the nearest set of double doors at the top of the auditorium with her hands over her face.

"I told you she'd be upset!" Barbara admonished as she moved away from her new husband. "We should have waited."

Indeed, she had, she most definitely told him that eloping was a bad idea and it would only upset his mother who would miss the wedding of her only child. She told him over and over that even if it wasn't a big deal to him—or to her for that matter, as Barbara had no family—it would be a big deal to his mother.

Watching his mother flee through the doors, he felt ashamed as he answered his father, "No, we're both doctors, we know how protection works." He took one long stride away from The General to go after his mother before stopping to grab Barbara's hand and drag her with him. The last thing he wanted, other than to make his mother cry was to leave his new wife to the company of The General where he would interrogate her like a POW.

It took quite a bit of doing and the promise of a real wedding on the farm before Claire calmed down. Richard had no idea how important something like that could be to her and if there was one person in the world that he never wanted to see cry it was his mother. Three weeks later Richard Mason and Barbara McKinney re-enacted their vows with one Judge James Rice presiding over the ceremony

Sitting in his chair with his half-empty glass, a child went down Mason's spine.

A month later, the Doctors Mason headed to the Mayo Clinic to take the medical world by storm. Michigan soon became nothing more than a faded nightmare.

Barbara had been the light of Mason's life, she was sweet, sassy, daring, and always challenging his inherent skepticism. Together they spent an entire year of wedded bliss together. For the first and only time in his life Mason was truly happy. He had a job that gave him purpose and paid very well, he had a woman who loved him deeply and whom he loved the same.

All Good Things Must Come to an End, just after their first wedding anniversary, Barbara was gunned down by a meth-head as she stood in line at the bank. Everyone told him how brave she was and how she tried to talk the tweaker down, that was so like her. The addled drug addict would have none of it and he shot her where she stood before making off with ten thousand dollars leaving her pretty face to turn ashen as her blood pooled on the marble floor.

Twenty-four hours after her funeral, Mason threw away his brilliant medical career and enlisted in the Marine Corps. That was the first and only time The General patted him on the back and called him a man.

Losing Barbara was the beginning of his no-holds-barred lease on life. It was the catalyst that led him to take chances others would never even consider not just with his own life but the lives of his patients as well. Whereas others would and did call him reckless, he considered himself bold.

As it turned out, Major Mason's military career was nowhere near as long and certainly not as distinguished as his father's. During Desert Storm, he was putting his talents to work in a mobile hospital unit when a suicide bomber attacked. Twenty-two men and women lost their lives that day and Richard Mason came home with a decimated hip. He spent four agonizing months in a crappy VA hospital where he became addicted to morphine as he fought like hell to stay out of a wheelchair.

After his Honorable Discharge, the budding brilliant medical career in civilian life that he'd left behind trying to drown the pain of losing Barbara came back to him along with seventy percent use of his left leg.

The physical and emotion pain never left him. Instead, it led to a very long relationship with his two best friends: Mr. J&B and Mr. Oxycodone. Those two guys never failed to pitch in and hold him up whenever he needed it which was far more often than he should like and nowhere near as private as it should have been.

Despite his whispered reputation for drugs, alcohol, and loose women Doctor Richard Mason was one of the mostly highly regarded physicians in his field. He was known the world over for his uncanny—nearly eerie—ability to diagnose any disease/condition/illness that came his way. Although he often resorted to very unconventional methods to reach his conclusions. That made him difficult to work with, if Mason learned nothing else from his father, The General, he learned how to make demands on those around him. Demands that were always questionable at best and dangerous at worst.

Yet, people had an inherent drive to live. They flocked to him from every corner of the globe when every other doctor had failed them.

For many lonely years, between four more marriages and not, he pulled in a one or even two million dollars a year in annual salary running his own private practice. During that time, the price for an office visit with him rose from a normal hundred and twenty dollars to over five hundred dollars an hour for his precious time.

That rate hike insulated him from the Real World from Real People with Real Problems that included financial woes and payments from the State that were always late. It let him see only those cases he found interesting even though the

17

patients themselves tended to be as boring as they were filthy rich.

He grabbed another quarter million a year when he agreed to do lectures. Although they were always Standing Room Only, his lectures were bitterly tainted by the memory of his father's absence during the three most important speeches of his life. While his brilliant mind attracted eager young doctors and older ones, his personality always put them off. He was rough, gruff, forthright to the point of cruelty at times and cynical to the bone

Today, as he sat here in his cozy one-bedroom ranch he reached for a half-empty bottle of Mr. Oxy and swallowed a fat pill dry before reaching for the bottle of Mr. J&B.

Doctor Richard Mason had four failed marriages behind him. Thankfully, none of which produced any offspring but did leave him with four bitching nagging ex-wives to whom he wrote four fat alimony checks every month.

There had been Ginny a spunky chubby redhead he'd been married to for all of ten months before she walked out on him while he was in another drunken haze.

Then there was Jenny, a skinny little blonde with green eyes who was so Narcissistic she couldn't see past her own nose or the Jaguar in the driveway. Three years into their marriage he caught her in bed with the gardener and summarily kicked her and the quarter of a million-dollar wardrobe he purchased for her to the curb.

After that there had been Tammy-Lee. He met her in a bar outside of Nashville. It lasted nine crazy months.

Two years after that there was Betty a truly sweet woman who'd loved him with all she had and for as long as she could before his constant sarcasm and cynicism wore her down to the nub. He still regretted losing her. Betty never asked him for anything other than some of his time, but his time was valuable too valuable to spend it lazing by the fire watching movies, eating popcorn, and making love on the sofa. She left him in the middle of the night while he was

18

working leaving only a note behind telling him how much she loved him but that she couldn't carry on this way any longer.

As for the private practice, well, fueled on by drugs and alcohol, his less than ethical ways had been the cause of more than one lawsuit. He didn't lose a single one, but his malpractice insurance skyrocketed so high that private practice was no longer feasible if he wanted to keep eating, drinking, and being friends with Mr's. J&B and Oxy.

It was lucky for him that two of his old friends, Scott Spaulding a brilliant orthopedist and Evelyn Sinclair an equally brilliant researcher and a woman he once had a heavy crush on back at Johns Hopkins but who wouldn't give him the time of day were growing disillusioned with the bureaucracy of medicine.

Five years ago, the three of them sat in a swanky Manhattan bar knocking back cocktails when Scotty broached the idea of opening their own private clinic. Six months later, they broke ground on The Mountainside Wellness & Research Clinic nestled in the heart of Willington, Vermont population 1,000 give or take a hundred.

Mason put up his entire lifesavings of five million dollars to buy-in as a full partner. With fifteen million dollars in cold hard cash between them and a whole host of rich benefactors behind them the state-of-the-art clinic opened with Richard Mason as the head of Exploratory Medicine.

Mason's salary plummeted to a rather healthy weekly paycheck along with a fat bonus every quarter. Still, it was far from the salary he once made but, in trade, the cost of malpractice insurance plummeted along with it. Not having a penny left to his name after buying in, Mason was lucky to be able to make those alimony payments and rent his current palace; a one bedroom ranch with a grand total of 800 square feet of living space. To be fair, the house had a finished basement but with his hip, he only ventured down there to fill the boiler. Mason even had the washer and dryer brought up to the small kitchen not wanting to navigate the stairs with a basket of clothes in one hand.

Today the Wellness Clinic was bustling along having quickly gained a 'cutting edge' reputation but 'with a personal quality of care unmatched anywhere'. That was according to the American Journal of Medicine, who, coincidentally, was unable to interview Mason for the article in the prestigious publication. He was busy that day, Evelyn made sure of it.

He could afford to move, to buy his own larger house but the landlord was laid back and the place was comfortable for an aging confirmed bachelor like himself.

Being one-third owner of the clinic gave him a lot of juice when it came to staffing. From the start he wanted his own private staff of five. In the end, he got three; John Steward a top-notch neurologist, Connie Wylds an endocrinologist who graduated at the top of her class at Yale Medical and she did so two years ahead of schedule. There was Martin Goodspeed a grade A cardiologist and cardiac surgeon.

With them at his side, to advise and rein him in from time to time, Mason continued his practice of pulling the correct diagnosis out of the air or bone marrow without anesthesia, whatever the situation called for. Overall, he still catered to the Rich and Shameless but Evelyn made sure he stayed grounded.

All the doctors on staff, including the three owners, were expected to put in fifteen hours a week in the Free Clinic.

The Mountainside was the only medical facility within a hundred miles up here in this part of Vermont. One of the conditions of purchasing the land and opening the place had been the Free Clinic. While Willington itself only had about a thousand people year 'round, there were plenty of families still living off the land in the mountains and hillsides. People that Society forgot. Evelyn and Scott readily agreed to the idea when he saw he was outnumbered at the table that day, Mason gave in.

He hated the duty. He hated the people. Not because they were poor, he just disliked people in general. He didn't save their lives because he liked them or because he felt for them ...they were puzzles to be figured out and nothing more. He thought that quality made him an excellent doctor. Others thought it made him cold, aloof, and above all else, uncaring. Three qualities a doctor should never exude.

Pouring another drink, he let the last of the papers, the **Terms & Conditions of the Trust Fund for the Benefit of Johannah Morgan Rice,** fall off his lap and onto the floor. It landed face up partially covered by the will that had fallen before it. Looking down all he could read was her name, Hannah.

"No, not me, Banana, you don't want me to take care of you." Bending down in the chair he scooped up all the papers and threw them into the nearest bin. "Not me. Not gonna happen." Cradling the green bottle of J&B as gingerly as he would a newborn baby Mason shuffled off down the hallway of the one-level ranch and to his bedroom where he finished the bottle and then passed out for the night.

That wasn't the last he would hear from Attorney Lawrence who would send him no less than a dozen certified letters over the next three months and ring his phone so often that Mason changed the number. When he stopped accepting the certified letters Lawrence sent three copies of the same letter; one certified and one sent regular mail to Mason's home and another to his office at the clinic. Mason ordered his secretary, Mary Higgins, not to sign for the letters and never to put through a call from the attorney.

It was the first time in his life that Richard Mason decided to ignore a problem in the hopes that it would just go away rather than meet it head on. All the while, his younger sister, Hannah Rice, lingered in the group home and then, after it closed for good, she sat alone in a motel room for two weeks. Day after day she waited for her big brother to come rescue her and was let down by the boy she'd once admired. She slipped deeper and deeper into her own mind and the clutches of depression.

Chapter Two

Other than the occasional trip to the movies and every Sunday for Mass, Johanna Morgan Rice hadn't been outside the walls of her group home in nearly five years, and it was almost three decades since she crossed the Michigan State Border. The train ride from Michigan to Vermont is so exciting that it's almost overwhelming for her. The whole time, from the short trip from the motel room to the train station and then the entire time on board the chugging train, Hannah couldn't stop looking out the window at the wide world speeding past her face pressed to the glass. Ten hours later, the trained stopped in Rutland where she disembarked with Mr. Lawrence and her social worker Miss Leavenworth. From there they took a car up into the mountains where Hannah gazed out of the window staring at the brilliant display of early fall colors. She tapped on the glass excitedly whenever a deer, moose, or other wild creature came into view, which was quite often. On the seat next to her was a basket of carefully baked cookies that she kept special watch on ensuring they didn't fall over.

At the end of their ride into the countryside, they stopped at a long building nestled into the mountainside. While it was long, it was only two stories tall. Whereas most hospitals she'd been too were just as cold and sterile on the outside as they were on the inside, this one seemed warm and welcoming with its wood frame and sparkling glass windows.

Ricky was inside.

That was all Hannah knew at that moment in time, her brother was behind those doors waiting for her. The excitement overtook her as she started bouncing up and down on the black leather backseat pulling at the door handle with all her might, but it wouldn't open. Frustration set in, she tapped on the window, pulled on the handle, and continued bouncing until her basket of cookies teetered on the edge of the seat.

"Argh!" She cried grabbing the basket just before it could tumble to the clean carpet.

"Hold on, Hannah," Attorney Lawrence said from the front seat, "Just wait, let me unlock the door and I'll help you out."

Trying to grab hold of herself, she held the basket tight and jumped a little when the automatic locks popped but then her door was opened by the attorney and she slipped from the car to stand in the parking lot. Breathing in the crisp mountain air her sallow cheeks flooded with color as her tired eyes lit up.

Taking her by the elbow to escort her inside Attorney Lawrence gauged her carefully, "Are you ready to see your brother?"

Holding one hand over her swiftly beating heart, she clutched the basket as she nodded. On legs that had been unsteady for decades, she toddled between the attorney and social worker to the front door. Her heart pounding so loudly it echoed in her ears.

Walking through the double doors a great reception area greeted them. It was big and full of bright sunlight from the tall windows and the skylight above them. The walls were a light gray and the tile on the floor a light blue with gold specks. Taking a breath Hannah found the place even smelled inviting, as it didn't stink of antiseptic but smelled rather like a field of wildflowers on a warm summer day. Silently staying the course between her handlers, Hannah made her way up to the big half-circle desk and the woman behind it.

In an authoritative but kind voice, Attorney Lawrence informed the woman with the big blue eyes of their mission, "We're here to see Doctor Mason."

"Do you have an appointment?"

Lawrence lied as the receptionist began punching buttons on her keyboard, "Yes. Attorney Lawrence, Miss Leavenworth, MSW...."

His name was certainly familiar to her. For the last few months, she'd been deleting his messages and throwing out his letters just as Doctor Mason instructed. Now he was here, she had to stay her ground, "I'm sorry, I don't see...."

"And Johanna Rice, Doctor Mason's sister."

His words stopped the receptionist cold. Eugenia O'Gara was an employee since the clinic opened and she was not known for letting strangers or those without appointments past her guard station. She had been fully prepared to get her back up if she had in order to turn him away. "Sister?" That made Mason's callousness regarding the attempts at communication seem quite odd. Up until this point, she figured he was being sued—again.

She glanced at the woman bolstered by the attorney and social worker. Her body was crooked as she stood there with a wicker basket in her hands. Her eyes shined with what could only be perceived as childlike anticipation. To her practiced eye the woman appeared simple. Maybe that was why Mason was ignoring her. Eugenia couldn't do the same, "I'm sorry I didn't know Doctor Mason had a sister. He's in the conference room." Pulling a small slip of paper off her desk, she drew the path on the ready-made map, "just follow the left corridor down to the third intersection, take a right and it's the fourth door on the left."

Taking the paper Attorney Lawrence nodded his balding head, "Thank you." He turned to the women accompanying him, "This way, Hannah, we're almost there."

From her place at the large desk bathed in bright sunlight, Eugenia watched the three of them make their way down the hall. She couldn't help feeling sorry for the woman in the middle as she toddled along. Just watching her put her legs down and out to the side as if she were a sidewinder crab was painful, she couldn't imagine how Doctor Mason's sister felt.

25

The second they were out of sight, she called up to Mary, Mason's secretary letting her know company was on its way. "You're not going to believe this, that attorney Mason's been dodging is here….with his sister."

Making their way along the marked route, the small troop finally came to the door marked Conference Room. Like the front area, this place was open; the Conference Room wasn't behind thick walls but a wall of glass windows. The blinds were mostly closed but the muffled rumblings of voices could be heard and the shadows of those inside seen between the slits.

Right next to it was a door marked Richard Mason Exploratory Medicine.

In an authoritative voice, Mary Higgins called out, "May I help you?"

Lawrence wasn't interested in being stalled by another secretary the trip had been long and, as far as he was concerned, totally unnecessary. "No," he opened the door. Hannah followed him through along with Miss Leavenworth.

Gripping Attorney Lawrence's hand tightly, Hannah froze in her tracks as Ricky came into her view. He was leaning over a big wooden table talking to eight other people in white coats. He pointed at them as his face turned stern. Yet even with the gray hair and the wrinkles, in her addled mind, Hannah would still know him anywhere. Her breath hitched in her throat as she let out a long low moan hoping that he remembered her and, most importantly, he wouldn't reject her now that she was so mangled and scattered. Hannah understood this was her last chance at a family and she wanted it with all her heart.

Smoothing her graying hair all tied up in a bun and looking down at her meager offering in its wicker basket tucked beneath a neat starched lavender napkin she hoped with all she had that Ricky would open his arms to her.

The Senior Staff fell silent as their eyes shifted from Mason to the people standing behind him. Without turning around Mason barked, "Don't you knock? Can't you see the 'Do Not Disturb' sign on the door?"

"Sorry to interrupt your staff meeting," Attorney Lawrence was unfazed he did his homework on Doctor Richard Mason and was well acquainted with how rude and downright insulting the man could be. This worried him. He wasn't at all sure Mason was the type of a man who should oversee this very delicate situation. "However, if you'd picked up any of my letters—besides the first one-- and then been kind enough to answer them, perhaps we could have handled this differently." Lawrence left Hannah's side only to have her shadow him as the attorney held out his hand, "I'm....."

"I'm a doctor," Mason slammed his open palms on the wood table, "I can *smell* a lawyer a mile away." Closing his eyes to wish with all his might that it would all just go away he opened them again to see the eyes of his colleagues staring at him in wide confusion. "Fuck," he muttered under his breath steeling himself to turn around. Grabbing hold of his cane, he let the breath go and turned to face his fate. Before him stood one man with his hand extended, a rather neatly dressed woman in her late sixties staring at him with shock and a third woman of whom he could only see her graying head bobbing from behind the attorney's shoulder.

Sucking air over his teeth, Attorney Lawrence forced a smile as he kept his hand outstretched, "For etiquette's sake, I'll do it anyway, humor me, what do you say? I'm Attorney Christopher Lawrence. This is Miss Helen Leavenworth, MSW. May I present your sister Miss Hannah Rice?" The attorney made a swift, nearly comical, skip to the right to reveal the aging woman standing behind him. For a second, he took in the similar deer-in-the-headlights look upon the faces of Doctor Mason and the mentally disabled woman behind him.

Ignoring the mutters from his colleagues at the table and finding it more palatable to shake hands with the attorney than look his childhood friend turned sister in the eye, Mason absently extended his hand to Lawrence, shook as he quietly remarked, "I can't believe you brought her with you."

Shaking hands firmly and then letting go Lawrence said with a warm smile, "Yes, well, as I said if you'd only picked up the phone perhaps, we could have avoided this awkward situation." Turning to look at his ward, he tried to encourage the mentally disabled woman, "Hannah, do you have something for Doctor Mason?"

Hannah was nervous, her little heart raced in her chest and a bead of sweat broke out on her full upper lip. Even before they left for the train station, the whole time she sat alone in that motel room, she practiced this moment so she could get it right and not embarrass Ricky whom she understood was a very important man now. He was a world-renowned doctor, a man of affluence and intelligence. He was a man who surely had no need for an idiot sister. Taking two hesitant shaky steps forward she held the wicker basket out to him as a token of love and friendship.

As she held out the basket, she glanced upward toward the strong but gentle voice in her head: *Nice and easy now, take your time, don't be scared. Its Ricky, you remember Ricky, you like Ricky.*

From near her feet, she heard the second voice answer in its mocking tone: *So, don't embarrass him you little moron.*

Struggling to ignore the second voice and to find her own so long silence and ignored, she stuttered, "I mah-may th-these ffor y-y-ou."

Lawrence was shocked taken aback, "Very good Hannah."

"Yes," Miss Leavenworth praised, "excellent." Leavenworth had been working with Hannah for over a decade and never once heard the woman utter more than a grunt.

Unfamiliar with Hannah's level of communication and her level of understanding Mason looked from Hannah to the basket she held out to him and back again. He didn't have to look at Attorney Lawrence, Miss Leavenworth, or the members of his panel behind him to know all of them were staring at him as they waited for the Good Doctor to give the proper response to his obviously challenged sister. Holding back all of the rude comments that wanted to fly off his normally sharp tongue, Mason took the basket and looked inside to see several dozen perfectly baked chocolate chips cookies. "Oh goodie, cookies," he clasped his hands together loud enough to make Hannah jump.

"Hannah loves to cook, don't you Hannah?" The attorney said and Hannah nodded her graying head as she waited for her big brother to take a bite of the chocolate chip cookies she'd baked for him just before leaving the hotel room where she had access to a kitchenette.

Mason picked up one of the perfectly baked cookies, each of them a delectable golden brown without a single burned spot. He found that quite an accomplishment for someone like Hannah. "Do you know who I am?" He asked as he held the cookie to his lips and watched her nod. Taking the cookie away from his lips he asked; "Who am I?" She just stood there staring at him with dewy eyes. "Tell me and I'll eat the cookie, don't tell me and..." he began to put it back in the basket even though it smelled so good it made his stomach demand that he eat it.

Leaning to the left and holding her hand by her knee she stuttered his name, "R-r-r—Rah-Ricky." Her nervous lips then felt uncertain as the people at the table began to smile and snicker uncomfortably. She began to panic thinking she'd gotten his name wrong. She leaned to the left and did her best to hold her hand by her knee without falling over.

The fine medical professionals behind him began to snicker not at Hannah's speech impediment but at his old nickname. "Shut up," Mason grumbled at them then he

29

turned back to her. He watched her hold her hand down by her knee. "That's right, I'm *Richard*." He returned the gesture of holding his own hand by his knee indicating that he understood she was trying to tell him that she remembered him from when they were children. Hannah gave a slight smile and her tearing eyes lit up a bit when Mason took a bite of the cookie.

He had expected it to taste like cardboard even though the scent told him otherwise, but it was just what it looked like, a perfectly baked cookie. "Very good," he muttered shoving the rest of the cookie into his mouth, "Anybody got any milk?"

"I believe we have some loose ends to tie up, Doctor Mason." Attorney Lawrence said satisfied that Mason was attempting to get off on the right foot with Hannah.

"Yeah," Mason agreed reluctantly. "What about you?" He said over his shoulder. "Seen enough of the show yet? Don't you all have patients to run expensive tests on or something?"

Those gathered at the table rose to their feet with uncomfortable stares and mumbles of 'right' and 'sure'. Picking up their charts and files, they made their way to the door where three of them exited without looking back but five others stayed behind to introduce themselves to the anxious woman.

Mason's immediate staff went first with Steward the neurologist in the lead.

A handsome black man in his late thirties, Steward was a pound or two overweight, but he wore it well as he peered out at the world from a set of light brown eyes. Extending his dark-skinned hand to her he greeted her warmly, "I'm Doctor Steward, and I work with— your brother." He glanced up at Mason still in shock over the news that his boss even had a sister.

Even though he wore a white doctor's coat, which Hannah didn't like, the happy smile on his warm face put her at ease.

Gingerly she slipped her hand into his and did her best to stutter her name for him. "Han-nah."

"It's nice to meet you, Hannah." Steward said kindly as he shook her hand and then let it go to step aside and let the others follow suit.

A man with a crop of sandy hair approached with his hand out. He had green eyes and very white teeth. "I'm Doctor Goodspeed. I also work with your brother."

"Han-nah." She said again as she shook his hand.

"This," Mason said in a voice loud enough to catch Hannah's attention, "is Doctor Wylds, she works with me too." He dug in his back pocket to produce his wallet. "Actually, that's not true. They all work *for* me. Except these two, they're my partners and they're leaving."

Doctors Evelyn Sinclair and Scott Spaulding paused long enough to introduce themselves to Hannah before making their way out the door and mumbling excitedly to each other all the way back to her office.

Inside the Conference Room, it was easy for Doctor Wylds to see that Mason wanted his sister out of the room for a while. Taking the twenty from his hand, she smiled at Hannah, "Hungry? Thirsty? We have a fantastic cafeteria."

It had been a long trip from Michigan to Vermont and she'd been too excited to eat on the train. Hannah was thirsty so she nodded then made a drinking motion.

"Not hungry?" Mason asked. "What did you have for lunch?"

"Hannah doesn't eat lunch," the attorney said as both men looked down at their watches. "She doesn't eat breakfast either."

"I didn't ask you," Mason snapped at the attorney as he noted that it was well past 3pm and the last thing she probably ate was dinner. "What's the matter? The group home was too low on funds to feed the residents? Owners too busy lining their pockets with all that government money?"

31

Hannah cringed at the sharpness in Mason's voice and the look in her brown eyes made him feel guilty although he'd never admit to any such thing.

"Take her down to the cafeteria get her something to eat. Mr. Lawrence and I have business to discuss." Leaning heavily on his cane he reached for another cookie and found it just as delicious as the first. "I'm in charge now and now you eat three meals a day."

"Come on, Hannah." Wylds said gently as she tried to take Hannah's hand but the woman pulled it away as though Wylds were trying to burn her.

"Go. Now." Mason said to her sternly.

Hannah grasped Wylds' still outstretched hand, she nearly tripped over her own feet as she turned toward the door and then toddled towards it as best she could on legs that hadn't worked properly since she was a young teen.

Once Hannah was out of the office, the attorney turned to him. "Are you in charge of her now? By your lack of response...."

Mason gritted his teeth and spoke through thin lips, "Looks like I am."

"In that, case Doctor Mason, if I was you, I'd be nicer to her."

"Why?"

"If nothing else, Miss Rice does come with a 3.5-million-dollar trust fund." He said with a sly smile, "One that you'll have access to as her caregiver." Attorney Lawrence placed his rather expensive leather brief case on Mason's desk to open it and remove a thick stack of papers. "These are her medical records I assume you'll be finding an appropriate physician for her in the near future."

"What? I'm not 'appropriate'?" Mason asked as he grabbed the stack of papers and shuffled through them.

Attorney Lawrence bit his tongue, "No comment. However, if you really don't want this responsibility this is your chance to say so. Just utter the word, I'll give you the papers and you could be rid of her."

"That's why you brought her here? So, I could turn her away?" Mason opened the files.

It was a cheap ploy and Lawrence knew it but, "Yes, after you'd seen her and had the chance to meet her. Yes. It's not as though you left me with a plethora of options."

With images of long ago summers traipsing through his mind, Mason shuffled through the medical files before looking to the lawyer. "There's only ten years of records here," he griped, "where's the rest of it?"

"That's all I have."

"Her accident was nearly thirty years ago," Mason reminded him. "I have patients that have been here two days and have files thicker than this. Hell, Rice's Will is bigger than this!" Mason shook the file at the attorney with an angry hand.

"That's what the last group home had. Speaking of, have you even bothered to look for a suitable group home since I first contacted you?"

Looking past the attorney to the social worker standing silent in the corner of his office he had to admit to himself for the last time that he'd been hoping the whole thing would just go away. That the lawyer would take his lack of response for exactly what it was, disinterest and then be on his way to finding another guardian and trustee for Hannah Rice. That didn't happen. He was still asking himself one question for which there didn't seem to be a satisfactory answer; why in God's name had her father—their father—made him, Richard Mason unrecognized bastard son, her guardian in his will? "I'm still working on it."

"I see." The lawyer said smugly. "In the meantime, where do you propose she stay?"

"I don't have to 'propose' anything." Mason said in the same smug tone. "I'm in charge, what I say goes. For now," he sighed unable to believe the next few words that were going to come out of his mouth. "I guess she'll just have to stay with me."

Miss Leavenworth spoke up as she neared Mason's desk, "You have a room for Hannah?"

Mason swallowed hard as he stared into the woman's cold eyes, "Not exactly but I do have a very comfortable sofa." Taking in the disapproving look in her narrowing eyes, Mason added, "After four failed marriages I'm a confirmed bachelor with no need for a spare room. Got it?"

Wishing very much that the gruff and rude Doctor Mason would just step aside and let her take care of Hannah, not for the money but because she honestly cared about the woman, Miss Leavenworth tried to keep her composure and remember she was here to act on Hannah's behalf. "I'll need to check out and then sign off on her living arrangements," Miss Leavenworth asserted. "Once that's done, I'll contact Vermont Department of Disabilities to have a new social worker assigned."

"Oh joy," Mason grumbled. "I can't wait."

Doing his best to hold his temper, Lawrence slammed his hand down over the papers in front of Doctor Mason, "I see now that bringing Hannah here may have been a mistake on my part. It isn't too late to say no, do you understand? If you really don't want this responsibility, I'll take Hannah back to Michigan and have someone installed who will take this seriously and who will act in her best interest. All you have to do, Doctor Mason, is to refuse the charge given to you."

Mason wanted to agree, he wanted to tell the haughty lawyer to go fuck himself and take Hannah with him. Yet the wafting scent of hay in late summer and open fields of wildflowers stretching out for what seemed miles under the bright sunlight wouldn't leave his brilliant mind. The memory of Hannah's grinning girlish face flooded behind his eyes and the echo of her titter filled his lonely ears.

"Hannah the Banana," Mason whispered.

"What?" Lawrence asked sharply.

34

"Nothing." Mason reluctantly signed documents that gave him full legal guardianship of Hannah and put him in charge of all her personal and financial affairs.

"You are going to have to account to the Court twice a year with regard to her funds and her health, you're aware of that, aren't you?" The lawyer asked.

"Got it." Mason agreed off-handedly.

"They take these things very seriously, Doctor Mason." Now the lawyer's voice left the smugness behind and took on an almost fatherly protective tone. "Even if you don't."

"Hey, 3.5 million is nothing to sneeze at."

"Neither is her well-being."

"I am a...oh what's that word again? Oh yeah....a *doctor*, that's right, so, ya know, I think I can handle it."

Glancing at Miss Leavenworth and seeing the same concern in her eyes that Lawrence felt in his heart, he drew a deep breath, "From what I understand, Doctor Mason, you work with people who have come to the end of their rope, is that right?" Pausing for a moment, he watched Mason nod with steely eyes. "People who've exhausted every other avenue available to them come to you when no other doctor can discern what's wrong them. You diagnose and then you fix them, is that correct?" He watched as Mason pursed his lips and nodded again. "Then the psyche isn't your forte. You can't 'fix' Hannah, she is what she is."

Always up for the toughest of challenge's Mason looked down at the closed file containing Hannah's medical records. "We'll see about that." Mason stood up. "I want the rest of her medical records."

"I told you I don't have them." Lawrence pointed to the file. "That's her records for the last ten years, which is the entire time that she spent in her last group home."

"What about before that?"

"If you really require it," the lawyer sighed, "I'll do some digging and see what I can come up. The truth is Hannah was in two group homes before the last one. The first burned down and the second, like the last, closed due to lack of funding. Personally, I think you're lucky to have as much medical information as you do."

"Yeah, well, I'm a greedy son of a bitch," he said with that razor sharp tongue, "I want it all."

A few moments later Hannah returned with Doctor Wylds. Leaning on his cane, Mason got up from his desk to come out from behind it and look at his new sister closely, "Did you eat?" Hannah just stared down at her feet as though she hadn't heard him. "Did she?" He asked Wylds in a sterner voice.

"Yeah," Wylds said with a slight frown, "if you call half a dozen sugar cookies and a carton of milk eating then she ate."

"I thought I told you to get her some real food."

"She wouldn't eat it. What was I supposed to do? Force feed her?" Wylds retorted then pulled back as her green eyes rolled in her young pretty head. "Never mind, look who I'm asking."

"That would be...me." Mason said as he turned to where Hannah had been standing only a second ago but she wasn't there, instead she was curled up in the chair by his office door. "What the hell?"

Miss Leavenworth looked at her watch, "It's four o'clock, Hannah takes a nap at four."

Out of habit, he looked down at his watch again to note that the social worker was right. It was a well-known fact that people like Hannah often got a little worse after 3pm. Doctors like him called it 'sun downing' and if that was what was going on then come 7am tomorrow morning she'd be the best she was during the course of a normal day. "Hannah?" Mason asked in a voice loud enough to be heard but Hannah didn't look up at the sound of her name. "Hannah!" That time she jumped and turned her eyes toward him.

"Hey, you don't have to yell at her." Wylds interjected.

"I'm not yelling," Mason corrected, "I'm cutting through the fog in her head." He turned back to Hannah. "Come on get up, time to go."

"Go?" Wylds asked. "Where? What about our patient?"

"That's your job, besides family first, right? Well, look at her," Mason responded, "I think it's time to get Cinderella home before she turns into a pumpkin."

Looking from the attorney to the social worker and back to her boss knowing Mason lived in a one-bedroom ranch; Wylds leaned in to whisper, "She's going to stay with you?"

"What? You think I'm inappropriate too?" Mason looked around for a moment as he waited for one of them to answer pursed his lips. "Unless you have a better idea then... yeah, she's staying with me." He limped over to where Hannah was nodding off and took her by the arm. "Come on, upsie-daisy, we're going for a ride." The fog in her head that was appearing in her eyes lifted for a moment and Mason determined that Hannah liked to go for rides in the car but— "How do you like motorcycles?" Being warm weather and his new guest unexpected Mason rode his Honda CBR 1000 into work that morning.

The haze in Hannah's eyes lifted as her face lit up and her heart began to race.

Staring at Ricky with a wide grin, she thought: *A motorcycle? Oh, it's been so long since I rode on a bike! Frank used to take me out every weekend on his bike; we used to ride down to the Dew Drop Inn for coffee or lunch. I still remember the sweet smell of the air as we zipped down the back roads and the wind on my face. Yes, I want to go on the motorcycle! Yes! Yes! Yes!*

All those thoughts ran swiftly through Hannah's befuddled head but she was unable to give them voice no matter how hard she tried. The best she could manage was to jump up and down with her fists balled and pumping.

"Looks like a yes to me," Mason quipped looking around at the disapproving stares that greeted him.

"You can't take her on the bike." Wylds complained. "She'll fall off if she can even get on it."

Mason thought it over. "It's a short trip, she'll be fine."

Attorney Lawrence couldn't hold his tongue, "Doctor Maso—"

Mason cut him off pointing two fingers at the lawyer and social worker, "You two follow and bring my cookies." The tone in his gruff voice was final. "Let's go Hannah."

Not letting the stern faces staring at her deter her in any manner, Hannah took his arm and followed him out of the office.

Walking out in the setting sun, Mason stopped next to the Honda and looked down at the small woman who forty years ago he'd thought of as a friend. "You can hold on, can't you? On the bike?" She looked at him with those blank brown eyes and he began to think he needed to call a cab. "Do you even understand what I'm saying? *Hold on*?" He put one fist inside the other.

Hannah took one step back to stand behind Ricky where she put her arms around his slender waist and laced her fingers together. Pressed up tightly against him, she made a low guttural noise like the sound of an engine as she gently leaned from one side to the next as the motorcycle in her throat shifting gears: *bruum-bruuummm-brrruuummmmm*. When she thought she'd gotten her point across without stepping out of bounds she toddled out from behind him to take his arm once more.

"You're smarter than people give you credit for, aren't you, Hannah Rice?" If that were true, then Mason reasoned she must get damn sick and tired of people talking about her as though she weren't in the room. He would have to watch that from now on, at least until he got her settled into an apartment of her own. If she could afford it—and she could— then why should she have to live in a group home? A small

38

apartment with a reliable full-time caregiver would be much better.

In answer to his question, she just shrugged her shoulders and gave him a wan smile.

Hannah hoped she was still something near intelligent, that the things she wanted to say were her own and they were not the delusional product of some sort of odd voices in her head, but she couldn't be sure. She couldn't be sure of anything at all since the accident.

Hannah had a great deal of trouble raising her mangled leg high enough to get it over the seat. She tried and she tried but to no avail. Mason had no choice but to help her and climb on then get on himself that made things rather difficult for him and his injured hip.

Starting the bike and glancing over his shoulder Mason opened his mouth to tell her again to hold on but he didn't have to. She slid right up next to him and put her arms around him without any hassle.

Gliding down the winding mountain road, Richard Mason was amazed and impressed by Hannah's ability to be a good passenger on his motorcycle. Most women—well, most people in general—tended to hold on too tight or not at all. They leaned too far into the turns or in the wrong direction but not Hannah. Her arms were snug around him but not cutting him off so tightly that he couldn't breathe. She didn't seem afraid as she leaned into the turns. Mason kept a keen eye on her in the rearview mirror where he could see her smiling and she lightly bounced up and down on the back of the bike as though she were actually jumping for joy.

Once they arrived at the small house in the middle of 'downtown' Willington, he pulled the bike into the driveway at the end of the postage stamp sized yard expecting to see boxes and packages containing the rest of Hannah's things waiting on his doorstep but there was nothing. Turning off the bike's engine and he carefully dismounted before Hannah so that he could help her off the bike. It wasn't easy for either of them, the two gimps, but they managed it. Mason took in her expression carefully as they made their way to the front door. He noted no surprise just the glow of fresh air. "Home sweet home," he announced sliding the key into the door. They entered the mudroom before turning left to open the door to the living room. Once inside Hannah just stood there as though she were awaiting instructions. "Go on, make yourself at home." He invited. Still, she stood there. "Time for the grand tour?"

No reply.

He took her around the small house, showed her the living room where she showed an interest in his piano by staring at it intently, but she didn't touch it. She stared at the guitars hanging on the wall behind the piano and the saxophone in its case but made no move toward them either. "Do you still know how to play?" Mason asked as he watched her stare at the piano while memories of those long-ago summers skipped through his mind again. Her mother, Adelaide Rice first taught Mason to play piano when he was still a boy. As he remembered it, Hannah had quite the talent for tickling the ivories.

Hannah didn't answer him she just stood there staring. He let out a sigh and from their spot by the piano pointed to every room in the house. "That's it, it's not much, but I like it."

A few moments later, Lawrence and Leavenworth showed up with Hannah's belongings one small suitcase and a garment bag. Lawrence also had the file, and Mason's basket of cookies. Astonished by the single suitcase, he couldn't help but turn to his new sister, "Hannah, don't you have more than this? Where are the rest of your things?"

Hannah gazed upward as her mouth dropped open as she stood there shifting from one foot to the other thinking: *The rest of my things? Did I forget something? Tell me I didn't forget something! I was so careful to pack everything into the bag. At least I thought I was.*

40

Then the nasty voice piped up again calling her eyes to the floor: *You idiot. You're dumber than fuckin' doornail!*

Letting her legs fly out from under her, Hannah plopped down on the floor next to the suitcase with a thud so heavy it made everyone around her cringe. She didn't notice the gasps and instead began rifling through the open bag inwardly cursing herself for being forgetful. Starting to groan in panic she looked up hearing the kinder voice reply: *Calm down, relax, everything's here. Just take your time and look.*

Feeling a little better, she breathed a little easier as she fished out a plastic shopping bag from the suitcase. Turning it over in her hands, she thought that it looked familiar. Biting on her bottom lip, she thought to herself: *I am supposed to do something with this. What is it?*

"Give that to your brother, Hannah," Leavenworth instructed over Hannah's shoulder. "I'm going to inspect the house now."

"Knock yourself out," Mason sneered without looking at her.

Sitting on the floor with the bag in her hand Hannah thought: *That's it! Give this to him. That's right; I'm supposed to give this to Ricky. To my brother.*

Rising to her feet much more slowly and carefully then how she had sat down, she held the bag out to him with a shaking hand making the contents rattle loudly. Mason took it from her, surprised by the weight of it, he didn't have to open it to know it was nearly chock full of prescription drugs.

Clearing his throat but trying to keep his voice light even as it oozed with wicked sarcasm he remarked, "This should be fun." Tossing the sack of pills to the couch, he looked to the lawyer wanting all of this to be over. "Are we done?" From the corner of his other eye, he watched Leavenworth open doors and go room to room in the tiny house the whole of which could be observed from the small foyer.

"Almost," Attorney Lawrence returned in the same snide tone, "Hannah has a storage facility in Victorville. It's full of the contents of the house." With a wary eye, he gazed around at the open living room with its sparse furnishings knowing Doctor Mason's home was a step up from her group homes but a big step down from the large house where she grew up with its antique furniture and stable of horses. "It's all in the inventory file. As for personal effects that's all she has." He pointed to the small open suitcase and the garment bag near it. "She received one hundred dollars per month for spending money while she was in the home. While she's with you, she'll receive two hundred. You of course will be paid a yearly stipend as Guardian and Trustee."

Mason took a step forward as he turned his lanky body to the side and away from Hannah who was staring at them with understanding eyes, "Yeah? How much?"

Lawrence groaned and ran hand across the top of his baldhead, "You didn't read any of it did you? I outlined everything and you..." Feeling his temper was starting to get the best of him, he reined himself in, "You'll receive fifty thousand a year as a standard fee. If she lives with you it doubles." He looked Mason up and down taking in the man's scruffy beard and wrinkled clothing, "Not that a world-class doctor like yourself would need the money, of course."

Scratching his graying head as he leaned heavily on the cane Mason wanted to tell the snotty lawyer that no, he didn't need the money. But then again, more money was always a good thing. Before he could say anything, Miss Leavenworth returned to the living room with three bottles of prescription pills.

"May I ask about these Doctor Mason?"

"War veteran. Bad hip," Mason returned defiantly as he slapped his side. "I have a prescription, wanna see it?"

"Did you write it yourself?" Miss Leavenworth shot back. "How about one for the empty bottles of scotch? Do you have a prescription for them too?"

Mason didn't skip a beat, "In case you hadn't noticed I am over twenty-one."

42

"I did notice there's only the one bedroom as you said. Are you going to make her sleep on the couch?"

"Well, there is a finished basement, but I don't get down there that much," he slapped his left hip again. Pursing his lips and nodding almost gleefully he continued, "Don't think hers are much better so making her sleep on the couch, well, that would be damn ungentlemanly of me, now wouldn't it?" Mason huffed knowing that was his intention. "She can take the bedroom until I find a suitable place for her."

Knowing she had the power to nix the whole thing right here Miss Leavenworth wrestled with her conscience for a moment. While she didn't find him to be a suitable Guardian for Hannah his home was neat, tidy, clean, and showed no signs of neglect or pests—other than its current resident. "Yes, well, until then," Miss Leavenworth said as she handed over a slip of yellow lined paper. "She'll need someone to stay with her while you're at work. This is a list of caregivers in this area and a list of group homes."

Not wanting to admit he felt a twinge of gratitude Mason snatched it from her hand, "I'll look into them. That it?"

"For now," Attorney Lawrence agreed, "I trust from this point forward you'll be opening and responding to my letters as well as those from the Michigan Court." He held out his hand feeling a bit uneasy at leaving the delicate woman in the care of the gruff doctor.

"Wouldn't miss 'em," Mason chimed shaking the man's hand. "Have a safe trip."

Hannah waved good-bye with a sad smile as they crossed the threshold and Ricky shut the door in their faces with a solid slam.

"Why don't you go unpack?" Mason suggested. "Clean out the bottom drawer of the bureau. You can have it." Looking at the open suitcase, he doubted she'd need even that much space. At his instruction Hannah obeyed, she picked up the suitcase and toddled off down the hall toward the bedroom at the end.

Sitting down on the couch, Mason opened the bag of pills. On the top were two weekly pillboxes, one clear, and one blue for her Day pills and her Night pills. Both were neatly filled and ready for use. Below them there had to be at least 30 bottles of pills in the bag along with new prescriptions for each. Within the prescriptions, Mason found a mindboggling thing a prescription for Oxycodone with unlimited refills. Part of him felt like he had just hit the Jackpot in Vegas, surely she wouldn't mind sharing now and then. Hell, she probably wouldn't even know, and his own bottle was running low, so he popped two of hers into his mouth.

Mason lined the bottles up on the coffee table and was utterly stunned and amazed by what he saw. Hannah had pills to sleep, pills to wake, pills to keep her calm, pills for arthritis, pills for acid-reflux, pills for ulcers, pills for kidneys, pills for high blood pressure (beta-blockers AND ACE inhibitors). She had pills for high cholesterol, anti-depressants, anti-psychotics, anti-hallucinogens, pills for osteoporosis and schizophrenia, blood thinners, cough syrup, allergy medicines, and pain killers of which Oxycodone was only first. She also had a steady supply of Percocet, Percodan and a, Jesus H. Christ!, a small bottle of morphine. Then there were the birth control pills that he couldn't stop staring at.

Seemed his sister was a walking—if not exactly talking—drug store. He just sat there staring at all of them with his mouth agape. "Doesn't anybody read drug interaction warnings anymore?" He mumbled shaking his head as he stared at the bottles that nearly stretched from end of his coffee table to the other. Fumbling with the envelope he pulled out the papers inside the top one was a letter addressed to him from Miss Leavenworth. It read:

Dear Doctor Mason:

I am Hannah's Case Worker and I have been helping to care for her for the last twelve years. I will miss her very much. It is my hope that you will take good care of her, as she is very special. I've taken the liberty of writing down Hannah's schedule along with a few of her likes and dislikes to make the transition to her new group home more comfortable for her. This bag contains all of her medications within it you will find two weekly pillboxes, the clear one contains her morning medications and the blue one contains her nightly medications. Hannah can put these together herself if you are watching to be sure she does it correctly. As you've probably noticed by now, Hannah isn't very vocal and she has trouble communicating her needs and thoughts to those around her but if you take the time to listen to and study her I'm sure you'll pick up on whatever it is she may be trying to convey. Hannah does best in a well-structured environment, when left to her own devices she tends to become easily bored which leads her to get into trouble. Supervision is the key to all aspects of her life, especially to her use of the oven/stove as Hannah loves to cook and is very good at it but often forgets to turn the appliance off. On the whole, she is very sweet and loving though, she does have 'bad days' when she acts up and lashes out. Such incidents are normally easily remedied with nothing more than patience and a little TLC. Being a doctor, I'm sure I don't have to tell you that. If you have any questions or need assistance with her please call me at 906-555-4896

Sincerely,

Louise Leavenworth, MSW

Accompanying the letter were several more pages each with a different heading. HANNAH LIKES, HANNAH DISLIKES, and HANNAH'S DAILY SCHEDULE, that one looked more like a regimen than a schedule. It informed him when she was to get up, when she was to eat, how much 'free time' to give her (11am-12pm), it even had her daily bathroom habits listed along with the information that Hannah's bedtime was 8:30. Seemed a little early to him. The last sheet of paper was marked "HANNAH'S MEDICATION". That last page was merely a list of the pills and the schedule for taking them.

The very first thing listed under "HANNAH LIKES" was; Hannah attends Catholic Service every Sunday and prefers the noon mass.

Mason read that twice and tried to restrain the giggle rising at the back of his throat, "That's gonna change," he muttered as he rubbed the stubble on his chin, "I'm not taking you to church." Richard Mason was a man of Science and as far as he was concerned, Science topped God who had no place in the Realm of Logic. God was a fool's game created to bilk the weak of mind out of their life savings. Hannah probably put her entire hundred dollars a month allowance into the damn collection plate. He read on and discovered that:

Hannah likes music, she loves to hum and dance, she plays piano when encouraged but will listen to the radio very loudly if not watched.

Dance? Mason wondered thinking of those stiff bowed legs. But, it was almost nice to know that she could still remember how to play a tune. Perhaps he'd try to coax one out of her later.

The very first thing under "HANNAH DISLIKES" was; Hannah doesn't like fire, I believe this is due to the fact she was present when her first group home burned to the ground. Please do not smoke around her, light candles, matches or lighters, or use a fireplace as the sight of flames can be enough to send her into a manic state.

"Fair enough," Mason grumbled knowing his days of leisurely smoking his Jamaicans in the house were over. He gazed longingly at his fireplace. It was one of the selling points when he bought the house five years ago. Every October through late April and sometimes into May, he burned it. Not only did it ease his oil bill but it the radiant heat soaked deep into his hip easing the constant ache that got so much worse when the cold weather set in. With a grunt, he continued reading.

Hannah is afraid of the dark. Please allow her to sleep with a small nightlight. Do not be alarmed if she attempts to crawl into bed with you, she is only looking for comfort. Please pass this information along to her next home manager as the last one tended to punish her quite severely for this behavior.

Wondering what said punishment might be, Mason caught the movement of a shadow and looked over to see Hannah standing in the bedroom doorway holding her stomach. At first, he thought that she was going to be sick but a quick glance at his watch and HANNAH's SCHEDULE told him it was way past her dinnertime of 5:00pm.

"Hungry?" He asked and turned the papers over so she couldn't see them. He wasn't sure she could read but just in case it was better to be safe than sorry. Hannah grabbed her stomach tighter and started toward the kitchen.

Mason remembered Lawrence saying that Hannah loves to cook.

Well, unfortunately for Hannah there was never an abundance of ingredients in his house. "I got some soup." He offered and met her in the kitchen where he took a red and white can from the cupboard. Hannah grimaced. "What? Don't like vegetable beef? It's my favorite but ok, I've got chicken noodle too."

She turned up her nose and rolled her eyes before opening the refrigerator. Looking inside she sighed deeply at the sight of the half-empty carton of milk, accompanying orange juice carton, mayonnaise, ketchup, mustard, and six-pack of Coors.

"Yeah, it's not much I know but usually it's just me and I tend to eat out of the can."

"Blllleeek." Hannah stuck out her tongue.

"We've got soup, take or leave it." Mason offered knowing he could order them a pizza or Chinese food or anything else they might want. She just stood there staunchly. "No soup got it." He put the can back in the cupboard. "Pizza? Do you like pizza?" Now her eyes brightened. "Pizza it is. Pepperoni ok?" Eyes bigger still. "Who wants soup anyway? Even if it is m'm'm good?" He cracked, Hannah let out a little snort that was almost a laugh.

As always, Mason planned to eat his dinner on his coffee table in front of his TV but it seemed Hannah had other plans. After he placed the call for delivery, she set the small dining table with two place settings. When the pizza arrived, she took it out of the box and put it on a serving platter Mason forgot he owned. Sitting down at the table, he reached for a slice and she slapped his hand lightly.

"What?"

Hannah scooted her chair up close to the table, put her hands together, bowed her head and closed her eyes in silent prayer.

"Oh Christ," Mason grumbled and promptly had his hand slapped again. "Stop that. I'm a big boy I don't have to pray before dinner, or bed, or anything else, if I don't want to and I don't want to."

Hannah gave him a sour glance as she watched him put a large slice on his plate.

"You want me to thank God? For what? The fact that *I* made enough money to buy this pizza? God didn't do that. *I* did." Mason took a big bite while Hannah rolled her eyes and then went back to her prayer. If Mason could have read her mind, he would have known she wasn't thanking God merely for the pizza but for her new home and for finally answering her long held prayer of being reunited with her brother.

When she finished thanking God Hannah dove into the hot pizza with so much zest Mason thought that he should have ordered two of them. Hannah devoured four slices of the pie without stopping then took her time with the fifth and last slice. Watching her with keen eyes, Mason figured that's what happened when you only ate cookies and dinner.

Without being told to, Hannah picked up the two plates and washed them in the kitchen sink before putting them in the rack to dry then she wandered back to the couch, sat down next to him, took his hand, and rested her head on his shoulder.

48

"Tired?" He asked noting it was 8:37 by his watch. "Your hand is freezing." He held it in his own and then picked up the other to discover they were both as cold as ice. "Come on, I'll put you to bed."

Hannah with her chilly little hand inside his warm one sat in her place as she pointed over her slender shoulder to the baby grand in the corner.

"You want me to play you a song?"

Tired eyes coming to life she smiled and patted his hand.

"Then ask me to play you a song. I know you talk, I heard you."

Yes, she did talk but it was difficult, and she always ended up stammering, stuttering, and tripping over her tongue like a drunkard whose feet wouldn't cooperate. Hannah pointed to the piano, wiggled her fingers in the air, pointed at him and smiled again.

"Yeah, I get you like Charades, but I don't. You talk so from now that's what you're going to do." Mason stood up abruptly and reached down for her cold hand to bring her to wobbly feet. "I'm in charge, remember? You want. You ask. Or you don't get."

Hannah didn't offer any outward resistance as he guided her down the tiny corridor to the single bedroom. She just followed along behind him with her tongue stuck out at the back of his head.

In the bedroom doorway, Mason stopped cold. "Hannah? What's this?" He'd told her to empty the bottom dresser drawer and put her things in it, but she'd gone a few steps further while he read through her medical files. She didn't empty just the one drawer but all the drawers and then she'd taken their contents folded, stacked, and lined everything up on his bed in very a precise fashion.

Every single pair of his underwear was folded in threes and then in half. They were sorted by color ranging darkest to lightest and by style before they were neatly stacked on the pillow with his socks and undershirts next to them making a

49

uniform row across the top of the bed. His blue jeans were next; each pair folded in half and then half again. Colored Tees were next, those with funny sayings or pictures were also stacked darkest to lightest. Just past those was a small stack of Gentlemen's Magazines he kept in the bottom drawer and next to those was the jar of Vaseline that he kept next to them.

The sight of them made Mason wince but then he grew intrigued wondering what she'd thought when she came across them. Had she looked through them? Did she know what the pictures were? Was she disgusted? On the other hand, had she felt nothing at all? He didn't know but, two things were for sure, the first; this what had taken her so long in here while he perused the files and second, with everything on the bed there was no room for Hannah.

"Nice work, now finish up and put it away."

With a huff, Hannah scooped up stacks of clothes and laid them in dresser drawers until she got to the stack of magazines. She stopped, pointed at them with a sharp finger and rolled her eyes.

"Put them back where you found them," Mason ordered.

"Ick," she let out a grunt of disgust, picked up the magazines and let them slip from her hands into the trash bin next to the bed.

"Hey! That's not what I said."

Hannah just dusted her hands together and left them in the bin as she crossed her arms over her chest.

"Ok, I can see we may have a few...kinks...to work out," he quipped snatching his Playboys, Penthouses, Ouis, and Swanks from the wastebasket. Slapping them down on the nightstand he added, "Feel free to look through them you may learn something although I'd try to avoid the sticky pages if I were you."

Her mouth dropped open in a little 'o' before she pretended to vomit on them.

50

"Oh, this is gonna be fun, alright little sister, let's go, it's bed time."

Hannah didn't hide her displeasure this time she stuck her tongue out right at his face.

"No thanks."

Hannah stomped a foot on the bedroom floor and shook a finger at him.

"Yeah, you understand everything, don't you? Sure, you do. Go brush your teeth." He hitched his head toward the bathroom door. Watching her go, he knew he was right she understood but getting her to communicate was going to be the challenge. As he listened to the water run and the sound of the brush scrubbing her mouth, Mason investigated the bottom drawer. Hannah had two pairs of slacks, one pair of jeans, two sweaters, one t-shirt, one pair of white slip-on canvas shoes, three pairs of undies—unattractive and fairly ratty—and one bra also ratty. She also had one very faded red and white St. Mark's High School sweatshirt that looked as though it had been through the wars.

No nick-knacks, no little dolls or big ones for that matter, no books, no photographs, she had absolutely nothing other than the nearly worn-out clothes. What stumped him most was her lack of a winter coat or a pair of boots. It was damn cold and snowed heavy in the Upper Peninsula. That got him wondering if group home residents were made to stay indoors October through April.

Hearing the water turn off he picked up the black t-shirt to ask her if she slept in it but was shocked when he looked up to see her toddling out of the bathroom. "Whoa! What the...."

Hannah stood there naked except for another droopy pair of underwear and an oval locket made of gold. She stared at him as though she were waiting for something. The first thing that caught his eye, after the initial shock of seeing her standing there naked, were her poor gnarled legs. They looked more like twisted broken branches of a tree with scarred bark. After the accident, the doctors flayed her like a flounder hip to

51

ankle on each leg as they tried to repair the damage. There were scars on her hips, knees, and shins, where the broken bones burst through from the impact of metal rolling over.

Just looking at them made him swallow hard as he tried to hold back the gasp rising in his throat knowing it wouldn't be very professional—or even brotherly of him—to let it pass over it lips. He reached down to his bad hip and absently ran his hand over it as he stared at her. Ironically, he found he was grateful for his busted hip because surely it couldn't possibly ache as much as her legs. If they didn't rate her all the painkillers she wanted, then nothing did. The second thing he noted was that he could clearly count every single rib, her hip bones jutted out like the fins on a '57 Chevy, and her skin was ashen almost scaly. Although she looked clean, she smelled all right, and yet still Mason wondered when she'd last had a bath.

His cranky disposition was suddenly wrangled into submission when Hannah put her hands up over her head and leaned in toward him like a small child. Mason raised the t-shirt in the air and slid it over her head. "I've got some work to do," he said easily and pulled the blankets back on his bed, "I'll be right out there, ok?" She did not answer him, but she complied when he motioned that it was time for her to climb in under the covers.

"Here," he put the remote control in her hand. "You can watch all the TV you want, ok? If you need me, I'm right out there." He pointed through the door to the living room beyond. The garment bag hanging on the door caught his attention. Already knowing he would find Hannah's Sunday-Go-To-Meeting dress inside he unzipped the bag. Pushing aside the light blue plastic, he took in a simple white dress that was well past the knee. It was almost sleeveless with a sweetheart bodice made of lace. There were no stockings to go with the dress and no heels. Looking at her legs again, Mason thought he could give her a pass on that fashion faux pas. Draped on the hangar was a wreath carefully woven of silk baby's breath and lily-of-the-valley. "What's this?"

Hannah piled her hair into a bun and pointed to the wreath.

"For your hair, huh?" A long ago memory jumped to the forefront of his mind. Hannah, little Hannah, sitting a big field with a pile of freshly picked flowers carefully weaving wreaths and daisy chains. "This goes in the closet," he said with a heavy voice as he zipped it again, took it down from the door, and then tucked it into his closet next to his suits. "Besides, you won't be needing it; you're not going to church anymore."

Hannah's eyes turned sad as she put her hands together in a gesture of prayer and then pointed upward.

"No, no more church. Organized religion is only for weak-minded fools easily parted from their money."

Hannah shook her head vigorously and made the praying gesture again but this time with urgency.

"You think God wanted this to happen to you? What kind of God would do that?" Mason shot. "There is no Gah—" the next thing he knew she clamped her hand tightly over his mouth before he could finish. Grabbing her wrist roughly in one hand, he pulled her hand away. "You don't shush me, got that? There is NO GOD."

Hannah couldn't believe what she was hearing such blasphemy! To her it was unconscionable as she slapped her hand over his mouth again tighter this time. With a very angry finger, she pointed upward then she pointed it at him.

Again, Mason took her hand away. "What? You think He's gonna hear me? Let him." He raised his cane to the ceiling. "NO GOD! God's a fake a big fat phony!" He said it louder and then paused before regaining her cold stare. "See? I'm still standing. No lightning bolt not even a tiny rumble of thunder. Know why? Because He can't hear me because He doesn't exist."

It was at that point that Hannah did something completely unexpected, she reached out with her frail arms, pushed Mason as hard as she could until he stumbled backward then she stormed out of the bedroom. She marched right down the hall and to the front door before Mason knew what hit him.

"Hey!" He hollered watching her put her hand on the doorknob and he limped down the hall as fast as he could knowing he wouldn't get there in time if she decided to bolt. "Where do you think you're going?"

Another unexpected turn of events came when Hannah flipped him the finger and opened the door letting the cold autumn air into the small house. Wearing only the simple black t-shirt, she took one toddle over the threshold.

"Don't you do it! Hannah! I'm warning you! Don't you walk out that door, little sister."

With her jaw clenched tight, she turned around as she held the door open and made one last plea as he limped toward her. Looking at him with sad eyes Hannah shook her head, sighed then she pointed upward to where the gentle voice emanated. The one that was always there to encourage, comfort, and calm her. Hannah knew it was God and that He was watching out for her. Nothing Ricky ever said or did would convince her otherwise. Yet, she didn't want to leave here and had no idea where she would go if she did. She wanted to stay with Ricky, with her brother, and have this last shot at her own family knowing so many other chances had been snatched away never to return. However, if Ricky wouldn't let God stay in his house then she couldn't stay here either. Staring daggers at him, she put her hands together again as her eyes started welling.

Mason attended St. Mark's High School for two to six weeks out of every year, but Hannah had been treated to an entire twelve years of Catholic school. He didn't doubt that the Rice's attended St. Mark's Church every Sunday and that Hannah had gone through every blessed sacrament save marriage and last rites. "You're brainwashed, you know that?" He snapped feeling the burning pull in his bad hip as he slammed the front door shut. Still, she stared at him with her hands together. "You want to pray? Fine, I won't stop you but you're going to do it here. IF there's a God—which there is not!-- then He can hear you wherever you are even if you don't actually talk. So… no more going to church. Now go to bed." He pointed off down the hall to the open bedroom door. "Right now. March, young lady."

The gentle voice called to her it caught her attention and made her look up: *Do as he says and go to bed. Just because he's blind now doesn't mean he will never see.*

The other voice, the mocking sinister one, countered God's proposal: *Why don't you go play in traffic? Get it over with.*

Hannah's mouth fell open and she let out a low wail as she started to cry. Then Ricky's arm wrapped around her shaking shoulders. It was warm and comforting, Hannah threw her arms around his neck with such force she almost knocked him to the ground.

Feeling a knot of guilt roll around in the pit of his stomach Mason knew he's been too hard on her. His mouth always got the better of him and, normally, he cut people down left and right with his rapier wit never giving it a second thought. "Don't cry," Mason huffed as he patted her bony back, "I hate it when people cry, they get all snotty and messy. Stop it." That was about as close to 'I'm sorry' as he could get right now and it seemed to soothe her a bit. When he turned her around and led her down the hall back to the bedroom Hannah toddled alongside him wiping her eyes.

"Alright, you go to bed now, no more foolishness tonight." Mason instructed and watched her nod. Then she did something absolutely amazing. Hannah put both hands on the mattress and sunk to her busted knees. "Ow," Mason grunted. Just watching her do it made his own leg hurt. "Hannah…"

On the floor by the bed, Hannah crossed herself and said her nightly prayers while her brother looked on in bewilderment and disgust.   She thanked God again for bringing her here and asked Him to help her be good and not to make Ricky angry anymore because she really loved her brother and she really liked her new home. She didn't ever want to leave it and go back to another lonely group home. "'Ahhhh-men," she uttered then she crossed herself again and tried to stand up.

"Yeah, Ah Men. We're great aren't we?" Mason put his hands under her elbows and helped her to feet then he pulled back the covers on the bed and helped her in. Snuggling down in the soft blankets Hannah's haggard face softened for the first time. She patted the empty space next to her then held her arm out to him.

"Did you share a bed in the group home?"

Staring at him, she thought: *Yes. No. Sort of.*   Remaining silent under the covers, she just shrugged her shoulders.

"Yeah, there's a definitive answer," he griped and sighed running the palm of his hand over the side of his short graying hair. "Not me, ok? Not me." He pointed at her, "You sleep here, and I'll sleep out there. Tonight. Tomorrow you take the couch." Mason hitched his thumb toward the partially open door but didn't take his gaze from her. "Got it?" Mason put the remote control in her hand, "You watch TV until you fall asleep."

Feeling confused and worn, she wondered why he seemed angry with God. The mocking voice that lives near the floor spoke in her head: *You're an idiot, you know that? A fucking idiot. That's why he's mad cuz he's smart, you're stupid, and he's stuck with your lame ass. God, really? God? Moron.*

Scratching the side of her head and giving her hair a tug just over her left ear she frowned. It took a few seconds but then she nodded at him and pushed the big red button on the remote. In Hannah's limited experience, it is always the big red button that turns the TV on and off.   Ricky's TV is no different.

56

With his old friend J&B to keep him company, Mason sat in the living room periodically glancing at the half open bedroom door as he went over Hannah's records. Drink in one hand, file on his lap, and a freshly popped set of pills making their way down his gullet, Mason started with the most recent report.

Two years ago Hannah had been assessed for the court in the great state of Michigan by the Radshaw Clinic. Glancing at his watch and knowing he wouldn't receive an answer at this hour, Mason popped the browser on his Galaxy . Within a minute, he found the address and telephone number for the Radshaw Clinic. Three hits down the Google page he also discovered the place closed 18 months ago.

"Great," he tossed the phone to the couch as he took a long sip of the warm amber liquid and began to read.

The scant one-page report stated that Hannah Rice, age 47, suffered from auditory and visual hallucinations. It noted that, although she seemed to enjoy her interactions with people, she was confused, withdrawn, and disconnected from her surroundings. The report further went on to state that her verbal communication skills were nearly non-existent, and the best Hannah could muster under the best of circumstances were usually 'yes' or 'no' answers to the most basic of questions. It went on to say that Hannah often appeared to stare upward at an invisible companion for assistance/advice when she became stuck, scattered, or possibly just bored. Her written skills were also non-existent as, when asked to write, Hannah would only stare at the pen or pencil before her as though she didn't know what they were.

That disturbed Doctor Mason, as he remembered it, Hannah used to love to write and she often passed her little stories or poems around school. Hadn't his mother told him, all those years ago, that she'd been accepted to Brown on a journalism scholarship?

He kept reading the report.

According to it, Hannah had no concept of abstract things or of money and finances. It also noted that 'she still continues to be overly and inappropriately affectionate with those around her'.

Mason glanced over the top of the report to the birth control pack on the table wondering just how 'overly affectionate' Hannah could get and just who might have been sleeping in the bed with her.

The report recommended that Hannah remain in her group home with her father, James Rice, as her guardian, conservator, and trustee. Looking at the signature on the report Mason cringed, it was signed by Kim Hanrahan, PA.

Physician's Assistant.

Whomever Hannah's doctor had been they just couldn't be bothered to examine Hannah or write the report. Not for what the State of Michigan paid anyway.

That shouldn't be the case with Hannah since she had all of that trust fund money meant for her medical care and her personal needs. So why was she sent to a public clinic instead of a private doctor? For that matter, why was she living in a group home when she could afford live-in care in an apartment of her own or, barring, that why wasn't she in an Assisted Living Facility? What did they mean she was 'inappropriately affectionate'? Or that the best she could manage was 'yes' or 'no'? She stood right here in his office this afternoon and said she made him cookies, she asked for something to drink, she said her name, didn't anyone else hear her? OK, it was difficult for her but she did it, she said it.

Maybe she just didn't like to talk to the PA or the group home manager.

Knowing he could put it off no longer, he reached for the phone. On the other end of the line, the phone rang three times before a female voice answered "Hello?"

"Hi, Mom, it's Richard. I really need to talk to you."

58

"Richard," she said softly on the other end of the line, "I know you're calling about Jimmy—"

"Not now, mom. Some other time," Mason wasn't ready to hear about the circumstances of his conception just yet. "Tell me about Hannah."

Claire was at a loss for words. When she saw him pop up on the Caller ID she steeled herself for one of his massive hissy fits and told herself she had it coming. This was totally unexpected. "Hannah? Why?"

"Oh, well, because, Mom, Hannah's the present Daddy Jimmy left me in his will." Mason chirped through gritted teeth.

"What?" She gasped in a whisper. There had been whispers around town that Judge Rice left his only daughter, demented as she was, to the town's most famous hometown boy. She'd gone so far as to call Attorney Lawrence and hint around but he was tight lipped on the matter. In silence, with her head spinning, she listened as her son quickly filled her on his current circumstances and his new sister who'd just become his house guest. When he seemed to have finished she was still in a daze when she muttered, "I don't understand what you want to know."

"Yeah, makes two of us, mother." Mason huffed and took a pull off Mr. J&B. "She's a goddamn mess so just tell me everything. Tell me everything you know about her and the accident."

Cute, precocious, gregarious and all things Sugar and Spice, that was Little Hannah Rice. He remembered the girl in the yellow dress who lived in Victorville with her father, James and her mother Adelaide. Well, until that summer day when Adelaide sat in a running car in the garage with the door closed.

Memories of Hannah's tenth birthday suddenly flooded into his mind with all of their colors intact. He tried to push them away and concentrate on what his mother was telling him. It wouldn't go. It was so strong he could almost feel the light breeze rolling in off Lake Superior as he sat on his living room couch.

It was a beautiful summer day for the grand celebration on the lakeshore. There were bright colorful balloons and a clown, a huge cake, a big cookout and damn near the entire population of Victorville.

Adelaide gave Hannah a golden locket and sunny yellow dress for the occasion. Hannah dashed into the Bath House and changed into it right away. She came sprinting out with a huge smile, hugged her mother tightly, and curtsied for her. She'd been so happy just like a little girl should be, laughing, smiling, giggling, without a care in the world. Not even the cast she had on her arm from falling off her bike the week before dampened her spirit.

Little Hannah Rice laughed and danced in the sun with balloons in her hands and ribbons in her chestnut hair. The memory made his heartache.

The next time he saw Hannah in that sunny yellow dress was at her mother's funeral. When happy, precocious little Hannah Rice was anything but.

After that, Hannah didn't take the dress off very often. She wore it until it was faded and torn. Until it was too short and she had to wear shorts or pants beneath it. She wore it until her body began to change from a girl to a woman and she was known far and wide as 'Hannah the Banana'.

Sitting here in the dark thinking about the woman in the next room a wave of guilt so deep it felt a like tsunami went through him. Poor Hannah, how many years did they taunt her and call her that?

Kids.

Strange things.

They decried conformity, said they wanted to be 'different' that they *were* 'different' when deep down all they really wanted was to be like everyone else and despised the fact that they were.

When one person in the group wasn't like everyone else, say they lost a parent especially due to a very public suicide when all the others still had theirs, then that person became an outcast.

Why?

Not just because Hannah was different but also because she reminded all of them that life wasn't perfect and they (and their parents) were all mortal but Death may not be the worst of all the Fates Life in in store for them. Teenagers didn't like to be reminded of such things.

He wasn't any different at that age he was right there with them calling her names because he thought it was cool. He knew it was wrong but he was the out-of-town kid—the Summer Kid—who desperately wanted to fit in anywhere.

"The accident, it was so long ago, Richard."

"I know." Mason agreed and pulled a fresh bottle of Scotch out from under the couch. "If I'm going to help her I need more information than I have. This is...it's...it's shit!"

Claire knew her son well and he liked to have as much information and details as he could get in order to put his lifesaving puzzles together. It seemed to her that his new sister had just become his latest puzzle. It meant that Hannah was in the most capable medical hands imaginable and the worst ones for compassion and bedside manner. Those were things someone like Hannah needed in her life, "Can't you get the accident report?"

There was an idea. "Maybe, I'll call that lawyer tomorrow and see if he can get me a copy."

"Lawrence? Why would he have it?"

Mason thought for a second before he led, "Because he's probably the one who handled the lawsuit."

"What lawsuit?"

What lawsuit? What did she mean what lawsuit? "Isn't that how Hannah got her money? They sued after the accident?"

"Sued who?" Claire asked as she tried to follow her son. "They never found the other driver, Richard. No one knows who drove her off the road that night. Hannah's money, whatever there is left of it, comes from Adelaide. Her family had money and when she died it all went to Hannah. Only the women inherited in her family, some type of tradition they brought from the Old Country. James Rice received a stipend as her spouse but the bulk of it has been kept in Trust for Hannah."

Yeah, the stipend. Mason was being paid to be his sister's keeper. He took another pull off the bottle. Then several more as his mother continued to speak. He'd have to get in touch with the hospital back in Victorville and get her original records from the accident, if they were still on file after all this time.

"Poor Hannah, you know she just graduated from St. Mark's," Claire said wistfully, "not two months before. She was going to Brown. She won a journalism scholarship. You were already off to the University of Pennsylvania by then."

Yes, he remembered when his mother called him about Hannah's horrible accident. The news was awful, of course, but at the time, he wasn't sure why his mother seemed so upset over it. Hannah was a nice girl to be sure and no one wished her any harm but she was just a girl from town as far as he could see. Yet he did his best to pretend to sympathize with her

"James was so angry," Claire said as the memories came back. "He wanted her to go to school here; he was really fit to be tied over it." She stopped there not wanting to discuss her son's biological father with him for the first time over the phone. "Anyway, Hannah had been dating Frank MacNeill, you remember Frank, his father owned the garage. They went together almost all of her senior year in high school, and everyone expected them to get married. Then she was in that terrible accident."

62

There was a name he hadn't heard since high school, "Frank MacNeill? That grease monkey? Oh I bet Judge Rice loved that."

"Richard, about Jimmy about the will and the trust and, well, everything..."

"Fuck Jimmy!" Mason shot and before he could rein in his tongue, "Oh never mind, you already did that, didn't you?"

On the other end of the line, Claire gasped loudly feeling as though she'd been punched in the gut, "Richard, please...let me explain...that's not..."

"Good night, mom." Mason hung up before she could say anything further.

Three shots later Mason passed out on the leather sofa for the night

Chapter Three

"Look, I said I can't go tonight, all right? Gimme a break already."

Hannah sighed and bit her bottom lip as she listened to Frank telling her he had to help his father in the garage. He couldn't go to the movies with her. She wasn't buying it. "I know you're mad, ok? I'm sorry. I didn't do anything wrong but I'm sorry you're so upset." She said sincerely. "Honestly, Frank, we didn't do anything."

"Yeah. Right." Frank huffed. "Whatever, Han. I gotta go." He hung up.

Frank was still angry over Ricky, Hannah wished she could explain but it was a secret that she wasn't ever to tell. Over the summer, Ricky Mason had come back to Victorville for what would undoubtedly be his last summer visit. He was off to medical school and wouldn't have time to come back here any longer. Hannah didn't know when she'd ever see him again. She understood how Frank got the wrong idea but it wasn't like he'd ever caught her kissing Ricky or even holding hands with him. "To hell with it," she sighed and put the phone back in the cradle. "Be that way. I'll go by myself." Hannah picked up the keys to her little Chevette from her night stand and then grabbed a fuzzy pink sweater. It was nice right now but it was supposed to turn damp and rain later. "I'm going out, Dad." She said as she made her way through the living room, pulling her long sandy hair back into a ponytail.

"Where?"

"I'm going to the movies to see *A Nightmare on Elm Street.*"

"Frank going with you?" He asked as he peered at her from over the top of his newspaper and picked up his ever-present glass of J&B. "You know I don't like that boy."

64

"I know, Daddy." Hannah said and walked over to him. "He's a nice boy, but no, I'm going by myself. He has to help his dad tonight." She gave him a peck on the cheek and felt the reek of alcohol make her eyes sting as it assaulted her nose.

"The boy comes from nothing and he's never going to amount to anything. Mark my words, he's just interested in your money, Hannah ...and...whatever other pleasures you might have to offer him."

Forcing herself to stand still, she thought; *Yes, Daddy I'm a slut, I know. A rich slut but a slut just the same.*

She said, "I'll be home around 10 or so."

Yes, I know you think he's only after my money but what are you after, Daddy? Why did you have the house and all of the bills put in my name after Mama died? Could it be so that my trust fund would pay all of your monthly expenses? I'm sure that couldn't be it, could it, Daddy?

"No later than ten-thirty." Rice sneered as he lit his pipe full of Captain Black tobacco.

"I know, Daddy." Hannah said.

Ten-thirty. She was going to be 18 next week and she still had a ten-thirty curfew when everyone else she knew either stayed out until midnight or had no curfew at all.

"I'll be waiting right here, young lady."

Don't I know it.

"See you then."

On the way to the movie theatre, a light rain broke out and Hannah turned on her wipers. Like the car, they were rather old and not in the best of shape but good enough just the same. Traveling down Winding Road she fished in her purse for the pack of Kools she kept hidden there, pushed the car lighter in, turned up the radio and rolled down the window. Sparking up the cigarette she felt the nicotine rush to her head making it light and fuzzy. That was just the start, Hannah had a baggie in her glove compartment and before she went into the movie—if indeed she even went to the movie!—she'd pull off the road, probably in the Dew Drop Inn parking lot, roll herself a nice joint and relax.

Frank was being such a dick about Ricky, she just couldn't believe it. How he could possibly be jealous of Ricky Mason? Sure, Ricky was smart he was always on the Honor Roll. Now away at college he was always at the top of The Dean's List. He was very handsome but he lacked a lot in the personality department.

Taking a drag off the Kool, Hannah figured that maybe Ricky came upon that honestly, after all their father wasn't exactly going to win any popularity contests. Both of them with that same razor sharp wit that kept you on your toes around them lest you get cut deeply. He was a nice enough guy once you got to know him but getting Ricky Mason to let you in wasn't an easy task. She should know, she'd been trying for the last seven years.

With the radio blaring and a light rain coming in through the open driver's window, she pulled into the parking lot of the Dew Drop Inn. To her it looked like things were getting started in there tonight. She saw Red Martin's car (black '69 Mustang he was restoring) and Jack Bennington's car (beat up old white VW), looked like Betty Andrews was in there too, her red Monte Carlo was out front. Like Frank, they were all two years ahead of her. Hannah graduated high school this past June and wouldn't turn 18 for another week. Not that it mattered, come October 1st they were raising the legal drinking age to 21 but until then, those inside the Dew Drop Inn would drink it up.

Parking in the back of the lot, turning off the lights and the car, Hannah fished the quarter ounce of weed from its hiding place along with a pack of orange Zig-Zags. "Just what the doctor ordered." She proclaimed as she crushed up the weed and then stuffed it into the paper.

Earlier in the day, Hannah and her father had another massive falling over her being accepted to Brown. He was so damn stubborn! She worked her butt off to get that scholarship. He said it was too far away and he didn't want her where he couldn't keep an eye on her. Well, after next week that would change. Hannah would be able to sign the admission papers herself and happily accept the scholarship. Then she'd be off to Rhode Island and far away from Victorville.

She hated the idea of leaving Frank behind but it didn't look as though things were going anywhere there anyway. If he kept digging his heels in over Ricky she didn't know what she'd do. He even wanted her to throw out her scrapbook.

Oh he'd been so angry when he found it tucked away under her bed. Hannah didn't even know what he was doing looking under her bed! She never showed anyone that scrapbook, even her father didn't know it was there, if he did she was sure she'd be in for it then. Oh yes she would. If he found it then he'd know that she knew the secret, she didn't know what her father would do then but it wouldn't be anything good.

Hannah tried to explain to Frank that the scrapbook was harmless, it was just a bunch of old newspaper clippings. Frank said Hannah had a crush on Ricky Mason and if she didn't get him out of her system right quick...it was over. The whole time they argued she just wanted to scream at him; *He's my BROTHER you fucking idiot!*

But she couldn't say that. She must never say that. She promised her mother she would keep the secret safe her whole life.

Hannah reclined the seat back as she lit up the freshly rolled joint, turning the key to the battery position she listened to the radio and the rain as it fell against the windshield. "I'm never going to get out of this town," she sighed and took another toke. "Oh screw that," she told herself as she held the smoke, "yes, I am going to get out of here and away from all of them." Coughing out the smoke, she waved a hand in the air at the cars in front of her, "Away from Dad and Frank and Red and Betty and all of those idiots."

Hannah thought she loved Frank but understood that she was only 17 and she didn't know enough about love to be sure she was in love with Frank. She liked hanging out with him and being around him but maybe he wasn't the right guy for her. How would she know if that was true or not if she never got the hell out of here? If she didn't go other places and meet other people? Rhode Island wasn't that far, it wasn't like she was going to Oxford and her father would have to travel across the goddamn Atlantic Ocean to see her. Brown was a fantastic school, she was lucky to get in at all let alone get a full scholarship for her journalistic talents. Why couldn't he see what a big achievement that was? Why couldn't he support her in this when she'd worked so hard for it?

"What are you talkin' about?" She grumbled to her reflection in the rearview mirror and took another hit off the joint, "he never supports you in anything."

James Rice had been hard enough to live with before her mother died but ever since then it had been nearly impossible. Nothing she did was ever right, it was never good enough—though things were often proclaimed 'good enough' *for* her, nothing *from* her ever qualified—not smart enough—full scholarship? Bah, what did that mean? Nothing. Not to him. Especially since it was from some 'Yankee liberal arts crap-llege'. Brown was an Ivy League School! And they wanted her! Why couldn't he be proud of that? All he cared about was getting drunk, reading his paper, talking gossip about those in town—not caring if any of it was true—including Ricky who he simultaneously praised and tore down for being good but for not being just that much better. He cared about whether or not his dinner was ready ON TIME and his HOUSE WAS CLEAN and his LAUNDRY DONE and his...

"And I'm getting the hell out of here and I'm never coming back." She said to that sad reflection. "I don't care what any of them want. It's my life, it's about what I want. Finally." Raising her eyes to the night sky she proclaimed, "I'm getting out, Mama, do you hear me? I'm getting out!"

Brown would pay the full tuition so long as she kept her grades up, they even offered her dorm space free of charge. All she had to pay for were books and meals, with a part job she could swing that even if he refused to let the Trust pay those expenses. She didn't need her Dear Daddy anymore and it was about time he realized that. By the time she graduated, the trust money would be all hers and she'd do whatever she damn well felt like with it! She wouldn't have her father holding it over her head anymore.

The joint nearly gone, only a small roach left, she dropped it out of the window to the wet gravel parking lot below. Reaching in her purse, she gave herself a good squirt of Obsession to get rid of the pot smell and then popped a stick of gum into her mouth. Just about ready to pull the seat up so she could reapply her lipstick, Hannah heard a familiar sound. From the below the steering wheel she peeked out at the parking lot to see Frank pulling in on his Honda. "You son of a bit--!" She growled. "Working with your dad, yeah...right...you son of..." Hannah put her hand on the door handle so she could let herself out and then give Frank a piece of her mind but Frank was expected.

Betty Andrews came sprinting out of the bar to greet him. She kissed him!

She ran her hands through his hair!

Sitting behind the wheel of her little Chevette, Hannah muttered, "You two-timing little jerk!"

Frank put his arm around Betty's waist then lowered the hand to her round buttocks where it gave it a good squeeze, she squealed as they turned to make their way inside.

"Working in your dad's garage, huh?" Hannah bellowed as she tore out of the car. "What the hell is this?"

"Back off, Hannah." Frank warned, she could tell by looking at him that he was already three sheets to the wind and he hadn't even gone into the bar yet.

"You're drunk," Hannah accused.

"Yeah, and you're stoned. So what?" Frank snapped and then gave Betty's firm hump   another squeeze made her squeal. "Why don't you go find Ricky? I'm sure he'll let you cry on his shoulder."

"Ricky! It's always about Ricky! This is RIDICULOUS! I saw you, you've done more with her in the *last thirty seconds* then I ever even thought of doing with Ricky in the last fifteen years!"

"I got further with her in the *first* thirty seconds then I did with you in SIX MONTHS." Frank shot back.

"That's because she's a slut!" Overhead the first rumbles of thunder were heard as the rain started to fall a little harder. "Every guy in this town's screwed her!" Hannah said as she began to shake. "Including Ricky," she added in a low growl.

Frank looked over at Betty and she raised her eyebrows with a nod of her head. "Yeah? So what?" Betty sniped as she put her around Frank's waist, "Jealous Banana?"

"Of what? You? You're a whore," Hannah spat. How she hated to be called by that old nickname, Hannah the Banana. It was stupid and cruel. It infuriated her. "Oh, no wait, that's right you're a *slut*! At least whores get paid!"

"Look, Han," Frank offered, "A guy can't live on blowjobs forever I think it's time I stepped up."

"Stepped up?" She didn't like having her sex life—what there was of it—called out for public consumption especially not in front of this Jezebel. According to St. Mark's and all of the dogma she'd been taught, Good Catholic Girls waited until they were married to engage in sex. However, outside of St. Mark's and the dogma, all Good Catholic Girls knew that a girl could not expect to leave her boyfriend unsatisfied night after night and not have him go looking for the town trollop at some point. Even though Hannah didn't like doing it, she never left Frank unsatisfied after they'd gone a little too hot and little too heavy . Obviously that was not enough for him. "Fine. You want that slut, fine, you can have her." Hannah yanked on the long silver chain around her neck ripping it and

Frank's high school ring from her body. "I'm done." Throwing the ring off into the distance Hannah angrily walked the distance to her the car, tore open the door, and then threw up chunks of wet gravel as her tires peeled out of the parking lot.

Shaking and nearly devastated Hannah drove through the rain to the movie theatre as she planned but she only sat in the parking lot for the next two hours listening to the radio and the rain and the wind, getting stoned, and thinking about her life. 'Freddy Kruger' would have to wait for another time, she had her own Nightmare on Black Rock Road to deal with, Elm Street's problems would just have to stay on hold. Just another few weeks, she kept telling herself as she smoked, just hold on another few weeks, that's all, Banana, that's all you gotta do, just hang on. She held on this long so what was two or three more weeks? That was nothing. She could do that standing on her head.

Behind her, through the fogged glass she saw the people coming out of the theatre and knew the movie was over. It was time to go home.

"Great," she mumbled, "he's probably plastered and pissed." Going home to Daddy was never any fun. "Just a few more weeks," she encouraged herself. "A few weeks, I'll be out of here, I'll be some place new and different, some place where they don't call me 'Banana' and I'm out from under Daddy's thumb. To hell with Frank MacNeill, if he wants Backseat Betty then he can have her."

Hannah waited until the movie goers had left the parking lot to start the car and waited for the defogger to kick in but it didn't. "Damn it, Daddy! I told you weeks ago to have this thing fixed! This car's a piece of crap anyway." Using her sleeve to clear the fog from the windshield she rolled down the driver's window before pulling out of the parking lot in the pouring rain to make her way down Black Rock Road where she was sure she'd see Frank's bike outside the Dew Drop Inn but not Betty's car. Hannah was sure that Betty would be driving him home tonight on account of the rain. He'd be putting it to her in the backseat long before she dropped him off at his door. "Slut."

Driving down the dark road, wiper blades slapping the sheeting rain away but unable to keep up, radio playing loudly and Hannah taking the last tokes off of her fourth joint of the evening, she rolled up the window most of the way. The rain was coming in too heavily, it was soaking right through her sweater and her Jordache jeans. As a result she had to lean forward often to clear the fog away from the windshield. "Jesus Daddy, I swear, can't you do anything I ask you to?" Still three miles away from the Dew Drop Inn Hannah slowed to a crawl. There were no streetlights on this part of Black Rock Road and with no moon to guide her, the sheeting rain, and fogging windshield, she couldn't see more than a foot in front of her. The little Chevette began to sputter as the engine always did when it got wet. In no mood to deal with a stalled car on such a stormy night, Hannah put her foot on the gas to boost her speed and keep the car from stalling out. "I can't see a damn thing!" She bitched as she reached forward to clear the glass one more time. The roach fell from her fingertips just behind the dashboard bent. "Oh crap." She complained as she fished around for it while keeping one eye on the road. "There is it," fingertips touching the paper she managed to scoop up the roach and bring the last of it to her lips before she pitched it out the cracked window. Turning back to the road ahead she saw headlights coming in her direction. At least she thought they were headlights it was damn hard to tell what anything was out there tonight. The lights went from one side of the road to the other and back again. "What is he? Drunk?" Hannah figured the driver must be coming back from the Dew Drop Inn. Keeping her foot heavy on the gas, she pulled her little car as far over to the right as she could get it and still be sure that she was on the road to give the oncoming drunk a wide berth. It didn't seem that he noticed her kindness as he kept swerving toward her and then away from her and back again. For a moment

Hannah thought she ought to pull over to the side of the road and just let him pass but the car would stall out and she'd never get it started again in this storm. "Get on your own side of the road," she complained to the driver who couldn't hear her. The two cars got closer and she honked her horn. The other driver swerved back to their side of the road and Hannah felt a bit of relief. It didn't last long. The next thing she knew she was blinded by the oncoming lights.

There was the loud grating sound of metal on metal as the drunk plowed into the front driver's side sending Hannah and her little Chevette flying off the slick road and launching it into the air. Hannah had just enough time to scream before the car landed heavily on the left front tire then flipped over and over and over again before it finally collided with a massive oak tree, crumpling the little car's front end like an accordion bringing the tree down on top of the car covering it from view. Her elegant legs snapped and broke like twigs in the storm, the dashboard pinned the steering wheel against her chest and the seatbelt caught halfway around her neck pressing tightly against her throat.

The drunk kept right on driving leaving her behind.

Hannah sat trapped in the car, in the ditch, in the rain for two days praying to God that help would find her before it was too late.

Chapter Four

With stiff joints, a numb yet burning hip, and a foggy head, Mason woke at 6am to the heavenly smell of frying bacon and brewing coffee. Tossing the blanket aside and trying to sit upright he wiped his eyes and saw Hannah puttering around in the kitchen.

He was stunned and amazed to see his small dining table set with every single plate he owned. Although they were crammed unnaturally close, each one was neatly displayed with a fork, knife, and folded paper towel.

Except for one, each plate had exactly four perfectly made pancakes sitting on it. The lone plate was empty. Next to two plates was a steaming cup of coffee with more in the pot. The other plates had glasses full of milk next to them and when she ran out of milk, she used water for the last three place settings. If it had been anyone else, Mason would have been outraged over the waste of food in his cupboards but her behavior fascinated him. "Good morning, Hannah."

Hannah was neatly dressed in her faded clothes with her hair combed she smiled as she motioned for him to come sit at the table. Hannah took her seat only after Mason did and then she made the sign of the cross, put her hands together, bowed her head and began to pray.

Instead of starting the morning with an argument, Mason waited until she was done before reaching for anything on the table even though the smell of fresh coffee and pancakes was making his stomach rumble. "Are we expecting company? Who's coming?"

Smiling and nodding she pointed to the table with all of its chairs and place settings that she worked very hard to find. "Yyy-ou," she pointed to him and then went to his left, "Rrrrr-Red."

74

That was the other plate with a cup of coffee next to it, "Red likes coffee?" He nodded toward one of the steaming cups.

Hannah nodded in answer to his question.

"Say it," he encouraged firmly as he took a seat at the table. "I know you can talk. I just heard you so stop trying to snow me, got it? Talk."

It was difficult, so difficult, but Hannah really wanted to make him happy so she gave it her best effort and stammered, "R-r-r-Red yike cuff-ee." She sat down in front of the empty plate.

"You don't like coffee?" He took a sip of the dark brew and felt himself start to greet the day. Just like the cookies yesterday, the coffee was delicious.

"I-I-I...yike cuff-ee."

"Well then," Mason put the full coffee cup in front of her.

She looked up at him as though she had just been caught with her hand in the cookie jar fifteen minutes before dinner. "N-nah-no, R-r-r-Red," hurriedly she put it back by the plate.

Mason passed his hand in the air around the table hoping to show her the seats were empty, "Red's not coming, remember? Just you and me." He picked up the cup and put it in front of her again. When she tried to move it away for a second time protesting fervently that the cup belonged to Red, Mason moved it back and let it sit next the plate designated for the man. Getting up from the table, he plucked a clean coffee cup from the cabinet and put it in front of her. She stared at the cup but didn't try to put it back, "Who's Red?" Mason took the pot off the burner and filled the cup in front of her.

Hannah's bewildered gaze turned from the steaming cup of dark brew sitting across the table to brother's narrowed eyes. "R-rrr-Red," she said in a definitive voice.

"Got that part," Mason nodded as he resumed his seat and sipped the coffee letting it warm him and raise him. Although he wouldn't admit it, he found it oddly comfortable to sit here sipping his morning coffee at his dining table rather than grabbing it in town on his way into work. That didn't mean she could stay. "Tell me who the others are. Who's that plate for?" He looked over to the nearest plate of pancakes.

Picking up the cup Hannah took a sip and then breathed a deep sigh as she did her best to cooperate, "Ahhn-nee."

"Annie? Annie doesn't like coffee?"

Hannah shook her head and waved her hand over the table gesturing to all of the plates, "No cuff-ee."

No coffee for any of them only Red got coffee. To him it seemed Red must have been very important. Maybe he was the group home manager and he didn't want the others to have coffee because the caffeine might have adverse effects like making the clients alert which would make Red's day much more difficult. "The rest, who are they?"

Although it took her some time and she got frustrated more than once, Hannah went around the table stuttering as she named off all of the people in her group home plate by plate.

Mason counted ten men and two women that included Hannah. Without saying anything, he slid Red's plate of pancakes in front of Hannah as he moved her empty plate to Red's spot. Hannah protested but not with as much vigor as she tried to push it back, "Red's not here, he isn't going to eat them. If you don't eat them, I'll have to throw them out. That would be wasteful. Good Christian girl like you wouldn't want to be wasteful, would she?"

Hannah shook her head but made no move toward the pancakes. "Nah-no. No brayfest."

"Breakfast," he corrected, "What do you mean 'no breakfast'? It's the most important meal of the day. You live here now. You eat breakfast. Go on. Eat."

Hannah just sat there with her hands in her lap.

"Jesus Christ," he muttered and listened to her gasp her disapproval. Letting out a deep exasperated sigh he complained, "Look, what are we going to do with all of those

76

pancakes if you don't eat some of them?" With a grand flourish of his hand, he gestured to all of the full plates and empty seats. "I'm in charge now, remember? Whatever I say goes. Eat your pancakes." He held out the fork and knife to her.

Although she remained confused, Hannah took the fork and ate the pancakes dry until he drizzled syrup all over them. She ate the whole stack and drank the coffee while it was still hot. Mason next to her eating and observing.

First and foremost, the pancakes were awesome just like her cookies and her coffee. Lawrence wasn't kidding when he said Hannah loved to cook. In the early morning light, sitting at his table having a leisurely breakfast Mason understood Hannah cooked for the group home. He would bet she made all three daily meals for every resident along with one or two snacks. "They must have loved you," he grumbled before realizing he'd spoken aloud.

Syrup dripping down the corner of her mouth, Hannah's pretty but hazy eyes widened, she pointed to herself and then crossed her hands across her heart. Hesitantly she pointed to him.

"I love you? No." He shoved another forkful of pancake into his mouth watching her face fall as she dropped the fork onto her plate, "The people who ran the group home. Why pay a cook when you can get a paying resident to do the job for free especially one who doesn't eat because she's too concerned with whether or not everyone else has enough to eat? That's why you don't eat breakfast, isn't it?"

He said it like it was a bad thing to want those you lived with to have enough to eat. Not wanting to disappoint him, Hannah just huffed a sigh and stuffed a forkful of pancakes into her mouth.

After breakfast, Hannah cleaned up the breakfast mess washing each dish and putting it away while Mason showered and dressed for his day. When he was ready to leave, he boxed the rest of the pancakes—two dozen in all—to bring with him. Hannah sat on the couch staring out the window with blank eyes. "Are you just gonna sit there? We gotta go. You're coming to work with me."

Hannah's eyes widened and so did her mouth as she looked up at him wondering what she could do at the clinic. Nothing.

Except.

Hannah folded her arms across her chest as she looked away from him with her chin high in the air and her noggin moving back in forth.

Mason grabbed her upper arm to haul her to her feet, "Oh, yes, it's Examination Day so let's go princess, find your slip-on shoes. We'll take the car today."

II

Just outside his big corner office, Mason stopped at his secretary's desk with Hannah at his side and spoke loudly so that anyone within earshot could clearly hear him, "I suppose you've heard about her. Yep, this is my sister Hannah Rice." Noting he drew the attention of those nearby with his announcement, he pulled a folder from under briefcase and continued in a slightly lower tone as he spoke to Mary his battle-hardened secretary. " I want you to call everyone on this list, you tell them you're calling on my behalf, that I'm Hannah Rice's brother and conservator and doctor...don't forget doctor...you tell them I want all of her medical records. Fax them my court papers if they ask for them. I've already signed all of the releases. Tell them I want the records yesterday." Mason pulled a second file from his brief case. It was thicker and contained all of the papers pertaining to James Rice's Last Will & Testament along with Trust For the Benefit of Johanna Morgan Rice. "This one fax over to my lawyer, I'm sure you have his number."

"He's on speed-dial," Mary chimed.

Unfazed, Mason continued, "Tell him I want a full breakdown of all of that and I want it in English by the end of the day. Think you can handle that?"

"I've been handling you for years, I think I can handle this," Mary snatched the files from his hand with a disapproving frown before turning to the startled woman at his side. "Hello, Hannah, I'm Mary," she held out her hand but the other woman didn't move to take it. "We met yesterday, do you remember?"

Although he was no prince of etiquette, Mason nudged Hannah with his elbow, "Go on, Hannah, don't be rude to the nice secretary. Say 'hello'."

With a furrowed brow, Hannah held her hand over the top of the desk to shake with the woman and then let go with a slight nod.

Doctor Goodspeed walked up behind his boss, "In case you're interested our patient..."

"Is recovering nicely from his bout of salmonella," Mason interrupted. "Doesn't matter we have a new case."

"We do?" Goodspeed uttered. He had been working under Doctor Mason for five agonizing years. This would be the first time Mason brought a case to them instead of the staff begging him to take on a case. "Who?"

Mason shoved Hannah between them, "Have you met my sister the loveable gimp?"

"Doctor Mason!" Mary admonished from behind her desk.

Mason whipped around with a cold stare, "Don't you have some faxing to do?" Leading Hannah away from the outer desk to his office, they walked through the double doors. Goodspeed, Wylds and Steward followed him. "While she's getting the old records we'll be updating them with new information."

"*You're* going to examine her?" Wylds asked in an unsure voice as she looked over at Hannah sitting in one of the chairs at the long table looking bored out of whatever was left of her mind and seemingly staring off into space.

Without even realizing it, all in the room suddenly felt very comfortable talking about Hannah right in front of her. She stared blankly but heard and understood every single word as the four of them began bickering.

Mason protested, "I *am* a *doctor*, why does everyone seem to be forgetting that lately?"

"And she's your sister." Goodspeed added heatedly pointing at Hannah without looking at her.

"Astute observation, what's your point?"

"Other than the creep factor?" Goodspeed asked. "You wouldn't do a medical examination on your mother, would you?"

"If I thought she was sick I would." Mason answered silently enjoying getting the three of them riled.

Goodspeed persisted, "You'd do a *full* medical examination on your own *mother*?" He waited to see if the others would back him up, he could tell by the expressions on their faces that they did but they weren't saying anything. Tossing his hands into the air, he surrendered, "Never mind, you would, yeah *you* would." Dropping his hands back to his sides, he turned to face his boss and appeal to him in another fashion. "If nothing else, you have to answer to the Court with her. They might see you acting as physician, trustee, and guardian as some type of, I dunno, conflict of interest."

Begrudgingly Mason admitted to himself that Goodspeed was right there were many other factors to consider. "Ok, Steward, you do it."

"What? Me?" Steward asked looking at the other two. "Let Wylds do it."

"Why? Because she's a woman?" Mason retorted. "But you're the neurologist and Hannah needs a neurologist, when she needs an endocrinologist I'll let Wylds know. Clear your schedule for the day I want the works. A full neuro-psych exam. Everything."

Not pleased at suddenly having to clear his busy schedule to do a full neurological work up on Hannah but thinking she could be the most interesting case he'd had in a long time, Steward agreed. "All right."

Mason didn't like the tone of Steward's voice so he made himself as clear as possible, "I want the whole nine yards, you got me, including EEG, EKG, MRI, CAT Scan, full body x-rays, a full blood panel and tox screen. Let's see what's going on or not going with her as the case may be." Limping over to the nearest medical cabinet with the aid of his wolf's head cane he pulled a swab from it, opened it, and ran it around in his mouth before capping it and handing off to Stewart, "And a DNA test. Compare it to that, we'll find out if she really is my sister or if this is just some cosmic joke."

Steward, like the rest of them, hadn't been made privy to the way Hannah came into Mason's life but, like the rest, he figured Mason didn't mention Hannah—not even once—because he was ashamed of her. Now, with Mason's DNA sample in his hand, he understood that might not be the case. "Including an—"

"An internal exam! Yes, there I said it!" Mason bitched. "She may be crazy but she's still female, she still gotta get a gander at the hoo-ha and she's on birth control pills. There must be a reason for that other than bilking her estate."

As all of their eyes turned to Hannah openly questioning why she should need birth control pills, Hannah and folded her hands neatly in her lap as she let out a wounded little sigh almost as though she were about to cry.

Mason quietly ordered, "If she gives you any trouble come get me." Pulling a plastic container out of his bag, he threw it down the desk. "If anybody gets hungry, Hannah made yummy pancakes this morning. Enough for the entire group home, you know, the one that doesn't live in my house."

Steward's interest was piqued, "Come on Hannah, come with me," he offered his hand to the woman in the chair and waited.

Mason's voice boomed in the room making his sister jump and her eyes to shift toward him, "You heard the man, Hannah, go with him. You do what I say now I'm in charge. You go. See ya later."

Hannah understood that now that their father was dead Ricky was in charge of her and she was to do what he said was best but that didn't mean she felt easy about it as she slid forward in the chair. With her hands firmly planted on the armrests Hannah pushed herself up to her feet but didn't take the outstretched hand. When the doctor opened the glass door, she followed him through it. From behind, she heard her brother shout out.

"She can talk and flip people off so don't let her fool you."

With a roll of her eyes and her hands balled in to fists as her sides, Hannah followed Doctor Steward down the hall out and out of Ricky's sight.

Wylds couldn't take it any longer, "You know that really isn't any way to treat someone like her."

"You gonna give me a lecture on ethics?" Mason quipped with narrowed eyes. "Or are *you* going to try to teach *me* how to be a good brother?"

Sometimes he could be so smug she just wanted to slap that self-satisfied look off his whiskery face, "Someone should," she uttered and took a step back from his desk. "What about the patient down in—"

"That's where you're going now and you," he directed his attention to Doctor Goodspeed, "Here's a list of group homes and adult care agencies, check 'em out let me know what you find." Mason limped toward the door, "I gotta go see somebody."

Glancing toward Mary on his way out of the office he saw her busily faxing his paperwork as he slowly made his way to the office of his long-time friend Scott Spaulding. Another confirmed bachelor. It had been a hell of a night and an even stranger morning. He needed to discuss it with someone in detail. Someone who would listen. Not believing in the ancient custom of knocking Mason stormed through Spaulding's door and plopped down on his couch with another container of pancakes. He threw them onto the coffee table as he fished a prescription bottle out of his pocket and down his second pill of the morning.

"Good morning to you too, Mason," Spaulding wasn't in any mood with put up with Mason's shenanigans today. "Thanks so much for introducing me to your *sister* yesterday."

Resting his chin on the top of his cane Mason replied an absent tone, "You're the one who scurried out you and Sinclair."

"You tossed us out besides I was too shocked to do much of anything else." Spaulding got up from his chair and crossed his spacious office to stand in front of his friend, "Twenty-five years, Mace, I've known you for twenty-five freakin' years and you never once uttered the words 'I have a sister'? What the hell is with that?"

Mason knew what everyone around was thinking since Hannah walked in yesterday. They thought he never mentioned her not even a single slip of the tongue because he was ashamed of her. "I didn't know," Mason offered staring up at Spaulding with puppy dog eyes, "not until a few months ago. I didn't know a lot of things. I still don't but I will. Steward's with her now he's doing a full work up on her including a DNA test."

"DNA?" Growing concerned, Spaulding sat on the coffee table in front of Mason, "How do you not know you have a sister? Oh, wait, oh my god, your father had an affair?"

Mason's beleaguered face lit up and he let out a hearty laugh, "That's one I hadn't thought of but, no, that's not it." Perched on the edge of the couch with his chin resting on his hands, Mason let the whole story fly from beginning to end without stopping or taking questions.

Letting it all settle in his head Spaulding sifted through the new information until he came to one conclusion, "Your mother didn't have an affair. She's far too sweet and, well, Catholic for anything like that." He hoped that would make his friend feel better after all Spaulding knew all about Mason's tumultuous history with The General and thought Mason should be relieved if not happy to know the man wasn't his father. The last time Spaulding visited the old homestead was for the funeral of one General Edwin Mason where his son, Doctor Richard Mason was anything but grief-stricken. Mason hadn't gone to say a tearful good-bye but to make sure his father was actually dead. Standing over the coffin at the view Mason openly took the corpses pulse!

"Don't bet on it," Mason grumbled. "Then again, I could be the thrown away bastard lovechild Judge James Rice."

"Adopted?" Mason adored his mother. Deep in his heart, Spaulding believed that other than his first wife Barbara, Claire was the only woman Mason ever loved. Claire was one of the very few people Mason even let in to his life and she was one of the elite, one of the few people that Mason felt could be trusted. Mason's Motto was simple: *People Lie.* He believed that with all of his Grinchy heart and Mason often went to great lengths to get to the truth no matter what it was or who didn't like it or what deep dark secrets he dragged into the light of day. People Lie, out of shame or guilt or fear, they lie even when their lives on their line. He applied that logic to everyone with meager exception. It was what made him a superb Exploratory Physician but a terrible companion. If The General wasn't his father that could also mean Claire wasn't his mother. If she wasn't his mother, if she'd lied to him all of these years, and he truly could trust no one when deep in damaged heart that was all Mason wanted then Mason's whole world collapsed in on him.

"Yeah, seems there's a possibility that not even my own mother wanted me. The real one that is."

84

"Claire is still your mother. No matter what happens or what the DNA test reveals she's still the woman who loved and raised you." Staring at Mason it was easy to see the confusion and underlying agony he was feeling. "Look, Mason, even if you are adopted, if James Rice—whoever he is—and his wife were your biological parents, so what? It doesn't change who you are. It doesn't change everything you've accomplished. Or the fact that Claire, your mother, loves you."

"What if Adelaide is my birthmother?" There were more than just trust issues at stake. His sanity could be hanging in the balance and he'd never been the most reasonable person on Earth. "She killed herself and Hannah's half out of her mind since the accident and then there's....me. How do you think that will play out? Doesn't matter I guess, full sister, half-sister, or no sister, we'll know soon enough."

"True you are half-crazy already," Spaulding offered with a grin, "that doesn't mean anything. You could just ask your mother."

"People lie. DNA doesn't."

Spaulding shook his head and bit his tongue. "How long ago was the accident?"

"Thirty years. I talked to the woman who purports to be my mother last night but she didn't say anything about severe head trauma and I got a funny feeling when her medical records start arriving they won't either."

Spaulding was still in shock and he could only imagine how Mason felt, "What are you going to do with her?"

"Do?"

"Yeah, I mean, let's face it, you live alone in that little house, you are the most unsociable person I've ever met, you're crabby, sarcastic, skeptical, and you can barely take care of yourself."

"Awww, stop, you're making me blush," Mason cracked, "I knew I was wonderful but that's a little over the top."

85

"See, that, right there, someone like Hannah doesn't need sarcasm even though you excel at it. She needs a loving, supportive, nurturing environment." Holding out a hand in exasperation Spaulding gestured to his old friend sitting there with his hair a muss, his face never clean shaven but always with a shade of stubble, he word baggy faded nearly ripped blue jeans, sneakers, and a t-shirt that read; F*CK AUTHORITY. He looked more like a vagabond than a world-renowned doctor. "You don't even know what any of those mean."

"I need a loving, supportive, nurturing, environment too, ya know!" The sharpness in his tongue surprised his ears and Mason took it down a notch. "So I take it you think I'm inappropriate too don't worry I've got Goodspeed looking into a list of group homes the Michigan social worker gave me. It isn't like I *want* her staying with me. This isn't the kind of inheritance I dreamed of getting when my father bit the dust." Mason rose too quickly as he fought to keep his temper and his bad hip paid the price making him wince as the pain shot from the hip to his flat ass. Leaning heavily on his cane he looked down at Spaulding, "You'll get to give me your opinion later tonight."

"Oh?" Spaulding rose with him. "Come again?"

For a while, his temper retreated as Mason grinned, "You're babysitting this evening and I've got a special mission for you."

Holding his hand over his heart and feigning shock Spaulding gazed upward, "Thanks so much for asking."

"Awww, shut up, we both know you're not doing anything anyway," Mason shot.

"You always know just where to jab," Spaulding huffed as he stood up. "What is it? What do you want me to do?"

The grin on Mason's aging face widened as his old blue eyes lit up, "Take her grocery shopping. Let her buy whatever she wants and don't try to advise her just take her there and home." Reaching into his front pocket for his wallet, Mason handed Spaulding a one-hundred-dollar bill.

Spaulding took it, looked it, and thought they was probably more money than Mason spent on actual groceries in a month. As far as he knew, Mason's cooking skills were limited to the microwave directions on a box of Stouffers. If he had that much cooking knowledge, that was. No, his old crotchety friend, Mason, preferred bar food and take out. Most of the time what he took out of the bar was a hooker or a lonely woman that he never even called again. "Why? Are you out of food? I see you had enough to make pancakes." He pointed to the plastic container.

"Hannah made pancakes. About fifty of them and they're delicious, by the way ..."

"Fifty?!"

"Yep, if stays with me much longer, between the pancakes and the cookies, I'm gonna need bigger pants." With that, Mason slipped out of Spaulding's office without as much as a 'see ya later'.

Chapter Five

Looking around the examination room with its cold white floor and walls, Hannah sat on the bed in a hospital Johnny not having to wonder why she was there. It certainly wasn't because Ricky or even Doctor Steward wanted to help her. No one wanted to help her; they just wanted her to be good and quiet and to forget about everything except making their meals and turning off the stove.

Other than that, no one cared what she thought, or even *if* she thought. They certainly didn't give a damn about what she wanted. Not even James Rice cared about his wayward daughter so why should his son give a hoot about his sister?

In her foggy mind, she felt confident that the coming examination was probably nothing more than a formality so that Ricky could place her in another group home. While the idea made her sad, silently Hannah hoped he would pick a nice quiet place nearby and that he would come to visit her often. That he wouldn't abandon her the way their father had leaving her in one group home after another never coming to visit not even on her birthday. If Ricky came to visit often then that would be something to look forward to and make her lonely life a little brighter.

"Hannah? I'm over here. Look at me, please." Steward said gently.

Another long sigh as the angry little voice in her head draws her eyes to the floor and tells her; *What's the point?*

"Hannah, is someone talking to you?" To that question, he got a little laugh but nothing else. "Ok, well, let's get the hard part over with first, shall we?" He rummaged in the cabinet and came back with a small plastic cup. "I want you to—"

Hannah grabbed the cup from his hand before he could finish. She slid off the bed and looked around.

To Steward it seemed she knew what he wanted she just didn't know where to go. "Behind that door," he pointed to one of the two doors in the room. "Do you need some help?"

Wrinkling her nose Hannah toddled off to fill the plastic cup with the contents of her bladder. Coming out of the bathroom, she handed it to him.

Most patients handed him (or the nurses) specimen cups that were wet on the outside but not this one. Hannah took a moment to dry it before coming out of the bathroom and he knew that because there were little tufts of lint stuck to it. "Thank you."

Hannah shrugged her shoulders and slowly climbed back up onto the examination table. Steward couldn't help but take in the trouble she had doing that with those legs so badly mangled. The color of the urine was a nice yellow and he was pleased with that. "Now we have to draw some blood...a good amount I'm afraid but I'll be as gentle as I can." Normally he would have her sit in the chair with the plastic arm but Steward did not want Hannah to have to crawl back up onto the examination table afterward. Instead he wrapped the tubing around her arm, told her to make a fist and the slid the butterfly under her skin. Hannah sat there watching vials fill up, some were skinny, and others were fat. By the time the fifth one was nearly fully she looked up at the doctor with a disgusted expression. "Not too many more, I promise," Steward said easily, "Mason insisted on a full panel, he's very picky. He just wants to make sure that you're alright because he cares about you."

"Ha!"

The suddenness of her short but meaningful outburst almost caused him to drop the vial of blood onto the floor. Fumbling to keep it in his grip Steward looked at her with cautious eyes, "Why did you laugh?"

With her arms folded angrily across her chest, Hannah looked down to the floor hearing the haughty voice gleefully telling her; *No one will ever care about you. Not even your* *brother. He even **said** he didn't love you, didn't he? He's just stuck with your stupid ass, that's all.*

Outwardly, all she did was let out a low sigh. She didn't even look up when Steward slid the butterfly stick from under her skin.

"There, all done." He put a bandage on the small round wound. "Wasn't so bad, was it?" With another shrug of her shoulders, it was plain to see that Hannah understood what people were telling her and even what was going on around her. He also understood that she could talk, they had all heard her yesterday, but giving a proper response was another matter. Whether there was something wrong with her vocal chords or her brain or if she just refused to talk was anyone's guess at this point. "Open up, say 'ahhhhh'."

"AHHHHH."

Gently Steward swabbed her mouth for the DNA test Mason wanted. Putting the vials neatly into a sectioned carrying tray he brought them to the door and gave them to the nurse to take down to the lab telling her he wanted the results as soon as possible before going back to Hannah. "Want to draw me a picture?" Steward asked and took a small pad and pen from his coat pocket. Hannah didn't look up her eyes stayed cast to the linoleum so he bent at the knee to get under her stare. "Anything you want. Anything at all." Her eyes shifted to him and seemed to focus but she didn't move to take the pen and pad from him so he tried a different approach. "Hannah, I want you to draw me a picture of something you like."

With hazy eyes, she nearly stared through him as she wondered why he would care about what she liked. Yet he kept holding the items to out to her until he was nearly shoving them in her hands. With a loud huff, Hannah took the items he was offering then turned her back to him so he couldn't see what she was drawing.

"No, face me, please." Steward reached out and turned her around. He wanted to see which hand she was using to draw so he could determine which hemisphere of her brain controlled speech. This would give him a clue as to where to start looking for the cause of this problem as, clearly, it wasn't a problem with her vocal chords. Hannah held the pen in her right hand and the pad in her left, which, for Hannah, meant that the left hemisphere was in control of language. He watched in amazement as Hannah drew what he considered a rather complex picture for someone like her. She drew a large circle then cut it in quarters with four lines and then into eighths with two more lines. At first, he thought she was drawing a pie but then, on each little triangle she drew three little circles. "Pepperoni pizza?" Steward asked as he took the pad back.

The smile grew wider and she gave him the thumbs-up.

"OK, now we're going to do some simple tests." Steward flashed his light in her eyes and watched as the pupils dilated properly then he stood a few feet away from her and asked her follow his finger with her eyes. She watched as he moved it side to side and then down but when it went up her entire head followed it. "No, Hannah, just your eyes, ok?"

One more time. Same result.

She knew his finger was moving in an upward direction but moved her entire head to follow it.

"Like this," he encouraged and rolled his brown eyes as high to the sky as he could raise them. "You try."

Hannah looked up by tilted her head back until she looked like the little cartoon guy in the Reach Toothbrush commercial whose jaw unhinged so his mouth opened like a clamshell to get the back teeth.

"Ok, that's enough; let's take your blood pressure now."

Hannah stuck out her arm while he put the cuff on it, pumped it up, and then frowned.

"Do you feel ok? Do you feel lightheaded? Like you're going to pass out or be sick?"

Staring into space she thought: *I always feel that way.*

"Hannah, I'm over here." Steward said again noting the way she looked off to the left when he asked her something. She brought her eyes back to him. "Your blood pressure is very low," he remarked leafing through the list of medications Mason gave him and seeing the high blood pressure medicine Lisinopril listed. He scratched it off the list before putting the buds of the stethoscope in his ears. "I'm going to listen to your heart and lungs now, all right? Just take a deep breath for me." Hannah breathed in and out as he asked. To his ears, her lungs were crystal clear and her heartbeat normal. "Hop— let me help you down," Steward corrected and held out his hand. Hannah took it and let him help her off the table. "Cold," he pressed his other hand over her icy one and rubbed. "Are they always cold? How about your feet?" Rather than ask her to hop back up on the bed he stooped down to feel her bare feet, which were even colder than her hands. "We'll get you dressed as soon as possible, ok? In the meantime I'll turn up the heat in here a little." After dialing up the thermostat, Steward asked Hannah if she saw the yellow lines on the floor and then asked her to walk them.

Hannah snorted, put her hands on her hips, and pursed her lips.

"I know it's difficult for you but just try, ok? No one's going to be angry if you can't do it." In fact, with those legs he was certain that she couldn't but he would judge her on her attempt. Hannah put one foot on the line and began to walk but she didn't walk, Hannah toddled, moving forward by shifting her legs side to side like a drunk rather than bending her knees—which probably didn't bend so well to begin with—and putting one foot in front of the other. She was careful to keep her foot on the line as she went. "Ok, good enough." Steward announced. It was clear that she saw the line; she knew what it was and what she was supposed to do. "Here's another one you're not going to like, can you stand on one foot and touch your ankle?"

92

Hannah rolled her eyes deeply as if to say; *you have to be kidding me.*

"I know but just—"

"TR-I!" Hannah balled her fists and shook them at her sides as she stuttered loudly, "TR-I, TR-I, TR-I!"

Steward was taken aback by the second outburst but didn't show it, "That's right, just try. No one's going to judge you if you can't do it."

Hannah did her best to plant her weight on one foot and raise the other but those mangled legs just didn't want to comply. Her knees didn't bend and her hips didn't push her legs forward. Trying to keep her feet on the line, she went crashing to the floor of the exam room. "Oooooo," she said and rubbed her sore backside.

"Are you all right?" Steward helped her to her feet. Hannah curled her lip and stuck the tip of her tongue at him. He realized the same thing Mason had, which was that while Hannah might not verbalize well she really had no problem getting her point across when she wanted to. "I'm sorry but I have to ask you to do these things even if I feel you can't...never know, you could surprise me." Steward had her stand straight with her feet shoulder's width apart and judging from the grimace on her face that was about as far as she could spread her legs. "Close your eyes, tilt your head back and---"

Hannah finished the maneuver before he could finish asking. She closed her eyes, tilted her head and touched her nose first with the right hand—no problem—and then the left—she missed the tip of her nose and toddled backward.

"Woops, are you ok?" Steward asked as he came forward and caught her before she could hit the floor. "Why don't you sit down for a few minutes?" He helped her back onto the examination table while he sat at the counter and made meticulous notes thereby putting off the last bits of Hannah's physical examination. "Ok, we're almost done with this part," Steward encouraged warmly. "I'm going to test your reflexes."

93

He pulled the small rubbed hammer from the same pocket that held the pen. Asking her to cross her legs would be cruel so he refrained and instead bent down a bit to tap her knee. "You have to stop swinging your legs for this, ok?"

Hannah looked down to see her legs leisurely swinging back and forth in the air. She tapped the palm of her hand against her forehead and then turned it outward.

The gesture surprised Steward as it looked like American Sign Language for 'didn't know'. "You didn't know you were doing that?" She shook her head then did something equally puzzling.

Hannah made a fist and then used it to make a circle around her heart.

"Sorry? You're..." he repeated the motion, "sorry?" His mouth dropped open just a little bit when she winked at him. Steward wasn't proficient in American Sign Language. It didn't look to him as though Hannah was either but rather that she may have picked up a few signs from some her companions in her group homes. Going back to the task he tapped on her knees and found her response was slow. The muscle tone was nearly non-existent. "You're brother—Doctor Mason—is insisting on this," Steward began, "I'm sorry." He made the sign to go with it. "I'll be very gentle. Can you lie back for me, please?" He pulled the stirrups out from their hiding place tucked so neatly into the exam table. Hannah grunted loudly and shot him a dirty look. "It's not my idea, I swear."

The dark voice near the floor spoke in an eerie whisper: *They're never gentle. They lie. You know what he's going to do. You know it's going to hurt. Don't let him do it.*

Hannah's brow creased as she nodded to the floor then crossed her arms sharply across her chest and made an honest attempt to cross her legs as well. She shifted on the edge of the exam bed, lifted one leg and brought it close to on top of the other as she could.

Steward cringed as he watched her knowing how much that had to hurt. "It won't take long." He coached. "Please?"

94

The gentler voice in her head, the one she knows belongs to God speaks softly calling her eyes to the ceiling and her face to soften: *Ricky would never send you to someone who would hurt you. Let him do this.*

The arms clamped over her chest dropped limply to her side as she threw herself backward onto the exam table. Grabbing the pillow out from under her head she put it over her face and held it there until Doctor Steward finished.

Steward kept his word; he was gentle and did the task with as much expedience as possible. Everything looked normal, although, maybe, there might be some abrasions but if so, they were old, not recent and could have any number of benign explanations from running into something to simply wiping herself too hard. "All done, Hannah, I'm going to take you down for some tests now then we'll come back here, you'll get dressed and we'll spend a little more time together."

Hannah took his arm as he helped her off the table and didn't let go of it. She held onto it as though he were her escort for the evening as they made their way down the hall and then in the elevator. She only let go of him in between tests. Other than that, Hannah complied with most of the tests and the beeping machines and the sticky things stuck on her head and chest. When it came to the MRI, she balked when Steward told her she couldn't have anything metal and needed to let him hold onto her necklace for the time being. Clasping her hand over it as though Doctor Steward meant to steal it and she meant to stop him Hannah turned away. It was only after he swore to God he would give it back to her that she handed it over and watched as he slid it into his side pocket.

No metal, he said no metal.

Hannah grabbed hold of the sleeve of Steward's white coat and yanked on it like an anxious toddler. When she had his attention, she patted her knees furiously and pointed at the machine shaking her head.

95

It took Steward a few seconds but he got the message she was trying to relay. "You have metal knees?"

Hannah nodded and stopped yanking on him.

"It's ok, don't worry, you can still have the MRI," he assured her but inside he felt a little foolish. He should have known that already just by the way she toddled or at least discovered it when he tested her reflexes but his mind was preoccupied with the thought of giving Mason's sister an internal exam. "It won't hurt."

Sitting in the monitoring room Steward watched the MRI come up on the screen. He kept close watch on her brain as the machine did its work. Glancing as the screen there didn't appear to be anything out of the ordinary, certainly nothing in the left hemisphere, which would indicate a speech problem. However, perhaps, there was something on the right, probably the damage done as a result of Hannah's car accident, but further investigation was needed. He wouldn't have a full understanding of Hannah and her condition until all of the results were in.

However, it was easy to see that Hannah was right when it came to her knees. She had two full replacements that were nearly thirty-years old. Even he could see the cartilage was worn away along with the tendon. The only thing holding those old heavy metal knees in place were what remained of the metal pins. Every time she bent her knees or tried to walk metal ground against what was left of the bone. It was no wonder she couldn't bend her knees. Not only were they old and outdated, whoever did the surgery so long ago used the wrong knees. They were far too big for the teenage girl Hannah had been at the time of her accident.

That was the common theme with Hannah when the scan went past her hips to reveal a full replacement on the left side a partial one on the right. Down each leg, from hip to ankle, were the rotting remains of several pins used to put the bone back together. Watching the screen, he hoped Mason was going to enlist Spaulding's help. With major corrective surgery, she might be able to put one foot in front of the other again but it would be a long hard road.

When the MRI was complete, Steward helped her off the table by taking her hand and noticing immediately that it was even colder than it was earlier. Looking down at it, he saw it had a slight blue tinge, so did her toes. "The good news is you can get dressed soon so you'll be warmer." He told her.

Feeling tired she climbed off the table, missed the small step meant to help people and went crashing to the floor. She cried out as she landed squarely on her left knee and then curled up in a ball squirming in pain.

Trying to calm her down, Steward called for a wheelchair as he looked at the knee. It wasn't swelling but it was quite red. "Well, X-Ray was the last stop anyway." He said cheerily and Hannah shook her head with a smile.

Thankfully her knee suffered more insult then injury and a while later Hannah was back in Doctor Steward's office grateful to be back in her clothes. Staring out the window she noticed it was getting cloudy, looked like rain. Hannah hated the rain. The clock on the wall told her it getting on 3pm, she had been at this all day, and it was time for a nap.

"Just a little longer, Hannah," Steward said as he took in her expression and the way she was looking up at no one.

Getting antsy and looking down she heard the cold voice in her head: *Ricky's left you here. He isn't coming back. He's abandoned you to this man who will run endless tests on you until you die!*

"What is it? What are you thinking about?"

She pointed up at the clock.

That prompted a question, "Do you know what time it is?"

Hannah's upper lip curled and she shook her finger toward the clock on the wall.

"Yes, that's the clock and it tells the time. Do you know what time it is? Can you tell me the time?"

Letting out a long puff of air that fluffed the hair hanging over her eyes she knew the answer was 'no'. Hannah told time by the positions of the hands on the clock but could no longer adequately interpret them. For instance, if the big hand was on the 12 and the little hand on the 6 she knew it was dinnertime. If the big hand was on the 12 and the little hand on the 8 she knew her favorite TV show, *Dancing With The Stars*, was coming on. Other than that, time was an abstract concept. Yet, when they came in the big hand had been on the 3 and the little hand on the 9 now the big hand was on the 6 and the little hand was halfway between 12 and 1.

Steward determined she could not tell time but she did use the clock as some sort of reference.

For the next hour, Hannah went through a series of tests designed to determine her mental status. At first, he just sat there making more notes and little check marks; her appearance was good, she was clean and so were her clothes even if they were a bit worn. She had been neat and clean yesterday as well. That told him she had some sense of self and her own well-being. Her behavior overall was compliant though she was growing restless now and any other patient might as well after being at this for the whole day. He noted that Hannah did not like to make eye contact unless he insisted on it. She preferred to look up and to the left or down and to the right giving the appearance that she wasn't paying attention to the person speaking.

Doctor Steward repeatedly asked her to talk to him but she didn't utter a word. Doctor Steward asked her if she could write. Hannah shook her head. He asked if she could read and she wasn't sure. Steward wrote; *shake your head if you can read this* on a piece of paper and put it in front of her.

The letters floated in the air as Hannah moved the paper closer and further, closer and further, from her face in an accordion motion that made her stomach turn.

He decided they would have to settle for pictures and put a sketchpad with colored pencils in front of her. "Do you know where you are?" He asked. "If you do, draw me a picture."

Growing more frustrated Hannah picked up the red pencil with her right hand and drew a square on top of which she placed a triangle. In the middle of the square, she drew a stick figure with a circle on its head and a triangle around its neck. Next to it, she drew a straight line and then a squiggly one over it. Tossing the pencil down she pushed it over to him.

Nope, not the world's best artist and she forgot the wings but that looked like a caduceus to him and the little stick figure wore a stethoscope, the ring on his head was a headlight. She knew she was in the hospital. "Yep." Steward agreed. "I bet you think this is pretty dumb, don't you?"

Hannah grunted and it almost came out "Ah-huh."

"Do you know what day it is?"

Hannah was good at remembering the date because there was a calendar in the kitchen at the group home. While she sat in the Motel 6 waiting for her brother she counted and checked off the days on flimsy motel calendar. Hannah held up all ten fingers, put them down, and then held up five.

"That's right today's the fifteenth." Steward turned to a clean page on the sketchpad and pushed it in front of her, "Draw something that happened today."

Hannah thought about it for a long time. She was growing tired. She knew she had done a lot today she just couldn't remember what exactly it had been. Steward watched her stare blankly at the page.

"Ok, draw me a memory, anything, whatever comes to your head first."

Hannah looked up at him, shrugged her shoulders, and turned back to the page picking up the brown pencil. She drew a half arc and then another one next to it

She colored it in with the brown pencil very careful to stay within the lines she'd drawn. When she finished she put down the brown pencil and picked up the dark green one to make a swirly half circle on top. Behind her Steward recognized it as a tree. She colored the top in just like the bottom, staying

99

within the lines before she colored the bottom the same green to indicate grass. Before he could tell her it was a tree, she started adding in lines with half-diamonds that soon became the stems of flowers. Dotted here and there all over the bottom of the page she drew little blue flowers with squiggly tops akin to that of the tree. Done with the flowers she picked up the black pencil. Laying the tip to the paper, she drew a stick figure in the middle of the page between the top of the tree and the ground. She drew three little dashes behind it running from the tree to the figure.

Steward leaned forward to note the figure was falling.

On the grass below, she drew another stick figure with its arms outstretched as if to catch the person falling from the tree. Above them, she colored the top of the page blue and added a big yellow sun. She put the pencil down and looked at her picture, Steward thought she was done but then she took up the red pencil and added in round red circles on the green tree.

Steward knew they were apples although he didn't know what the entire image stood for. He was uncertain if she were the one falling out of the tree, if she were the one on the ground trying to catch the falling person or if she had just been a witness to the scene. At some point in time—last week, last month, ten years ago—on a bright summer or spring day with flowers all around someone had fallen out of an apple tree. The detail told him this was something that Hannah remembered very well.

Clearly the woman was in there somewhere not too far below the surface, she just couldn't find her way out. Taking his eyes from the page, he looked at her only to find her staring off into space with sad distant eyes. "We're done, Hannah. Let's go find Mason."

Chapter Six

"Geez, it's about time," Mason groused as Steward brought Hannah into his office. She was holding onto his arm and looking tired. "I've got places to go, you know."

"You said you wanted a thorough neuro-psych exam; you know how long they take." Steward offered unapologetically as he noticed Spaulding sitting in the chair in the corner. "I'll get you my findings in the morning." All those tests it was going to take hours for him to sort through all of it and he didn't want to stand here giving a preliminary diagnosis in front of her.

"Good enough, it's been, what? 30 years? Another night won't kill her." Using the cane to push himself up Mason came out from behind his desk. "Hannah, this is Spaulding."

"Hi, Hannah," Spaulding said grinning at her from a boyish face. "It's very nice to meet you." He got up when he saw she was holding out her hand.

"Well now that we've all met let's get going." He ushered everyone out of the office and into the hall where Hannah took his arm as he explained the plan for the evening and the fact that Doctor Spaulding would be staying with Hannah while Mason ran some errands.

The taunting voice in her head called her eyes to the floor as it spoke: *Errands? Yeah, right. He's already found a place to stick you. Just got some paperwork to sign and you'll be off to points unknown. He won't have to deal with you, the family idiot, the big shameful embarrassment any more.*

Letting out a long deep sigh Hannah has a thought that she knows is her own: *I wish Frank were here. I hope he finds me again one day now that father's gone.*

"That ok with you, Hannah?" Mason asked for the second time before she looked in his direction. "Can you hear me?

Earth to Hannah come in please. Is it all right if Spaulding takes you grocery shopping while I go out?"

Hannah pursed her lips as she lightly shrugged her shoulders and let go of Mason's arm. In front of her were the huge picture windows of the emergency room. The clouds that earlier had been gathering and turning the nice day chilly issued forth rain. She rubbed her arms and hugged herself as they walked. Over the top of her head, the two doctors passed a quizzical glance.

"It's settled then," Mason said as they walked through the emergency room to the front doors. Hannah went through the first set and but stopped staunchly at the second set of doors. Mason looked out at the rain with his mother's voice ringing softly in his head. "Spaulding, why don't you go get the car so the lady here doesn't get wet?" He barked.

"Umm...sure." Spaulding was befuddled it wasn't like Mason to show such concern, but he left the two inside while he pulled the car around front.

"Not much in the manners department, is he?" Mason said to her, but Hannah kept her stare on the falling rain. He wondered what she would do if it started to thunder. Out front, Spaulding's car pulled up to the curb. Mason had to tug her along to get her to walk out into the rain. "Come on, it won't kill you." On the curb, Hannah stood by the car as Mason opened the passenger door, but she stepped back from it as she gazed off down the parking lot toward the street and then up at the sky. Mason just knew thoughts of the accident were going through her mind and here he was asking her to get into a car with a man she didn't know from Adam on this rainy night. "Back seat?" He shut the door and opened the one in the rear. "Get in before you catch a chill."

Hannah climbed into the back seat of Spaulding's car and put on her seatbelt as Mason closed the door. He stood there in the rain watching the car depart.

"Hey, Mason! Aww, damn, did I miss her?"

102

Mason turned around to see Steward standing behind him. "What is it?"

"Give this to her, I forgot about it." From his side pocket, he produced a small gold locket. "She didn't want to take it off for the MRI I promised to hold on to it for her." Mason took it from his hand. "You got a second?"

No, he didn't, he was running late already for his appointment with Elysium Care Assisted Living but, "Sure." They stepped back in through the first set of double doors where Steward produced a file from beneath his white lab coat.

"As part of the exam I asked Hannah to draw me a few memories." He shuffled through the papers in his hands and came up with one of her drawings. "At first I asked her to draw me a picture of her favorite food and she drew this," he handed over the rather rudimentary drawing of a pepperoni pizza. "Then I asked her to draw me something that happened today...she couldn't do it."

"That doesn't bode well for her short-term memory, but it does explain the excessive number of pancakes this morning." Mason acknowledged as he looked at the crude pizza. "She's no Van Gogh."

Steward ignored the remark as he plucked another piece of drawing paper from the file. "Then I asked her to draw any memory just the first thing that popped into her head. This is what she drew." He handed over the picture of someone falling out an apple tree. "Do you know what it is? Other than someone falling out of a tree, I mean."

"Yeah," Mason rubbed his stubbly chin and tried to hold back the grin breaking out on his face at the long-ago memory but couldn't quite manage it. "That's me," Mason remarked, "the one falling. The other one with her arms out is Hannah."

One summer when he was 12 or 13, he and Andy Avery had been hiding up in an apple tree, sequestered behind the thick branches they pelted passersby with apples. Hannah had been one those people unlucky enough to enter the field that afternoon. For some reason young Richard Mason got it into his head that it would be more fun to jump from the tree and tackle her then it would be to throw apples at her. He moved to the edge of the limb and waited for the opportune moment but before that happened the branch snapped under his weight and he was falling to the ground right on target. At the last second, Hannah looked up, she saw him falling and, instead of moving out of the way to avoid him hitting her, she put her arms out as though she could catch him safely. She gave it a hell of a shot and certainly broke his fall. Luckily, neither of them was seriously injured.

Steward was puzzled by the distant look in Mason's eyes and the little grin turning up the corners of his mouth, "How old is this memory?"

"Oh," he stopped as the thought hurt his brain, "about forty years, give or take."

"Look at the detail, compare it to this one when I asked her if she knew where she was." He showed Mason the crude drawing of the hospital. "Short-term can't be that bad but it isn't as detailed. There's a lot to go over here and her test results, blood work, MRI, CT Scan, they won't be back until morning. I'll let you know more tomorrow."

"Right," Mason wandered back to the doors. "Hey, Steward." He turned around. "She make a pass at you?"

"Excuse me?"

"Are you deaf? Did she make a pass at you?"

"Why would you even ask me that?"

"I'll take that as a 'no'. Did she talk? Say anything at all?"

"Not really," Steward replied, "she's cognizant, she understands what everyone says and what's going on around her, but she didn't say anything. However," he tapped Mason's arm in a sign of encouragement, "she does seem to know some American Sign Language."

"Great," Mason griped, "I'm fluent in seven languages but that's not one of them."

Mason walked through the doors and into the rain with his notion of Hannah just not wanting to talk to strangers or people she didn't like reaffirmed in his mind. In his car, he noticed he was still holding on to the locket as he reached for the keys in his pocket. He turned it over in his hand to note the engraved cross on the front and the strange dullness of the gold there. Running his finger over it, he felt a very slight indentation almost as though Hannah continually ran her thumb over it like a worry stone when she was nervous, upset, or maybe even frightened. His curiosity engaged Mason opened it to reveal a picture of Adelaide Rice on one side. On the other was a picture of Ricky Mason aged 12. Smiling under the summer sun, he had his arm slung around the shoulders of Hannah Rice in a lemon yellow dress.

It was her 10th birthday.

Opening the car door so that the dome light would come on he took a closer look at it. Near the bottom of the picture of him and Hannah, he could just make out the top of the cast on her arm. Mason clearly remembered Adelaide calling them over to her just before they served the cake and she'd snapped this picture of them. Looking at it now with adult eyes, Mason wondered how he'd missed the resemblance between him and Hannah. She was nearly a carbon copy of him. In his heart he knew what that meant before the DNA test could confirm it for him. They had the same jaw line and cheekbones. She got their mother's eyes and he got their father's nose but other than that, it was clear to see they were related.

Closing the locket and turning it over he read the inscription; *Happy Birthday Hannah. Love Always, Mom.*

"If you loved her so much you wouldn't have sat in that car five days later and killed yourself. Selfish bitch." He snapped the locket closed and shoved it in his pocket before backing out of the parking space.

Chapter Seven

While Spaulding, Mason's oldest and dearest friend, took Hannah grocery shopping Mason drove all the way to Stony Brook to the Elysium Assisted Living Facility. It wasn't on the list Leavenworth gave him rather it had been suggested by Goodspeed after he went over the list and reported it was full of places he wouldn't house a stray dog.

Elysium, as it turned out, was a modern facility on the banks of a small river. On the outside, it looked like a mansion set on top a small rolling hill rather than a place for old folks waiting to get sick enough to move into a nursing home. On the inside, it was filled with brightly colored artwork hanging on neutral colored walls and soft, comfy places to sit and relax when one got winded. Unlike most places of this nature, there was no overt or underlying stench of urine and/or feces. The carpets were new and clean, in fact there didn't seem to be so much as a single speck of dust anywhere. As he took a short tour of the facility, he noticed that everything about the place said seemed to say that it was safe, clean, and friendly. The facility had what passed for a gym considering that mostly those over 70 were using it. It included an indoor pool, if he remembered correctly, and he had every reason to believe he was, Hannah loved to swim. Although the pool was open a few hours a week for 'free swim', mainly it was used for water aerobics classes. Gotta keep the old people moving, Mason thought as he wandered around on his guided tour, the best part of which was the cute little thing taking him around. Her name was Mindy and she was an evening liaison at Elysium— whatever that meant.

There was a large dining/activities room at the center of the facility. As they walked through it, Mindy informed him the Residents had three meals per day in this room, but it was voluntary. Those Residents who could or wanted to cook for themselves had rooms with small kitchens suitable to making small meals for one. If one wanted to eat alone or have something that wasn't on the day's menu that was fine. In addition, the kitchen was open eighteen hours a day and Residents were free to order Room Service at any point during that time.

It was in this large common room that Elysium daily activities for Residents ranging from entertainment such as magic shows and movies to arts and crafts. Again, Hannah's attendance would not be mandatory, but she would be greatly encouraged to join them. The Staff, all seemingly kind and conscientious, would play to Hannah's strengths, whatever they were, they would help her work toward more independence, and a more leisurely style of living then what her group home setting had allowed. They would work on her weaknesses but never emphasize them.

She would have her own little studio apartment completely furnished with all the items she would need but she was welcome to bring in items or furniture of her own if it made her feel more comfortable in what would become her new surroundings. If she qualified, she could even have one with one of those small kitchens. Mason almost laughed at that then reminded himself that he really needed to take her shopping and get Hannah some new clothes.

Most of the exercise activities took place outside in the nice weather on the rolling lawn by the babbling brook. Those activities included yoga and tai chi classes that were available in the early morning and early evening. There were weekly Nature Walks. There was also Bocce ball, croquet, and shuffleboard anytime someone wanted to play. Lastly, there was a tennis court and equine therapy for anyone the staff felt might benefit from such a thing.

As he remembered it, Hannah loved horses. Why shouldn't she? The Rice's didn't own an old and still limping along vegetable farm, they owned a horse farm. Hannah had her own horse; it had been solid black, although sitting here in Elysium deciding Hannah's fate the horse's name escaped him.

The staff appeared competent and assured him that, although they were accustomed to elderly folks, having someone like Hannah around would not be a problem for them. The only real concern expressed by staff and administration was whether Hannah was violent. Mason assured them that she was not even though he wasn't sure at all. She had only been with him a little less than 48 hours but so far, she was the meekest thing he had ever come across.

"You're very lucky, Doctor Mason," the administrator, a woman by the name of Kelly Murphy said to him as they sat in her office going over the admission forms.

"How's that?"

"Normally our waiting list is very long sometimes people wait more than a year for an opening, so your timing is impeccable."

Yeah, old people die all the time, he thought but didn't say. "Great. When can she move in?" This place was better than his one-bedroom ranch and it was definitely better than any of the group homes that Goodspeed checked out for him. From the small amount of research he had been able to do, they discovered that the group homes on Leavenworth's list were overcrowded with waiting lists up to five years if they weren't closed down for neglect. There was one group home in Peekskill, New York that had an opening and would be willing to take her if Doctor Mason could get her to upstate New York in the next 48 hours. After that, they expected the slot would be taken. It looked good and the Internet reported no problems with it other than Peekskill was just too damn far away for him to be able to oversee her care. Elysium was a mere twenty miles from his house.

"When was her last neuro-psych exam?"

"Today."

"Do you have the results with you?"

"No, I'll get them tomorrow."

"Well, in that case, after you get us the report and if everything checks out then I don't see why..." she looked down at the paperwork in front of her, "Hannah," she read and then looked up again, "shouldn't be able to move in and be happy in her new home by the end of the week." She looked down again. "Oh, you forgot to fill out the insurance information." She passed it back to him but Mason pushed it back to her.

"No, I didn't. Hannah doesn't have insurance," he watched her grimace a moment before uttering the words every medical administrator loved to hear; "This will be private pay."

Sure enough, across the desk, Ms. Murphy's green eyes lit up. She hardly ever heard those lovely words 'private pay' anymore. What a refreshing change it would be to have the full price paid monthly rather than having some corporation prorate everything down to the barest dime. Then again, that could be a problem. "We'll need to see financial records in that case. We will also require three months upfront and an immediate deposit of seventeen-hundred dollars into her Resident's Trust Account. Why doesn't Hannah have insurance, Doctor Mason? Is she uninsurable? Has she had too many past incidents or hospitalizations?"

No, you idiot, she's rich, he thought. Again, he bit his tongue and looked off to the side. It was important for Hannah that he not mouth off now. "Uninsurable?" He asked. "I don't know. I'm new to this." Although, in the end, Hannah probably was uninsurable. She couldn't get Medicaid because of her trust fund and it was unlikely that a private insurance carrier would take her due to her plethora of pre-existing conditions. Mason doubted anyone tried to apply for Obamacare on her behalf. That was his job now and he'd get Mary Higgins on it first thing in the morning. "She won't have any trouble making the monthly payments. I'll get you her financial statements; my next stop is my lawyer anyway. What's the seventeen-hundred for?"

"For whatever Hannah might need while she's here. We have an onsite hair salon where the ladies like to gather and

109

gossip. Vendors come in with clothing or books or other assorted items for sale several times a year. While the kitchen is open eighteen hours a day, if any Resident orders more than three meals and two snacks per day they're charged for the extra. We also have scheduled outings." The administrator explained.

"Outings?"

"Yes, Hannah wouldn't have to attend, of course, but if she wanted, she'd be more than welcome. We go into New York City three times a year for shopping and twice more for dinner and a Broadway Play. In the spring, just before tourist season, there's a weekend trip to Cape Cod. In the fall, there is a weekend trip to Sleepy Hollow to view the foliage. Hannah will require her own money for these trips if she's to join us." She said almost off-handedly.

The Legend of Sleepy Hollow.

Suddenly Doctor Richard Mason was no longer sitting in Administrator Murphy's office.

He was fourteen and sitting the auditorium of St. Mark's High School watching a play, *The Legend of Sleepy Hollow.* He couldn't remember who the other players were now, but Hannah Rice had been center stage as 'Katrina Van Tassel' and she had been pretty damn good. Funny, the long-forgotten things the mind could recall on a moment's notice or no notice at all. He remembered the way stage light hit her chestnut hair and how she spoke so clearly even when she whispered the entire audience could hear her.

At the end of the play with teachers, faculty, and parents in attendance (including his mother) Hannah Rice received a standing ovation. She blushed and curtsied as she looked out the crowd for her father.

Standing up there, all of 12, with the whole audience clapping, she tried not to let the disappointment show on her face as she smiled. Other than him, the rest of the people in the crowd probably thought those misty brown eyes of hers were filled with bubbling tears of joy. Not him. Why? Because

110

he looked around for Hannah's father too and came up empty. What had the man been doing that was so important he missed his only daughter's shining moment in the sun?

"Doctor Mason?"

"Humm?" The sharpness in her voice brought his attention back around. "What? I'm sorry I was thinking about a patient."

"That's what I was asking you. Who is Hannah's attending physician?"

"Steward, Doctor Steward, he works with me at The Mountainside Wellness & Research Clinic."

Ms. Murphy leaned forward in her chair and cocked her head to one side, "All right then, once you get all of her affairs in order why don't you come back and sign the paperwork? Say Friday around four?"

Friday. Two days away. He wouldn't even have to have Hannah around for a week.

"Works for me."

Wandering back through the facility to his car he couldn't help but notice all of the wrinkled faces staring back at him. They were all smiling, they seemed happy but then again maybe that was just the Thorazine. Overall, it seemed like it was a good place and Hannah would be happy here. Climbing into his car into the pouring rain, he asked himself if that were true then why did he feel like crap? Why did he feel like he was just shoving her off onto someone else so that he didn't have to deal with her? "Why the hell should I feel guilty?" He grumbled aloud as he started the car and headed for the lawyer's office. "None of this is my fault."

Reaching into his pocket for his cell phone as the first of the lightning streaked across the sky, he called home. "Don't say my name," was the first thing out of his mouth when Spaulding picked up the phone. "How's she doing?"

"At the moment she's sleeping." Spaulding looked down at Hannah curled up in a ball on the couch under a blanket.

"Wake her up."

"What? Mason she's exhausted. I found her schedule on your piano; it says she takes a nap between---"

"I know what it says I'm trying to get her OFF that schedule. Wake her up when I get off the phone."

Spaulding glanced at his watch. The schedule said Hannah would wake on her own around 5:00 and that was only ten minutes from now. If she didn't wake up, then he'd wake her but until then Spaulding would let her sleep.

"I want to get her into a routine and out of that regimented thing that passed for a life." Hannah spent so long in group homes that he felt some her behavior was more of a result of institutionalization than any actual illness or affliction. If he could get her to ease up on that predetermined schedule a little bit, offer her some flexibility, then she might do better when it came to communicating. That seemed to be what the people here at Elysium thought too.

"So how was...the place?"

"'The place'? I thought you said she was sleeping."

"Fine, Elysium. How was it?"

"It's nice, neat, clean, tidy, all the modern amenities."

"Then why don't you sound happier?" Spaulding asked but didn't get a response. Was Mason starting to take an actual liking to his sister? She was definitely a puzzle to him and if Mason had to do one thing in his life it was to solve every puzzle that came his way. That didn't mean he wanted her living with him. No, Mason was a loner from the get-go and he'd probably die that way. Spaulding never understood why the famous (and often times infamous) Doctor Richard Mason found it necessary to push everyone away other than he didn't want to get hurt and be lied to. Hannah was incapable of lying to anyone. That was a point in her favor. Unsure if Hannah was sleeping or faking and deciding not to take a chance, Spaulding walked into Mason's bedroom with the cordless phone in his hand. "I did what you wanted we stopped at the grocery store on our way here." He said shutting the door slightly.

"And?"

Like Steward earlier, Mason was trying to determine if Hannah could read and so he gave Spaulding $100.00 to take her to the grocery store and let her buy whatever she wanted.

"Well, your house is full of food."

"On a hundred bucks?"

"Hannah is a very efficient shopper."

"What'd she buy? Cookies?"

"No, but you've got plenty of ingredients to make cookies now. Meat, vegetables, soups—she seemed fixated on Vegetable Beef for some reason."

Mason smirked and shook his head. "She remembers I like it." That factoid did bode well for her short-term memory.

"Well, you've got plenty of it now." Peeking through the crack in the door to see Hannah still dozing on the couch, Spaulding went on to detail his shopping experience with Hannah. "I did just what you wanted." He started. "I didn't guide her, I didn't influence her, and I just watched her."

When they first pulled into the parking lot, Hannah just sat in backseat staring up at the sign as Spaulding watched her in the rearview mirror to see if she showed any sign of knowing where she was. He did not think Hannah could read the words Shop & Save but she might have recognized the word 'shop' which she would see on any grocery store logo. When he opened his door and got out, she followed him.

Once inside, Spaulding handed her the hundred dollar bill Mason gave him earlier and told her that was what she had to shop with.

Hannah looked at the money in her hand then her eyes wandered around her surroundings for a minute before she stuffed it in her pocket and grabbed a grocery cart.

Hannah began down the produce aisle. Picking up fresh fruits and vegetables, in great quantities. Although he wasn't supposed to interfere in this little experiment, Spaulding quietly whispered to her that she was buying groceries for her and Mason...no one else.

Hannah put three heads of lettuce, two bags of carrots, and two bags of celery back on the shelf. She went back to the cart, pushing it with one hand, she suddenly and quite naturally looped her free arm through his, and they began their shopping trip in earnest.

They began the first aisle, which was the Budget Aisle, several different items on sale that week. Nothing was in any sort of order. She went up the aisle quickly picking up nothing as she went.

The second aisle held cookies, crackers, coffee, creamer, tea, and the like. Hannah stopped in front of the coffee and then just stood there. Spaulding watched and waited until he thought there was something seriously wrong with her. Just before he finally broke down and said her name, Hannah picked up a yellow and blue can of coffee. She put it in the cart. A few steps down and she stopped in front of the non-dairy creamer. Several long moments passed before she picked up a yellow and blue jar of the stuff.

It soon became apparent to him that Hannah could not read. She was shopping by the logos and going through a rather complex process of elimination behind those distant eyes.

To the other shoppers, who weren't paying attention to what was going on, she probably appeared to be just some zoned out scatterbrain standing there lost and confused as she lightly rocked back and forth on her feet.

She wasn't.

Standing there in the aisle, product by product, her mind eliminated all of the logos, colors, and fonts that were not in yellow and blue packaging. Then, when she found the yellow and blue, she looked for the appropriate pictures for what she wanted.

Spaulding didn't know what stores she shopped at in Michigan and doubted there was a Shop and Save there but it didn't take her long to discover that yellow and blue were the Shop n Save store brand packages. Anyone who does a lot of grocery shopping knows that nine out of ten times the store brand is the cheapest. Hannah certainly did.

When they finished their trip, Hannah's cart held nothing but yellow and blue packaging...except for the milk, which she could only get in red. Spaulding deduced she realized that was whole milk and even though he would like to stop her and give her the one with the blue cap he did not.

With the last aisle finished, she headed for the checkout where she carefully put her items on the conveyor belt from heaviest to lightest. Spaulding added the items up in his head and was very surprised to see the final total, which included sales tax and bottle deposits, was $98.52.

He just stood there staring at the total in amazement while the bagger put the groceries back in the cart and the cashier stood there waiting for payment. Hannah handed it over to her. When the cashier gave back the $1.48 in change, Hannah promptly held it out to him.

"Oh, no, that's ok, Hannah you keep it." He said with a smile.

Hannah frowned deeply. She looked at the money. She looked at him with narrowed eyes. Then she grabbed his hand harshly and slapped the change into it with a loud huff.

"I gotta tell ya, Mace, the way she looked at me, for just that one second, it gave me chills. What do you make of it?" Spaulding asked Mason over the phone.

Mason's mind wasn't on any odd expression Hannah made in Spaulding's direction, that wasn't interesting to him right now. What was interesting was the conclusion he reached when she cooked but Spaulding confirmed for him today. "Not only did she do the cooking for the group home, she did the shopping too." They must have loved Hannah at her old group home. From what he was gleaning, she was probably the most capable resident they had, and she was private pay. They got her to work, to cook and to clean and to shop—probably even look after some of the other residents— all while they bilked her estate for an astounding $5,800.00 a

115

month. If you were the Group Home Manager, you couldn't beat that deal with a stick. "I've got one more stop to make; I'll be home in an hour or so. Wake her up." Mason clicked off the line.

III

The last stop was Mason's lawyer, Attorney Londregan, did not have good news for Doctor Mason. "What do you mean the trust won't pay for Elysium?"

"I mean, it won't pay for Hannah to live in an assisted living facility or an apartment or a house or anything of her own. Not even with twenty-four assistance." The lawyer said for the third time. "It will cover her living expenses only if she's in a group home or living with a relative. Her medical expenses are another story; the sky is the limit there. It will pay for anything her physician deems medically necessary."

"What kind of moron would put something like that in the trust this size?" Mason leaned forward with his chin on his cane as he fished in his pocket for his ever-present little amber bottle.

"Her father," the attorney said flatly and flipped through the legal papers concerning the Johannah Morgan Rice Trust—it was 23 pages long. "Originally, when her mother died, everything was left to Hannah in Trust until her eighteenth birthday. At that time, she was to inherit a quarter of the trust with the remainder being given to her when she turned twenty-one. Up until then her father was Trustee and he watched over the money. Hannah's mother died before Hannah became incapacitated and at that time, James Rice added this addendum to the Trust. He must have been trying to look out for her well-being knowing she couldn't be left alone."

No, no, no way. James Rice died less than a year ago and unless he was the world's biggest idiot, he was aware that there were better places for Hannah than group homes. Why would he want to restrict her like this?

116

"So, when he died, he named you..." the lawyer looked down at the pages in front of him and read, "' the most noted and honorable Doctor Richard Mason' as Trustee of the Johannah Morgan Rice Trust."

Creep. He just left Hannah to him as though she were a piece of furniture. "That's right, I'm Trustee, so don't I get the ultimate say on how the money is spent?"

"No," the attorney shook his head, "you're the immediate overseer. All money dispersed through the Trust actually will come through the Lawrence Law Firm in Victorville. You submit the bills, and they pay them. Hannah receives a $100.00 a month in personal spending money; it'll automatically come to you for her."

"Two hundred if she lives with me."

"That's right."

A hundred bucks a month. Big spender, James Rice must have been. That explained why Hannah's clothes were worn and why she could not afford new ones. If she did the cooking, cleaning, and general care taking at the group home, Mason was certain that group home manager was bilking Hannah out of her monthly pittance as well.

"When Hannah dies the Trust will distribute to you."

That got Mason's attention. "Excuse me? Are you saying if she dies, I'm rich? That is what you're saying, isn't it?"

"Every penny goes to you free and clear." Attorney Lawrence agreed. "However, if Hannah is ever restored to capacity, then it all reverts to the original conditions of her mother's trust and the money is Hannah's to do with as she sees fit."

Yeah, like that was likely to happen anytime soon. "So, you're telling me I'm stuck with her."

"Surely you can find a setting for her."

"The nearest group home is two hundred miles from here."

"There's the Burlington Psychiatric—"

"Over my dead body," Mason grumbled loudly. "I'm not going to stick her in a place like that, Hannah doesn't belong there."

"Just temporarily until you ca—"

"No." Mason could not stand the thought of Hannah locked away in a state hospital even if the State of Vermont did proclaim it 'safe'. He knew what kind of lunatics ran around there and she was not one of them. People tied to beds or screaming in straightjackets. People walking around like zombies zoned out of their minds on meds. They'd eat her alive in a place like that. "The Trust will pay her expenses as long as she's living with me, right?"

"As her brother, yes," The attorney reiterated.

"I could get a bigger place to live." He mused aloud.

"The Trust would pay for that."

Well, didn't that just figure? Maybe James Rice wanted to force his closeted lovechild to have to live with her. Why? The man left her in one home or another for the last twenty years, why the hell would he care? He didn't care enough to keep her with him.

"Too bad, I like my house." Yes, he did and he did not intend to leave it. "What about my fifty grand? I can spend that anyway I want, right?" The lawyer nodded. In that case, since he didn't need the money, he could use it to pay for several months of care at Elysium, but he would have to shell out for the rest each year. If he paid for four months or so up front, maybe by the end of that time, a slot would open up in a group home closer than Peekskill, New York. Then what? Then yank her out of her new comfortable modern surroundings with the pool and the horses and dump her back into some shabby group home? That did not seem fair. Even if he bit the bullet and doubled his clinic hours—oh, wouldn't that make Sinclair giddy—he would still have a hard time coming up with the other $75,000.00 a year. Assisted Living wasn't cheap. He could take the twenty-five grand and get her an apartment close by with a live-in assistant that would be easier and cheaper than Elysium.

"I see those wheels turning, Richard, before they really get rolling, I should tell you that if you put her into the community, in an apartment perhaps, and the boys in Victorville find out, Hannah will forfeit the Trust. It will become Null and Void."

"And the money?"

"Don't shoot the messenger," the lawyer began, "it will all go to some horse charity in Victorville. Every dime."

"Guy was a real prick," Mason bitched. He thought his father had been an ass. Well, James Rice was turning out to take the cake on that one, wasn't he? The man had his daughter pigeonholed and he wasn't going to let her go not even in death. Why? Mason didn't get the feeling he was trying to be a good father and look after his daughter but that he was trying to control her. Well, the lawyer was in Michigan, it wasn't likely he was going to be popping by for inspections or anything. Mason could just tell the court that she was living with him. He could get all of the bills in his name instead of hers and do it on the sly. Who would get hurt? Hannah would probably benefit. "What if I deem it medically necessary for her to live at Elysium? They'll have to pay then, right?"

The lawyer moved forward in his chair much like the administrator had done. "Tell me, you're not her attending physician, Richard." Mason just stared at him. "You can't oversee her care. You can't be her Guardian, in charge of making her healthcare decisions and be her attending physician." He began. "Surely you see the problem there, not to mention—"

"If I kill her, I get everything, yea, got it." Mason griped.

"So, who shall I list as her attending physician?"

"On what?"

"You're to report to the Victorville Court within a week of receiving her. You really didn't read any of this, did you?"

119

"I have to go to Victorville?"

"No, you just have to submit a report and list her new attending." He led.

"Damon Steward," Mason said uneasily. "Put that down."

"And he is?"

"A doctor at The Mountainside."

"His position?"

Mason grunted and rolled his blue eyes. "He's a neurologist and he works for me. Is that conflict too?"

"You're playing this awfully close, Richard. If there's even a hint of impropriety when she dies..."

"She isn't dying." He said sternly. "You think I'm after the money?" Mason snorted. "You can bury it with good old Jimmy Rice for all I care."

"And your medical license? What about that? If someone should start to whisper that perhaps you did not take the best care of Hannah, did not take steps or risks that you should have and that you, my friend, are well known. The Medical Review Board should get wind of it, what then?"

"Just put Steward down." Mason pushed himself up on his cane. The damn rain was making his hip ache like a bitch. Soon, if the rain didn't stop, it would turn into a screaming harpy from hell. "Get the report together and I'll sign whatever you want."

"You must have a place for her to live. What will I put down for that?"

Elysium was out for the time being.

No on the group home in Peekskill.

Definitely not in a million years to the Burlington Psychiatric Hospital.

"Give them my address."

Before he went home, Richard Mason made one phone call and one stop. The call to Home Care Angels went well. They would send someone over in the morning to stay with Hannah throughout the day while he went to work.

120

Opening his front door, the intoxicating heavenly scent that his mind recognized as lemon chicken wafted over to greet him and make his stomach rumble. Hannah was cooking. Something else greeted him as well; 'The Joker' by the Steve Miller Band was playing on his stereo. Walking into the small house, he found Spaulding sitting on the couch keeping an eye on Hannah who was busy in the kitchen.

"She's amazing," Spaulding commented. "Look at her. From the taste of the pancakes and the cookies, I thought she used a recipe book but—what? What's so funny?" He asked as he saw Mason grinning at him.

"The fact that you think I own a recipe book."

Hannah cooked as though she had always been in that particular kitchen and she had always made this particular meal. "Hannah?"

At the sound of his voice, she stopped stirring her lemon sauce and turned around.

"I've got something for you." From behind his back, Richard Mason pulled out a large white teddy bear. "You like him?"

Hannah wiped her hands on the dishrag before coming out of the kitchen with a happy grin. She took the bear from him, hugged it, and then wrapped her arms around Mason's neck to give him a big squeeze.

"Mason, that was—" Spaulding shut up when Mason shot him a cold stare. That was downright sweet of you, was what Spaulding was going to say. He sat there with his mouth closed watching brother and sister. Then he thought of something that Mason should see. Hannah woke up about an hour ago, turned on Mason's stereo and began making dinner. When it was on its own she did something he thought was amazing, "Hey, Hannah, would you like to play the piano for your brother?"

Hannah looked back at the dinner bubbling away then went to the piano where she sat down and waited for the next

121

song to come on the radio. Mason went to turn it off, but Spaulding stopped him. He had tried that already, she wouldn't play if the radio wasn't on. After a short commercial break, *Send Her My Love* by Journey came through the speakers. Hannah began to play along note for note. The only thing off about her playing was that she didn't use the foot pedals instead her legs were crossed at the ankles and swinging back and forth in time to the tune. Spaulding nodded at Mason then to the electric guitar in the corner. "Plug it in," he whispered.

Quietly Mason walked behind Hannah, turned on the amp, and plugged in the old Les Paul guitar. He didn't really know the tune but thought he could play along with it just the same since, like everyone else in his age bracket, he'd heard it a thousand times or more. With his head lightly bobbing on his shoulders and his good foot tapping on the floor, Mason waited until the song's refrain to join in. When he hit the strings to pluck out the lead which echoed the words 'send her my love' Hannah turned around, she didn't take her hands off the keys, in fact she kept right on playing up until she realized he intended to finish the song with her. At that point, she took her fingers from the piano to clap a little before they both continued the song. At first, Mason thought it was a quirk, something stuck in that long-term memory of hers. However, the more they played the more feeling Hannah found in the keys and soon they weren't just playing a tune they were jamming.

Spaulding was bopping around as he watched them. If he didn't know better, he would say that Mason almost looked happy.

After going through two tunes on the radio, Hannah returned to the kitchen without warning to finish making the evening meal. She didn't say a single word or make a single gesture through dinner, in fact, sitting there chowing down on the scrumptious meal she made both men might say Hannah

122

looked as though she were winding down, like a watch somebody forgot to wind that morning.

Spaulding insisted on doing the dishes and Mason decided to help him. By the time they returned to the living room Hannah was sound asleep on the couch.

"Been a long day for her," Spaulding remarked.

"Yep, and she made it until 8:45," Mason glanced at his watch, "a whole forty-five minutes past her scheduled beddy-bye time."

"I don't know why you want to get her off this schedule or change her whole life around, hasn't she been through enough?"

"How's she supposed to live her own life that way?"

"Live....good night, Mace." Spaulding patted his old friend on the arm as he made his way out the front door.

Mason pulled the blanket over his sleeping sister and slipped the sneakers from her feet before making his way down the hall for a hot shower and the siren call of his bed.

Chapter Eight

After another 6am wake up call, this time to bacon and eggs made for two along with Morning Prayer, Mason was the first of the Senior Staff in to work.   Stopping by Steward's office, he found what he was hoping for when the bin outside the door was overflowing with manila envelopes containing Hannah's test results. They were just sitting there waiting for Steward to do his job but, undoubtedly, Doctor Steward was still snug in his bed with Mrs. Doctor Steward.

Reaching his office, he was pleasantly surprised to find more envelopes waiting for him each one marked RUSH DELIVERY MEDICAL DOCUMENTS.   He was even more surprised to see they were from Cheboygan General. He didn't think they'd still have her records, but sometimes long shots paid off and when they did, they paid big. Unfortunately, this was no exception.

With a fresh cup of coffee steaming on his desk he knocked down a painkiller and put three sets of Hannah's X-rays up on his lighted board. One set from yesterday, one set from four months after the accident just before she was discharged and the other set taken upon arrival at Cheboygan General after being trapped in a smashed car for two days.

Leaning against his desk studying the images for one of the few times in his life Mason was dumbstruck. If someone asked him his own name at that moment, he wouldn't been able to answer. All he could do was stand there staring at the mangled mess that was Hannah's skeletal structure.

Thirty years ago, the job of putting tiny pieces of broken bones back together wasn't the intricate task it is today. Hannah was paying the price for that little lapse in modern medical technology. From the first two sets of X-Rays, it was clear that, whatever happened with Hannah's accident, she'd taken the brunt of it on the left side.   Hannah suffered compound fractures of the left femur along with the left and left patella and fibular. Her knees nearly exploded from the force of the dashboard impacting with her soft body. It crushed her chest, collapsing the left lung and breaking every rib on that side as she was thrown into the driver's door. The left clavicle and humorous also compounded. Left mandible and maxilla did not compound but they did fracture. Hannah's head hit the driver side window hard enough to leave spider cracks in her skull that probably gave her a nasty concussion. From the X-ray he couldn't tell if it also left her with diminished language capacity.

There were interesting things on the right side as well but to his well-trained eye, it was easy to see that none of them was the result of the car accident. At some point, the metacarpals in her right hand were crushed. Her right arm had been broken and he remembered the birthday party, the cast, and the story of Hannah falling off her bike. It was a lie. That wasn't an impact fracture of her radius and ulna. Those were stress fractures of the spiral variety and those only occurred when someone twisted another's arm up behind their back with so much force that the bones broke. Hannah didn't fall off her bike someone broke her arm. The last interesting thing to catch Doctor Mason's attention was her left foot, which had somehow escaped injury during the accident along with most of the left side of her body. That right foot and those busted metatarsals, four of them half between there and the sesamoids. Did that look like a U pattern hiding there in those fractured bones? Like someone had repeatedly stomped on her foot.

Then there was her head above the jaw. There was a fracture in the skull from the accident but there was another one on the right side. These breaks and fractures remodeled by the time of the accident with the broken arm being the only one tended by an actual physician. It seemed to him the other breaks were left to mend on their own. Mason picked up his cane and held the handle up to the X-ray near the right

125

side of Hannah's head. "Perfect match," he mumbled in disgust, "you bastard."

They say that Every Picture Tells A Story and Mason didn't like the one forming in the back of his head, so he thought he'd make it a bit more concrete by drawing on the Differential Board. He started with a crude image of a pyramid.

"What are you doing here so early?" Steward walked up to the lighted X-rays. "Are those Hannah's? I'm supposed to get those first."

"Yes, these are Hannahs', and you would have gotten them first if you'd been here to do your job."

"It's only 9 o'clock." Steward said as he sat down. "For your information, I've been here since 7:30 getting my report ready for you."

"Great." Mason said brightly. "Save it until the others get here." Then he turned back to the dry-erase board. "I think he was drunk."

"Who?"

"The guy who put the pieces back together," Mason hitched his thumb toward the X-rays on the lighted board.

Steward nodded, "Yeah, not the most talented surgeon but, hey, the good news is he's probably dead by now."

"You're a real silver lining kind of guy, you know that?"

Steward's pudgy but handsome face broke out in a genuine smile, "I learned from the best."

"What have you got for me?" Mason snapped.

Steward thought he'd start with the most innocuous fact, "Did you know she dyes her hair?"

That wasn't something Mason expected to hear, and he shook his head hard as if to clear his ears of water after swimming, "What? She got a lousy hundred bucks a month to spend however she wanted, are you telling me she spent it at the beauty parlor?"

126

Steward pursed his lips, he wasn't an expert in hair coloring but that wasn't his line of thinking, "No, more like she bought a home kit and probably someone helped her with it. Maybe the group home manager or someone else who worked there..."

Behind them Goodspeed and Wylds walked in to say their good mornings.

"Yeah, yeah, yeah, it's a lovely day." Mason grumbled looking at the happy couple who'd said their 'I dos' just last spring. "Sit down."

"Where's Hannah?"

"Home with the babysitter I can't drag her everywhere besides, we don't want her sitting in on this differential."

"What's with the pyramid?" Goodspeed asked. "What's all of this?" He started picking up the amber bottles on the table, all of them had Hannah's name on them.

"That's what I said." Steward said as they watched their boss continue to write. "3.5 what?"

Mason stepped away from the white board. "Ok, everybody ready to play 3.5 Million Dollar Pyramid?"

"Excuse me?" Wylds asked taking a sip off her morning coffee. "3.5 million?" She noticed letters on either side of the pyramid. "BSS? What's that? What's SF?"

"Baby Sister's Symptoms and Steward's Findings," Mason explained. "See we start at the bottom by eliminating everything Steward's about to tell us isn't wrong with her and we work out way up to the 3.5-million-dollar question...that's little triangle on the top...where we hope to hell we have the 3.5 million dollar answer. Cuz that's what Baby Sister gets when we restore her to capacity. So....Steward you're up, come have a seat in the winner's circle!"

"Wait," Steward interjected. "You didn't say anything about restoring her to capacity. I don't even know if that's possible at this point."

"Why not?" His eyes scanned the room jumping from place to place and person to person.

Goodspeed leaned forward. "How many cups of coffee have you had?"

"Don't know, why?"

"Are you on something?" Wylds asked lightly and scanned the line of pill bottles.

"Nothing more than usual," Mason cracked. "C'mon, c'mon, we don't have all day here, people."

"I haven't even told you what's wrong with her yet." Steward complained. "What is the hurry?"

"Anyone ever see that really overly cute and sort of annoying video with Will Ferrell and the baby?" Mason asked. "The one where the baby wants her rent or so she'll throw him out?"

"Yeah," Goodspeed said apprehensively. "What of it?"

"Well, Hannah can't go to Elysium...."

Goodspeed was visibly upset at the news. He'd spent hours researching nearby facilities for Hannah yesterday and he knew Elysium had an opening. "WHAT? Why not? Look, it's a wonderful place, they have kind competent..."

Mason cut him off. "Staff, lovely grounds, horses, a pool, and Hannah can't live there. The 3.5-million-dollar pyramid won't pay for her to live anywhere other than in a private or state-run group home. Oh yeah, she can also live with a relative and that would be...me. Sooo....since there aren't any decent group homes we either restore her to capacity or she lives with me for the rest of her life." That a lot of low grumbling greeted that idea along with disapproving skeptical faces. "Yeah, nobody wants that." He stumbled over to the board. "Now, does anyone have any ideas?"

"Let's start with what's not wrong with her." Steward began and opened the folder he brought with him.

"Wait, these came over yesterday, last night and some by FedEx this morning." Mason hobbled over to his desk and came back with a heft stack of papers. "Some for you," he dropped a third of the stack in front of Wylds, "some of you," another third in front of Goodspeed, "don't wanna leave out

128

the black guy, somebody might cry 'racism' or something so here's yours." He dropped the last stack in front of Steward.

Nobody fully understood what was going on, but it was clear that Hannah Rice was now their newest patient. Goodspeed spoke up." Is Sinclair ok with this?"

"Why wouldn't she be?"

"Just asking, I mean, you know, Sinclair doesn't like it when you start doing your own thing on clinic time."

"My time? No, it's our time now and Hannah's on the books, so cheer up, Steward, she's private pay. That bill you're going to submit for the neuro-psych exam and all those tests will be paid in cash and in full, no deductions. You did run tests, didn't you?"

"Hey," Steward said with a smile, "I figured you'd want me to run every expensive test we have so I did."

"Good man." Mason stood at the board again. "Let's start playing the elimination round." He pointed to the pills on the table. "Are any of these medications unnecessary according your expensive tests?"

"Almost all of them," Steward opened the folder.

"This is for you." Mason put a list of Hannah's medications in front of Wylds without explanation. "I'm listening." He said to Steward.

"Well, ok, for one, her blood pressure is low, very low..."

"You, cross high blood pressure and the pills off the list." Mason barked at Wylds. "You, throw them out." He said to Goodspeed. "See how this is going to go?"

"Got it." Wylds crossed off Lopressor and Vasotec from the list. Goodspeed tossed the bottles into the trash.

"All right, now that we know the rules, would you like to let me talk?" Steward inquired. "Maybe somewhere in all of...that," he pointed to the folders in front of each of them, "you can find a reason she was put on them, but I can't. Do you know if congestive heart failure runs in th—her—family?"

"OK, she's my sister," Mason said glibly, "I even put it on the board...see?" He pointed to where the initials BSS were written and underlined them as he spoke again, "Baby Sister."

Steward swallowed as he fished through his findings and brought back the test he knew Mason was most interested in, "Yes, she is your sister, your full-blood sister." He handed over the preliminary findings of the DNA test.

Mason didn't even look at it; he just tossed it to the table in the Conference Room. Family Matters could wait right now there was a puzzle to solve. "I'm fine with it, really. So, it is ok to say 'our family' when asking for the medical history and no, as far as I know, our dearly departed father, James Rice didn't have heart problems. Her mother didn't live long enough to find out." That wasn't very good and if some patient tried to feed him that, he would be off digging into their background. Begrudgingly he added, "I'll get in touch with my mother and see if she knows more." He said slowly and watched them all stare up at him from just the tops of their eyes before lowering them once more. This was going to be fun. Now that their long-held suspicions of their boss being a bastard—in the metaphorical sense if not the literal-were confirmed, they thought they were going to torture him about it for a while. Mason wasn't going to give them that chance.

Looking at the faces of his immediate staff, he realized they heard what he said but hadn't meant to say. His little Freudian Slip as he referred to Rice as their father but separated their mothers. He'd have to work on that even though he lacked the desire. Mason cleared his throat before he spoke again. "By the way, Steward, you'll be listed as Hannahs' attending physician in my report to the Victorville Court."

Everyone at the table had the exact same thought. Mason? Giving up control? Over his own sister's case? No way. It was Steward who spoke, "You're not going to be in charge of her case? I thought you just wanted me to do the exam."

"Yeah, well, turns out there *are* conflicts of interest being brother, guardian, healthcare representative, trustee, possible beneficiary, AND doctor. Who knew?" He shrugged his shoulders trying to make light of the situation, but the truth was, "My lawyer insisted."

"Ok," Steward agreed thinking that being Hannah's attending physician would mean he had a little sway over Mason. One could always use a little something up their sleeve in that department. "So long as you remember you're consulting. I should make you sit out there and be just another family member." He pointed to the hall beyond the glass wall.

"Umm, yeah, got it." Mason mumbled. "But since this is my office and I'm third owner of this place and well, you're not... I don't think I'm going out there," he pointed to the hall. A more serious thought struck him as he brought his gaze back to Steward. "Did you find something wrong with her heart?"

"No, as far as my expensive tests could see, it's fine but I'd like to get her in here for a stress test to be sure and since you're paying..." his voice trailed off with a smile.

Mason interrupted him, "I'm a generous guy, I'm gonna spread the dough around. Goodspeed, the cardiologist, will administer the stress test and any other big expensive tests he deems necessary."

Goodspeed glanced at his wife, Doctor Wylds, and they just passed a silent stare of WTF between them. Working with Mason wasn't a joy, it was always challenging and never dull but not joy filled. Both could only imagine what the Good Doctor in Charge was going to be like when he wasn't in charge. Trying to ease into his new place as Hannahs' cardiologist, Goodspeed spoke cautiously, "There are other uses for these medications. The Lopressor could have been prescribed because she was having unexplained chest pain."

"If that's the case then it's your job to explain them. However, Vasotec wouldn't be prescribed for that." Black dry-erase marker in hand Mason turned back to Steward. "Continue, what else can we get rid of?"

131

"The Coumadin is really hurting her circulation, have you noticed how cold her hands are? Not to mention her INR was only .95, she's hardly getting enough blood flow to keep herself warm. Whatever you do, don't let her near a knife with that level if she gets a paper cut it could kill her. It'll never stop bleeding."

As Mason recalled there had been a good deal of pink in the sink yesterday and today after Hannah brushed her teeth.

"Here," Goodspeed said and turned the folder around, "look, in 1998 Hannah had a blood clot in her left arm. That's when the Coumadin was prescribed."

Mason stopped writing on his board, "Ninety-eight? She's been taking that shit for over twenty years. What idiot keeps a patient on Coumadin for twenty-years with an INR that low?"

The faxed copies were blurry, and Goodspeed struggled to make out the name, "Doctor...doctor, I can hardly read this at all, Doctor Hansen?" He pointed to the name. "He prescribed the Coumadin and the Lopressor. He's at the---" Goodspeed didn't want to finish.

"At the what?"

"Victorville Free Clinic."

Mason hung his head. "Alrighty then," he swallowed hard and bite back his anger. Hannah could afford the best care in the world but that bastard Rice wouldn't let her have it. What was the point? Trying to focus on the 3.5 Million Dollar Pyramid he let out a puff of air, "Let's keep going. Don't suppose it notes she may have already been on the Vasotec?"

"No, sorry." Goodspeed said and reached for his coffee before grabbing the bottle of Coumadin and tossing it in the trash while Wylds crossed it off the list.

"She doesn't have arthritis. I don't what the Celebrex is for. Did you find anything on colon polyps or heavy menstrual cramps?" Steward asked Goodspeed and Wylds.

"Maybe it was her knees." Mason suggested. "They're pretty bad."

"Yeah, they are." Steward agreed and put up the X-Rays he'd had done yesterday next to the ones already on the board. There was noticeable deterioration in the bone structure and ligaments. "You should call Spaulding in on this, you know, while you're throwing money around and all. I think he can replace those old knees. It won't be a perfect solution considering the condition the rest of her legs are in, but it would give her much greater mobility."

With clotting scores that low, for Hannah surgery was off in the distance nine months to a year. Still, the news was better than he had anticipated. "Good. The 3.5 Million Dollar Pyramid there won't pay for her to live wherever might be best but anything that, well, all Steward here has to do is deems medically necessary is a go."

The Celebrex hit the wastebasket and was crossed off the list.

"Throw out the cholesterol meds too," Steward said. "Her HDL is only 38, probably from the other meds; they help inhibit good cholesterol as well. Her DL is only 170. So again, I don't know why they put her on it."

Goodspeed and Wylds scanned. "Doctor Hansen again," Wylds said, "prescribed it in 1996; at that time, it says her HDL was 43."

"Hardly enough to warrant that kind of medication when diet and exercise would have been just fine," Mason remarked as he began to wonder how Hannah survived in the State Run Medical System all these years.

Another bottle in the trash and crossed off the list.

"You can probably ditch the kidney pills too; again tests were low, too low."

"Didn't this guy get anything right?" Mason asked.

"One thing," Steward said, "she does have an ulcer."

"Is that any wonder?" Mason huffed. "How bad?"

"It's pretty advanced."

"She hardly eats anything."

"There's your cause, she doesn't eat, and the stomach acids have no job to do so they just sit around eating her stomach lining. That, the stress she's under, it must be so damn frustrating to be her, not to mention the blood thinners and meds, they're not letting enough blood flow get to the stomach lining so it can renew itself. Or any other part of the body for that matter, her blood's closer to the consistency of water thanks to all that...stuff." Steward pointed to the filling trashcan.

"Frustrating?" Mason asked. "You said it must be frustrating to be Hannah, why?"

"Clearly the woman knows what's going on around her, she's completely cognitive, Mason but she does have long-term brain damage, it's mild but irreversible. Hitting her head, the collapsed lung, and the seat belt clenched around her throat didn't add up to a good combination. I think all of that is what's affecting her ability to talk."

That added up to everything Mason was already thinking, and he was glad they were on the same track. "What else? What about the crack on the other side of her skull?"

Steward looked down at his notes knowing the injury did not come from the accident he found it hard to look at his boss as he spoke, "I think it's affected her visual memory. Hannah doesn't always see what's in front of her."

"Visual hallucinations," Mason echoed the PA's report.

Steward disagreed, "Not exactly, more like, like, a time warp in her head. Sometimes things get all jumbled and, while she might be able to know *where* she is, she might not be able to know *when* she is. If it's today or ten years ago doesn't always register with her."

"Her attentions span is about that of a gnat." Mason returned.

Steward knew that this was something Mason didn't want to hear. He also knew that there were going to be a lot of those things coming this was just the start. "I think she hears voices."

134

Mason's jaw tightened and his lips barely moved as he spoke, "She's schitzo."

"I didn't say that. If she were schizophrenic, would she have drawn a picture like this?" Steward produced the drawing of a young Richard Mason falling out of the tree. "Look at it, schizophrenics use bright bold colors, she's used almost all pastels and she used them appropriately, the sky is blue, the grass is green, the flowers are yellow and purple. If a schizophrenic drew it, the sky might be orange and the grass red. Haven't you watched her?"

"Intently."

"So, you've seen her, the way she tilts her head up and to the right or down and to the left when you talk to her. She seems to look past you if she looks at you at all."

"Yeah, it's annoying, she never looks at me." Standing there scowling Mason thought, that's not true either, she looked me dead in the eye right before she kissed me this morning.

"That's because the voices have her attention."

"That doesn't mean she's schizophrenic," Goodspeed added, "It could be a result of her accident or it could be something affecting her audiology sensors."

"Or the fact that her brain isn't getting enough blood flow." Mason offered staring at the wastebasket filling up with unnecessary medications.

"Her whole body isn't," Steward interjected, "My bet is the voices she's hearing are her own she just doesn't recognize them as such. So, watch her, watch for the signals if she looks up and to the right the voice is her higher brain function, positive thoughts. If she looks down and to the left, the voice is her lower brain function, negative thoughts." He explained and then tried to sound encouraging. "I think we'll see a marked improvement in a few weeks just from taking her off the unnecessary meds and getting her onto a healthy diet. The woman is deficient in every single nutrient most notably calcium and vitamin K both of which are probably adding her to state of confusion. What about pain? How much pain meds are you giving her?"

Everyone waited for an answer to that one. If there was one person in the world who would sympathize with Hannah and the amount of pain she was most likely in, it was Mason. "Why is everyone looking at me like that? Do you think I'm over medicating her?"

Sitting back in the chair Goodspeed answered for the group who'd been working with Doctor Mason so long, "We think that maybe you don't know where the line is. Maybe it's a little blurry for you."

Mason looked down at his bad hip knowing he took too many pills, but it never affected his judgment or his ability as a physician. Insofar as he was concerned, it did wonders for both even though others might heatedly disagree. "So she takes her pain meds according to the directions on the bottle. I give her one Oxycodone every six hours."

"She doesn't ask or indicate that she'd like more?" Steward asked.

"Not so far."

"Well then maybe like the other meds, Hannah doesn't really need them." Goodspeed suggested. "Maybe she just takes them for the buzz or because people keep giving them to her."

"The buzz? Was that a snipe at me?" Mason asked.

"You are related." Goodspeed reminded him.

"Have you seen her legs? There's no way they don't ache like a bitch." Mason insisted having firsthand knowledge. He threw open a file folder and tossed X-rays and MRI images onto the table. "Look at those. Look at the butcher job they did putting her back together like Frankenstein's Monster and tell me that doesn't hurt 24/7."

No one at the table could disagree and so they all held their tongues.

Behind them, Spaulding walked into the office. "Mason, I got a message saying to be here at 10 for a consult? What's going on?"

"Tell them about your shopping trip with Hannah." Mason told him. "Go on they're waiting."

In a bit of a state of confusion himself, Spaulding sat down and relayed the details of his trip to the grocery store with Hannah. Mason pulled out the very first folder he had been given on Hannah Rice. "According to this, Hannah has no concept of money or financial affairs but obviously that's not true either."

"No, it isn't." Spaulding agreed. "She knew how much money she could spend. She must have added the items up in her head, and she didn't go over the amount."

"So she can add but she can't read. That's interesting." Steward remarked. "Any other interesting abilities or quirks?"

"She cooks, she plays piano," Spaulding said, "but only with the radio on."

"She mimics the tune on the radio." Steward echoed. "Is it any song or..."

"Eighties music," Mason interjected. "That golden age of classic techno-crap." Hannah turned the radio on this morning as she made breakfast and she tuned the dial until she found music that was familiar to her stopping on 'Da ya think I'm sexy?' by Rod Stewart.

"Funny, I don't remember you being quite so crabby when the two of you were jamming together last night." Spaulding said as he crossed his arms over his chest.

It was just past eleven o'clock, they had been at this for two hours, and Mason felt a massive headache coming on. Still, there was one more thing he had to know. "Is she a virgin?"

"Mason!" Wylds admonished.

"Well, is she?" Mason asked Steward ignoring Wylds and her thinking he was rude.

"No," Steward said softly and shook his head. "This brings me to my last bit to report," he sighed. "Do you want me to say it in front of everyone?"

"We're all working on this, go for it." Mason fished in his pocket and popped an Oxy.

Steward rummaged in his folder and produced a slip of paper along with another X-Ray that he put on the board. "Uterine polyps?" Mason asked before Steward could begin his explanation. "Not all that uncommon in a woman her age."

"Look closer," Steward advised. "Look below the polyps."

Leaning on the cane Mason stood up and went over to the board.

"Do you see it?"

"See what? What am I looking fo—oh my g—are you kidding me? Is that real? This is a joke, right?"

"Congratulations, Mason, you're an uncle." Steward informed him.

"Family's getting bigger by the day." Mason chimed. "Where's the kid?"

"Don't ask me," Steward held his hands up. "Those scars are old; she gave birth maybe twenty-five or thirty years ago."

The rest of the team got up and came over for a closer look. "Are those..." Wylds asked pointing to the X-Ray.

"Yeah," Steward said, "you can take her off the birth control, Mason, Hannah's sterile probably the result of a botched abortion. Not to mention the fact she's well into menopause." He pointed from her cervix to the uterus and their eyes followed a long jagged line. "Doctor Hansen?" Steward offered.

"Anything else you have to tell me? Anything else I'm not going to like?" Mason grumbled and pulled back when Steward came in close as though he were about to whisper in Mason's ear. "Tell all of us damnit, we're all doctors here."

"Ok," Steward agreed, "but you're right; you're not going to like it. Baby Sister's got Gonorrhea."

Although outwardly he tried hard not to show it, Mason felt his stomach turn. "How advanced?"

Steward shook his head. "It's recent."

"How recent?" Mason inquired gruffly.   He wanted another pill but didn't want to suffer the stares of his colleagues for doing so soon after the other one they watched him take. That didn't count the one he downed on his way in or the one he swallowed just before Steward walked through the door this morning. Best to wait until they left, then he might have two. "Within the last, oh say, six to eight months recent?"

Goodspeed looked up at him with his mouth half open. "Six to eight months? You think her—your—father gave it to her? That's disgusting."

"Well, when you stop and think about it," Mason said smugly, "there isn't much about the clap that's actually attractive now is there? Well," he tossed his head, "contracting it can be fun but other than that—"

"It's very recent." Steward interjected. "Like within the last month recent. Completely treatable, it hasn't gone far at all." Those abrasions he found on her were not from running into anything or wiping herself too hard. They were from forced entry but, for the time being, he decided to keep that information to himself knowing Mason would surmise it on his own.

Standing there starring at the X-Rays the only thought that echoed in Richard Mason's mind was that the Gonorrhea hadn't come from James Rice but those broken bones sure as hell did. The baby? What happened to Hannah's baby? Where was his niece or nephew? Suddenly he felt a small warm hand on his back—Wylds—and another on his shoulder--Spaulding. He looked around at the concerned faces starring back at him. "While your concern is touching—and for once I actually mean that—don't worry about me," he grumbled, "worry about her. Go on, don't you have patients to see? Get outta here."

"Mason—" Wylds began.

"I'm fine...go do some research; bring me back some answers other than dumping those meds and changing her diet."

Picking up their items to leave the office no one argued with him.

Pulling the shades on his glass doors, Richard Mason helped himself to two extra Oxies. Looking around to be sure no one was standing on the other side of the glass, he turned on the computer on his desk. "This should be interesting." He said to himself and cracked his knuckles by lacing his fingers together and bending them outward. "What are you up to today, my dear?" He leaned in close to the screen.

"Mason, I thought—"

Spaulding was coming through the door, Mason glanced at the screen, and up at the good doctor with pursed lips.

"Internet porn at this hour of the morning? After that differential?" He waved a hand in the air to where files, papers, MRIs and other assorted goodies were scattered on the table.

"Nope, not Internet porn," Mason admitted as he waited for Spaulding to make the discovery and wanting to see the reaction.

"Then what is it? You want me to guess, is that it?" Not wanting to play Mason's little game, Spaulding walked over to the desk to get a look at the screen. "What is that?" He stared at it a little more and saw what looked like a bedroom, looked like a familiar bedroom, hadn't he seen that TV before? What about that crumpled bedspread? Yes, that looked familiar and..."You're spying on her?" It was Mason's bedroom. "Oh, no, oh come on, Mason, don't tell me you bugged the teddy bear you gave her last night!"

"Who? Me? Would I do something like that?" Mason said coyly. "Of course not." He said sternly then almost grinned. "Bear came with the bug...it's a Nanny Cam. Time for a little Hannah TV, you want to watch?"

140

"Here I was I thought you were being nice to her. I'm an idiot."

"That goes without saying."

"I don't believe you're spying on her."

"I'm not spying on her...not exactly...I don't know either of the women currently sitting in my house so forgive me for wanting to keep an eye on them. They make these teddy bears for a reason, ya know?"

"Yeah, so overprotective mothers can spy on their kids." Spaulding protested.

"Or so they can spy on the babysitter and make sure little Johnny or little Hannah isn't being mistreated." Mason insisted.

Spaulding stood there speechless for a moment trying to process what Mason had just told him. "Are you saying that you actually care about your sister? That she isn't just some enigma?"

"Someone has to stand up for her and it looks like I got the job." He reached out and turned the knob on the speakers. "This thing's cool, it's even got sound. There's a camera in the eye and another one in the butt," he chuckled. "No matter which way she's holding it I still get a picture."

"What's that sound?"

"You call yourself a doctor?" Mason grumbled as he looked up at Spaulding. "It's her heartbeat." He looked back to the screen. "You wanna know something else that's really cool? It's even got a speaker in it so mommy can talk to baby while she's at work."

"Mason, don't! The woman already may believe she's hearing voices the last thing she needs is a talking teddy bear."

"Aww, c'mon, let's have a little fun."

"Don't you dare." Spaulding warned as he watched Hannah. From this angle, she was sitting on Mason's bed, holding the bear tightly in arms while her finger laid on the remote control. The channels on the TV went from one to the next to the next. "Leave her alone."

141

"How am I going to make her better that way?"

"Fine but don't talk to her through the bear, ok?"

"Killjoy."

Spaulding shook her head one last time. "So, you're just going to sit here and spy on her through your laptop?"

"Oh, hell no," Mason reached into the pocket of his slacks to produce his phone, "I got it here too. I can watch her from anywhere there's an internet connection."

"You're hopeless, do you know that? Hopeless."

"What'd you come in here for anyway?"

"Hannah's X-rays," Spaulding snatched them off the desk and walked out the door shaking his head.

Chapter Nine

After a dreadfully long day of going through Hannah's records and throwing away meds, Mason was happy when he opened his front door and the smell of pot roast greeted him making his stomach rumble. There were definitely good points to having Hannah live with him. Not only was there the gourmet quality food she cooked but when he stepped over the threshold and she saw him her face lit up. Hannah toddled over to him as fast as she could as she motioned with her hands; she pointed to herself, put her index finger on the side of her chin, and then pointed to him. She did this twice before she reached him and threw her arms around him to give him a hug.

He didn't understand the sign, but he understood the gesture, "I missed you too," Mason whispered as he gave her a light hug. Letting go he hung up his coat on the brass rack near the door. "How'd we make out today?"

Betsey smiled genuinely. She was a cute little thing who just graduated nursing school and who was getting her feet wet working for the non-profit agency. "She's a pleasure, Doctor Mason. We watched TV and she played the piano for over an hour. She had a nap, she cooked, she seemed very happy when I found *Dancing With the Stars* on your ABC app, she really liked that. She watched several episodes."

"No trouble? None at all? Did she *say* anything?"

Betsey frowned as she reached for her coat, "No. I tried but she didn't seem to want to talk to me. Maybe tomorrow, huh, Hannah?"

Hannah shrugged her shoulders and waved good-bye. It wasn't that she didn't like Betsey but Hannah didn't understand why she needed the babysitter when she'd never had one before. She was the one who looked out for the others in her group homes. Betsey's presence made her feel small and completely incompetent.

After dinner, Mason introduced her to the new medication schedule. Hannah was not happy as she shook her head and then her hands in a 'no-no' gesture. Mason thought that for years someone told her that she needed all of that crap and here he was, back in her life less than 72 hours, tossing all of that out the window. Mason tried to explain that all those pills weren't helping her they were making her sick. "If you stop taking some of them, I promise you'll feel better in a few weeks." He assured her but she just huffed and rolled her eyes at him.

The voice near the floor crept up to her ears and whispered: *He's trying to kill you. You know you need all of those pills, you're weak in mind and body, the doctors all say so. If you stop taking them you'll die, he knows that, he's a doctor.*

"Hannah, I'm over here," Mason put a hand under her chin and tilted her face upward, he forked the fingers on the other hand and made a line of sight between her eyes and his. "*Look* at me." In the distant haze of Hannah's brown eyes, he was certain he saw distrust. "I'm trying to help you." He sighed knowing there was another little problem that she needed help with. Still holding her chin he reached into his coat pocket with his other hand and produced a syringe full of penicillin for Hannah's other little problem she balked at the sight of the needle. He wasn't sure what he should tell her, what reason he should give as to why the injection was important, but he wanted to know how Hannah contracted the clap. He just couldn't find a way to ask her if she'd been having sex lately—which she obviously had been doing—and with whom. Even his straightforward, just-put-it-the-fuck-out-there approach was failing him as the words simply stuck in his throat. Bottom line there may be that he just didn't want to know when, with whom and under what circumstances. Not doctorly but it was very brotherly. "You're sick," he told her, "this will make you better."

144

Problem was for the anti-biotic to help her best, Hannah had to let him inject her in the upper thigh. Those eyes staring back at him told him that one of the very last things he should say right now was; drop your pants, no matter how doctorly of a voice he used.

"It'll just take a second," he assured her, "come on, stand up; this has to go in the butt." He was instantly sorry for his poor choice of words, but it was too late. The chin he was so gingerly holding dropped suddenly and she slapped his hand away. "The needle, the *shot*" he corrected quickly, "I have to give you the shot in the butt." He attempted to smooth things over. "Come on, you've had plenty of shots, we all did as kids. It's just like that."

She couldn't drop her neck downward because he was still holding onto her chin, but Hannah's eyes still cast down to the floor.

The voice whispered louder this time: *See that! He's going to poison you. He couldn't find another place that would take your retarded ass so now he's just going to kill you.*

Outwardly, she started to tremble, and the palm of her hand ran over the top of her thigh with increasing speed and force. Hannah rocked back and forth, as she gazed down at the floor.

"Up here!" Mason barked suddenly and with enough force to make her jump. That hand didn't stop rubbing her thigh and now her feet started to wiggle. They moved in opposing circles against each other. He found that to be a rather complicated maneuver for someone like her. That damaged brain, it was doing something, and he wanted to know what it was. "Come on, damnit, look at me." He forked his fingers one more time and drew that line of sight in the air until her gaze came back to him. "You're sick and this is going to make you better. Stand up and drop your pants." Now the palm grabbed the thigh and rubbed the muscle deeply as those little feet picked up speed. Knowingly or not, Hannah was trying to calm herself by activating the nerve endings

145

signaling the brain to release chemicals and to detract it from the panic rising inside her. Mason told himself to just spit it out, damnit, see what happens. If it were any other patient he wouldn't hesitate in fact, he'd probably take a perverse joy in it. Biting down on the part of him that was rising up to tell him to shut up he uttered, "You have Gonorrhea."

As though someone flicked a switch, Hannah stopped rocking, she stopped rubbing her thigh and her feet slowed their rapid pace but they didn't cease their circular motion.

"Do you know what that is? You do, don't you?"

The hand that had been rubbing her thigh so intensely came up under her chin and she wiggled her fingers rapidly to the side. It looked like part of some crazy secret handshake. "Ddddd-dda—"

Mason wondered if that was her attempt at indicating a beard as he thought; *Oh, if she says, 'daddy', I'm going to lose it. Don't say, 'daddy', Hannah, please, don't say 'daddy'.*

"What? Slow down, tell me."

"Da-da-daaa", her voice started to rise and those fingers wiggled wildly in the air, "-dar-tee." Higher still, " Dur-tee. Dirty!" In that instant, her eyes were so clear and so bright he swore they'd burn a hole right through him.

Several thoughts ran through Mason's mind, the first of which was; *thank you for not saying 'daddy'* and the second of which was, *St. Mark's, good Catholic girl.*

Good Catholic Girls didn't get The Clap.

The third thought involved the comical gesture she was making. Sign language, Steward said she knew a few words. "You're not dirty," he told her and made the same motion with his hand under his chin as he tried to find his way down this rather rocky road. Hannah lowered her hand. It looked like his guess was right. "Just let me do this and it'll be over. All over." He held up the syringe. He still wanted to know who, but it didn't look like she was going to volunteer that information. A few moments later, she stood up, undid her jeans, and let him poke the needle just below the left buttocks. There were several good valid medical reasons he should just come right out and ask her who she had been sleeping with, all of them practical and appreciated by places such as The Vermont Board of Health. Mason found that in such short period he might have grown too close to the situation to retain any objectivity. That wouldn't be good for her in the long run. He was suddenly glad that he'd been forced to put Steward in charge of her medical care.

Pants pulled back up, Hannah curled up in the corner of the couch and drew those crooked knees up to her chin. "Who have you been sleeping with?" The words were out before he could stop them, they seemed to linger heavy in the air between them. Mason discovered he didn't want the answer to the question, but he had to have it just the same.

On the couch next to him Hannah put her forefinger to her lips; "Shhhhh"

He could go into a hundred medical reasons why she needed to share that information as best she could, but he tried a different approach; "Brothers and sisters don't keep secrets from each other," Mason offered. "It's ok to tell me, you're my sister. Who?"

Hannah refused to answer him. She just sat there with her finger to her lips shaking her head. No matter what tactic he tried, she would not give up the information. Rather than upset her, reluctantly he gave up after ten minutes or so and turned to another tactic that Hannah accepted easily, the piano.

No more mention of The Clap or other unseemly things they just played along to tunes on the radio until Hannah began winding down again. She missed notes and seemed confused. It was just past eight o'clock and although it was recently upsetting, they day had not been long and hard for her like yesterday had bee. Mason decided he'd try to keep her up for another hour or so. "How about some cookies?" He suggested.

147

Hannah looked up at him as she hugged the bear that he gave her and her eyelids grew heavy.

"You wanna make me some cookies? The last batch was so good I ate them all." If she stayed up a little late making him cookies, then maybe she'd sleep past 6am and he'd appreciate that. He watched as her head tilted up and to the right for a few moments where something in the corner of the living room ceiling seemed to be holding her attention.

The voice near the ceiling, the one she is certain belongs to God whispered sweetly: *Just one batch, it will make him happy. It won't take long.*

Just when a smile began breaking out on her thin lips, the lower voice countered God calling her eyes downward to the floor and she cringed: *You're tired, aren't you? You don't wanna make any stupid cookies; tell him he can make his own damn cookies!*

"Hey! I'm over here," Mason said sharply when she didn't give him an answer. "Cookies?" He watched her stare come back to his but only for a moment before she looked up and right again.

Just one batch. God encouraged in her head.

"Hannah, I'm over here." Mason waved his hand in front of her face. "Over here, *look* at *me*."

She didn't look at him and she didn't answer him. Instead, Hannah put the bear down and got up on wobbly legs as she wandered off toward the kitchen.

Sitting on the couch, he watched her pull the eggs from the refrigerator and then gather the other ingredients she'd need and put them on the counter. By memory, she retrieved flour, baking soda, and baking powder. She put them into a bowl without measuring. Well, she couldn't have measured the ingredients anyway as he didn't have any of those kitchen utensils because he did not cook.

She put two sticks of butter into the microwave for just a few seconds before unwrapping them and putting them into a

148

glass bowl. She mixed the beat the butter with an electric mixer he'd forgotten he owned. Once it was nice and creamy, she added in sugar, brown sugar, eggs and vanilla. Next, she added the flour mixture and then the chocolate chips. After carefully placing 12 spoonfuls onto a cookie tray, she turned toward the stove and then stopped as her gaze dropped to the floor.

Rubbing the back of her hand over her temple and smearing flour in her hair, she caught a whiff of the lingering scent of the long hard day she had yesterday. Instantly. she heard the nasty speak loudly and derisively. It frozen her in front of the stove. *You stink. You need a shower. What do you think you're doing anyway? You think cookies are going to make him let you stay here? HA! You're out the door, sister, no bones about it. Tomorrow morning he'll take you for a ride and that'll be the last you see of him.*

Standing like a stone, Hannah began to shake as she let out a long high-pitched whimper. The tray in her hand wobbled as much as her legs.

"Hannah?" Mason got up from the couch to make his way over to her leaning on his cane. She didn't look up at him or even seem to notice he was standing there. Maybe he was pushing her too hard. The last few days had been traumatic enough for her, maybe he should leave her alone, let her stick to her schedule, have her shower and go to bed. "Give it to me." He put his hand on the other end of the cookie tray to steady it. "Let go, Hannah."

Her hazy distant eyes came up to meet his, but she didn't let go of the tray.

"You go have a bath or a shower, ok?" Did she have a shower this morning before he got up? He didn't know but he remembered she passed out on the couch last night without washing. She looked like she could use a long soak in a hot bath. "I'll bake these." He didn't have the slightest clue how long to leave them in the oven but, hey, if he could diagnose

149

the rarest of diseases certainly chocolate chip cookies couldn't present too much of a challenge.

Eyes distant and hazy still glued to the floor Hannah spoke in a very clear, serious, and oddly gravelly tone, "Don't burn them."

Mason almost dropped the tray as she let go of it. Her eyes were as hazy as Los Angeles at sunrise, but her voice had been clear as the Liberty Bell. "What did you say?" But Hannah turned away and toddled off toward the bathroom. "Hannah?" He watched her open the door, step inside, and turn around to shut the door behind her but her eyes never left the floor. The crease in her brow only got deeper.

Tossing the cookies into the oven he waited and listened for the shower to come on and when it didn't, he limped down the hall and stooped to look through the bathroom keyhole. Instead of a shower, Hannah was planning on a bath. She stripped and had a clean towel waiting on the closed toilet lid. Hoping the warm water would calm her down,

Mason went back to his place on the couch to look over some of Hannahs' medical records that came over via fax before he left the Clinic. Mary informed him others were on the way and would arrive by FedEx in the morning. Pouring himself a glass of Scotch and popping another Oxy he thought he'd get in a few puffs off a Jamaican while she sat in the tub.

Outside the rain was picking up and the temperature was dropping, settling on the couch to go over her records again, he pulled a blanket over his legs to keep the chill away now that he couldn't use his fireplace for fear Hannah might go ballistic. Before Mason knew it, he was absorbed in the medical jargon and technical information. He was so lost that he didn't smell the cookies when they began to burn.

In the bath, behind a veil of steam, Hannah did smell them burning. With haste, she tumbled out of the claw foot tub and then scrambled to her mangled legs as she bolted for the closed door. Hands high over her head her throat letting out a panicked grunting she rushed out of the bathroom naked and dripping wet.

Before Mason could comprehend what was happening let alone stop her, Hannah blew past him, toddled into the kitchen as fast as she could and reached her bare wet hand into the oven to grab the hot tray. "Hannah!"

Too late, she let out a scream of pain as the hot pan seared her wet skin, but she didn't immediately let go. Instead, as the heat burned her, she took the time to throw the pan onto the countertop with so much force the charred cookies bounced off the metal sheet.

"Jesus Christ!" Mason exclaimed and Hannah shot him a nasty angry look. Rising to his feet, he limped over to her. "Let me see it," Mason ordered.

Holding her wounded hand close to her body her face gnarled, she shook an angry finger at him as she shouted, "NO BBURNNED CCOOOKKIES!" Hannah stomped on his foot with her heel, her face red as she huffed and puffed. "NO! BAD!" With the unburned hand, she grabbed his wrist so hard it made him wince as she pulled him to her. Bringing the burnt hand, palm open, up to her lips she brought it down fiercely slapping the back of his hand. "BAD!"

"OW!" Mason cried in pain as he stumbled backward.

She kept hold of his wrist and went on lost in her rage. "NO," she brought the fingers of the burnt hand together until the index and forefingers met her thumb then she slapped his hand and stomped on his foot, "NO," index and forefingers to thumb, slap the hand, stomp the foot. "NO!" She screeched letting one last round of slap and stomp fly. "BBBBAAD!" Letting go of him she put one hand on her hip and shook a finger at him before she pointed to the cookies steaming on the counter. "NO!" Her index and forefinger snapped down onto her thumb with all the force of an alligator taking its first bite of a hard won prey.

"Stop it!" Mason shouted and pulled his hand away. "What's wrong with you?" The pain in his foot was radiating

151

up his leg, he thought of how lucky he was that she wasn't wearing shoes. If she had been, she could have broken his foot with the force of those little stomps. "They're just cookies."

Standing there naked and angry she stood on her tiptoes and brought her nose close to his lips to take a few sniffs of the alcohol on his breath and the cigar stench in the air. Not liking the hauntingly familiar smells, she tossed her hands up in the air in frustration as she turned on her heels to toddle away from him.

"Where do you think you're going?" Mason reached out and grabbed her injured hand.

Something in those distant eyes shifted from anger to fear. Hannah flinched and tried to yank her hand away, but he was too strong.

The voice near the floor growled; *He's always too strong. You can't fight. It will only make it worse.*

Hopping up and down in place as she pulled, she started making a circular pattern around her heart with her free hand. Her throat emits a deep guttural whimper.

If he were more on the ball or if Steward had taken five seconds to tell Mason about Hannah's limited sign language abilities, he'd know she was trying to tell him that she was sorry but none of that happened. "Answer me, what's this all about?" Mason demanded his face getting closer to hers.

The whiff of alcohol and smoke in her face is stronger and more offensive.

Hannah's mind transported her back to a distant place and time until Ricky's face faded away and become her father's angry glare.

He's drunk again. I burned the damn cookies and he's drunk again!

Outwardly, she wriggles and cries, "Gggggggooooo!"

"Go where? Where the hell are ya gonna go?"

"Ggggggggoooo.....meh....ME!" Hannah kept pulling and pulling her arm away from him, the more he yanked it forward the more she yanked it back. Her skin was wet and so was the

152

floor where they were standing. She slipped out of his hold and went sprawling onto the floor. Mason hadn't realized how dependent his own balance had become on the situation and when she went down, she took him with her. Reflex kept him holding onto his cane as he crashed down on top of her. Beneath him, Hannah squirmed and tried to push him off as she tried to slide out from under him.

Hannah screamed, "Gggggoooo ME! HUFFF MEEEE!"

It all happened so damn fast that he didn't realize what was going on in her mind. He was trying to get up but between his bad hip, the wet floor, and the hysterical woman below him, Mason wasn't having much luck in that area. Each time he managed to push himself up a small way his foot slipped, and he fell back on top of her.

Hannah started slapping him as she wailed incoherently. Grabbing at those wildly flying hands slapping his face making his cheeks sting and turn red, he pinned her hands to the floor behind her head with the length of his cane. "Be quiet, Hannah." He hissed. "Stay still."

Staring up at him and whimpering she heard the dark voice; *Yes, be quiet, Hannah. Be still. Don't move. He's drunk again. You know what will happen if you don't be a good girl. Stay still. Hush.*

As though someone had flipped a switch in her mind, Hannah stopped fighting. She laid perfectly still and began to weep.

At first, Richard Mason was very relieved. It seemed her little episode was over, and it was only as he started to get up he realized what a precarious position they managed to achieve during their little tousle. Realized it so much hat dread settled into his heart.

The image of her X-rays flashed behind his eyes. The image of mended but untended broken fingers and broken toes along with the crack in her skull undoubtedly from the blow of a cane wouldn't let go of him. Then, very slowly, as though dawn were peeking over the mountains, he again realized the precariousness of their position.

She was naked, sprawled out beneath him and he had her hands firmly pinned to the floor. If he reached down to unzip his jeans—which he had half a mind to do just to see her reaction—then things would get mighty messy, wouldn't they? His heart and mind racing, Mason eased up on the pressure in his hands as he grasped the cane with one hand and used it to roll off her. "Hannah?" He lay on the wet kitchen floor for a moment with his heart and mind racing.

Hannah floundered as she twisted and nearly convulsed until she was on her stomach where it was easier for her to scramble to her feet. Holding one hand over her bare breasts and the other, the burned one, over the patch of graying hair between her legs she toddled off down the hall as fast as she could. Reaching the bedroom, she slammed the door behind her.

He stood there waiting for his own heart to stop racing with the smell of burnt cookies assaulting his nose. It took quite a while for the normally fast-on-his-feet Mason to gather his wits about him. He just stood there, shaking, feeling the pain in his hand and his foot radiating throughout his body and seeing those X-rays flash in his mind like the cameras of paparazzi chasing some hot sexy celebrity. The U-shaped breaks on her toes and the crushing fractures on her fingers. It was easy to understand that, at some point long ago, Hannah burned the cookies and Daddy Rice didn't like that.

His heart still racing and his mind swimming with the black knowledge that Hannah, in her addled memory impaired mind had just relieved that particularly nasty event. And she could thank him for that.

Those eyes, wild and distant, in them she hadn't seen her brother but their father. Taking the amber bottle from the pocket of his jeans, Mason swallowed an Oxy dry before limping down the hall to the bedroom. Laying his hand on the knob and expecting to find it locked he wasn't sure if he was happy or sad when the knob turned easily in his hand and the door opened.

Locking the door against Daddy Rice was probably a very very bad idea.

Peering into the open door he looked at the bed but it was empty. He heard her whimpering and looked hard into the darkness until he saw Hannah in the far corner of the bedroom beneath the windows where the cold rain sheeted against the glass. She was still naked as a jaybird with her knees drawn unnaturally up to her chin she was trembling, and wet. Her feet kept rubbing against each other as she rocked slightly hugged her naked body and trying so desperately to soothe herself.

Mason's cheeks stung from her repeated slaps and he felt certain she'd bruised two of his toes when she stomped on his foot with her bare wet foot. The damp weather hurt his hip made it ache like a bad tooth. She needed him that much was painfully clear. He was altogether unsure of how to approach her in her manic state. Soundlessly Mason crouched down in front of her and hovered there until her foggy eyes found their way to him. "I'm sorry, Hannah. I promise I won't burn the cookies again."

Drool ran down her chin as fast as the tears fell from her hazy confused eyes, she looked up at him from beneath a tuft of graying chestnut hair. She pointed to herself, crossed her wrists over her heart, and then pointed to him. Hannah pointed her index fingers at each other, twisted them around a bit, pointed to herself as she waved her index finger in front of her face.

Mason was unsure of what she was trying to convey but felt fairly certain she was trying to tell him that she loved him as she was begging him not to hurt her. "I'm sorry." He held one hand out to her and made a circle over his heart with the other. "It's ok now, I promise." He offered but she just kept circling her heart as she stared at him from beneath a lock of

155

graying chestnut hair. "It's me," he whispered feeling a cold steel hand wrap around his heart and squeeze, "it's me, it's Ricky, your brother. I won't hurt you, Hannah."

Without any warning, Hannah grabbed his extended hand like a drowning man grasping for a life preserver in open water. She pulled him down to her, threw her arms around his shoulders and sobbed on the floor like a baby.

It took him nearly a half hour to get her up off the bedroom floor and into the bathroom where he cleaned and bandage the second-degree burn on her left hand. Sitting on the toilet with her hand over the sink Hannah watched him but she didn't seem to notice anything that was happening. She didn't say 'ow' or try to pull her hand away. She just stared at him the whole time while she moved the other hand in a circular pattern over her heart. Below her on the fuzzy throw rug below the bowl, her feet intertwined, crossed, and rubbed against each other without stopping in a very flowing motion.

Mason swabbed her upper arm with a cold cotton ball dipped in alcohol. Hannah didn't blink. He drew up an injection and slid the sharp needle under her skin. Hannah didn't flinch she just kept staring into space with her feet going round and around. Putting his arm under her armpit and reaching around her back Mason helped her to her feet and Hannah offered no resistance she just followed along as though she were on Autopilot. Guiding her back into the bedroom, Mason turned down the covers, Hannah climbed in without realizing she was doing it.

When he covered her up and went to the door to leave, she made little whimpering sounds that tore at his heart. Hoping the shot of Lorazepam would soon have her sleeping deeply Mason turned back to the bed and climbed in next to her. Hannah latched on to him, her head on his chest and her arms around him. In the soft moonlight streaming through the bay window, he saw the tears rolling down her cheeks and they landed on his t-shirt until it was soaked through. She didn't make a single sound she just laid there with her eyes wide open and sobbing silently until she couldn't fight the drug any longer and mercifully, they closed. Her sleep was not peaceful as Mason held his sister throughout the night. She trembled in arms and let out little whimpers until the wee hours of the morning.

All night long the only thing he heard echoing in his head was her screaming; "GGGGGGOOOO MEEEEE!"

Let go of me!

"GUFF MEEEEE!"

Get off me!

All night long the only thing he saw in his mind was that snapping alligator motion Hannah made at him each time before she slapped his hand. How many times had he seen Rice do that to Hannah to shut her up? His brilliant mind couldn't count that high.

"That's how you train a dog," he muttered angrily to the darkness.

Come morning, she was up before him, she had his breakfast ready; cold cereal, fruit, and coffee. Sitting at the table together, they ate in silence. Hannah didn't even look at him.

After his breakfast, Mason headed for a hot shower, when he came out of his bedroom dressed for the day, Hannah was standing by the front door with her suitcase in her good hand and the teddy bear clutched tightly in the other. He asked her where she thought she was going.

Hannah made a circle around her heart, looked in his direction with dewy eyes and whispered, "Way...Ay-way."

After her outburst last night, she expected him to send her away but to where? "Why?"

Hannah made the same motion she'd made last night as she slapped his hand and screamed 'BAD!' Holding the white teddy bear tightly she reached for his hand with her bandaged one.

157

"You're not bad and you're not going anywhere," Mason whispered. "You stay with me, ok?"

Hannah's heart leapt as the voice of God near the ceiling announced; *You heard him, he said you could stay. You heard him.*

Hannah threw her arms around him and started to cry. She hugged him so tightly she damn near choked him and he had to push her away. Her gaze shifted downward as the voice near the floor chimed in.

Yeah, see how long that lasts, sister. Wherever he went the other day, he didn't like it he's still looking. He's still going to get rid of you you stupid stupid bitch.

"What are you thinking? Talk to me, Hannah, I know you can."

She stared straight at him and without warning, she reached out to cup his face in her hands, nuzzled her soft cheek against his whiskers and then she kissed him. Not a little peck on the cheek or a simple kiss on the lips, no, it lingered slightly longer than a sibling smooch should.

Mason thought; *Hannah is overly and inappropriately affectionate.*

But, then again, maybe that was the way she showed her gratitude. As far as he could see, it surely beat a simple 'thank you' any day.

"Listen to me" he said still holding her bandaged hand, "I want you to do whatever it is you want to do today. You got that? You want to watch TV, go ahead. You want to play my piano or the guitar, go ahead. You want to sleep all day, that's fine too." He reached in his back pocket and took out his wallet to hand her twenty dollars. "If you want to order a pizza or something," he pushed the money into her hand. "There's no schedule today, it's Hannah Day, ok? Whatever Hannah wants to do that's what Hannah will do today." He wasn't sure she understood but she did slip the money into the pocket of her ratty jeans and Mason told himself that this Saturday they were going to the mall over in Killingworth and

158

buying new clothes if it killed him. "Take your bag back into the bedroom. You're staying with me."

A short time later, there was a knock on the front door. Betsey, had arrived for the day. Mason informed her that Hannah had a bad night and that she was to be allowed to do whatever she wanted for the day. Feeling guilty about leaving he left Hannah to the nurse while he went off to The Mountainside.

Arriving at his office with a pounding headache, Mason knocked down two painkillers as he collapsed into his chair. Just as the headache began to subside and he was enjoying the blessed solitude his door opened and Spaulding walked in with Steward.

Intending to discuss procedures for repairing Hannah's legs when her blood was thick enough for surgery Spaulding walked up to the desk with his head down scanning his notes but when he looked up he could only see one thing. "What happened to your eye?"

"Got into a little altercation with Hannah last night," Mason explained off-handedly.

"Wonder what she looks like this morning," Steward mumbled.

"What did you say?" Mason leaned forward.

"Just wondering what started it and which one got the worst of it. We all know you have a gift for pushing people's buttons..."

"And you think I'd actually attack a physically and mentally challenged woman? Let alone the fact that she's my sister?" Mason was utterly insulted by the open insinuation. He looked to his dear friend Spaulding for back up, but the man's eyes suddenly found something amazingly interesting on the table in front of him. "Thanks, both of you thanks a lot. Listen up, I did not and I would not hit her," Mason began. Then he went into the tale of his tumultuous night with Hannah Rice. "I didn't attack her I was trying to restrain her, and she kept slapping me."

159

"What set her off?"

"Burnt cookies."

"You threw her down on the ground over some burnt cookies?" Spaulding admonished even though he found it hard to believe his own ears.

"I didn't throw her down on the ground," Mason insisted angrily, "she fell and brought me down with her, aren't you listening?" This brought him around to another point but back to an older one first. "She burned her hand grabbing the cookie tray out of the oven without a mitt."

"Ow!" Spaulding exclaimed.

"She was in such a rush to get them she just reached in and grabbed it." Mason explained. "Hannah didn't flinch over it not even while I was bandaging her second degree burn after I finally got her off the bedroom floor."

"Maybe the pain receptors are shot." Steward suggested. "Other than that," Steward began, "her outburst could be a result of her long-term memory which we know is intact and you are a big part of it. She probably learned how to play piano at a young age, you said her mother died early in Hannah's childhood, so she probably helped with the grocery shopping, maybe she cooked for her father—"

"Our father," Mason corrected and felt his heart sink as he wondered what else she did for him, other than serve as a punching bag from time to time. He glanced over at the X-Rays still hanging on the lighted board with a sigh.

"Look, out of the five senses smell is the only one that comes into actual contact with the brain and therefore tends to be the strongest trigger for emotion and memory." Mason was strangely silent, and Steward didn't like the deep look of concentration on his face. "What? What is it?"

"Smell," Mason mused with something akin to sorrow in his voice, "like alcohol?" He remembered the way she leaned forward last night and those few flares of her nostrils as she took in the scent of his breath. He wondered if James Rice was a drinker or became one after Hannah's mother died.

160

"Most definitely, especially if it's associated with something bad like someone being drunk and angry. Why? Were you drunk last night?" They all knew how much Mason loved sitting in his cozy little house drinking his J&B, popping a few painkillers, puffing on a cigar and jamming away on his piano. That was when he wasn't frequenting the local bar looking for a little warm company for the night.

"You know," Mason said with a false grin, "it just warms my heart to know how little you guys think of me. Your *boss*. No, I wasn't drunk, but I did have a few sips of Scotch that she might have smelled on my breath."

Chapter Ten

The first week with Hannah was an adventure. According to Betsey the home aide—and the teddy bear—Hannah did a lot of sleeping the first few days. Hannah's frail body was detoxing from years of unnecessary medications built up in her system and only God Himself (and possibly the social worker) knew how much sleep Hannah got at her group home. There people probably cried or screamed in the night. His place was quiet. If Mason could read Hannah's thoughts, he would know how much she appreciated that fact. After so many years of people screaming or blabbering nonsense around her the silence in his house was heavenly. So was the fact that his house did not smell like a public bathroom.

It was the mornings when Hannah was most like the girl he remembered. Every day she was a little brighter, a little more alert, a little more...there. She was definitely more communicative in the morning. Over breakfast, after Morning Prayer if he asked her questions, she did her best to answer him verbally. No one was going to give her any awards for her great oratory skills, but she got her point across with less stuttering and frustration even though she relied heavily on hand gestures to accompany her muddled words.

In the evening she didn't even attempt to talk, she only gestured or used her limited knowledge of American Sign Language to communicate with him. He figured out that she knew several basic signs, chief among them being; hello, good-bye, thank you, sorry, please, no, yes, don't, dirty, bathroom, go, stop, music, I know, I hope, I love you and his personal favorite, bullshit.

It was almost as though Hannah wanted to talk in the morning but in the evening, she did not.

Unable to break her of the afternoon nap, when he came home in the early evenings, she was wide-awake and smiling at him. No matter how grumpy or pissed off he might be she always seemed genuinely happy to see him and that made him feel good. He tried to get her to stay up later at night and sometimes Hannah might make it as long as 9:00 or 9:30 before she just nodded off without warning. Mason did this by playing piano with her. Hannah loved it and, if forced by fire or something to admit it, Mason would say that he did too. She would play anything on the radio that was popular between 1960 and 1988 or so. If he tried something a little less popular such as the jazz that he liked so much she would tap on the keys without much success. However, Mason soon found that if he played a few bars of something she didn't know then asked her to repeat it on her side of the piano she could accomplish it with a fair amount of ease. He would spend an hour teaching her a song bar by bar and she would play it beginning to end once or twice. When he switched to a song she knew and then came back to the new song she had just learned Hannah couldn't remember it. Mason became convinced that her ultra-short-term memory was gone. If something—an event or an encounter-- didn't make a major impression on Hannah, then it was as if it never happened.

Before going to bed, even if she had already passed out on the couch and he had to wake her up, she washed her face paying special attention to behind her ears. After that, Hannah brushed her teeth for two minutes. Hannah could not tell time and she didn't count to one hundred and twenty in her addled head. Instead, very softly, she hummed *Happy Birthday* six times, as she scrubbed and foamy toothpaste ran down her chin.

After that, she turned down the bed and dropped to her knees to say her nightly prayers. The routine was familiar and one he thought he would never see again, and he never wanted to. However, when she did it, as asinine as he felt the concept of God to be, it was quite endearing. Hannah crossed herself, kissed her thumbnail, put her hands together, closed her eyes closed, and knelt on those wickedly warped knees she prayed. Mason watched her face; sometimes her brow furrowed deeply causing the vein in her forehead to pop out. Sometimes her face was completely serene. Sometimes her face was home to one of the most beautiful smiles he'd ever seen.

Night after night Mason stood there wondering what she was praying for or what problems she had that she would only share with God—who, if He existed, should already be fully aware of them. He wondered what secrets she told Him, what guidance she asked for, and what it was that made her smile that way. Mason figured he would never know.

Over the course of the week as Hannah seemed more alert, Mason took the opportunity to try several experiments with her. Steward said smell was probably Hannah's biggest memory trigger and that got him thinking about his old pal Mr. J&B. If he remembered correctly, and he believed he did, James Rice drank J&B Scotch while he smoked, not a cigar, but a pipe. That got him thinking about the night the cookies burned and just who her broken brain told her she was seeing, she was confronting and fighting against before submitting so quickly. Mason racked his memory, but images of Judge James Rice eluded him. All he could do was wonder just how much he resembled their late father especially now that so much time had passed.

Wednesday night after dinner, Mason asked Hannah to play him a song while he sat on the couch. When she started playing *Joy the World* he took his bottle of J&B from the space between the couch and end table. Mason put it on the coffee table before sneaking one of his fine Jamaican cigars from the end table drawer. Hannah stopped playing; he glanced up to see her staring at him with veiled disapproval.

Leaving the unlit cigar in the ashtray and the bottle on the table, Mason got up and made his way to the bathroom. When he came back, the bottle and cigar were gone. He looked back in its hiding spot between the couch and end table, but the bottle was not there. However, the piano bench seemed to be having a problem staying closed even though Hannah was still sitting on it and smiling innocently at him.

Limping over to the piano and motioning for her to get up, he opened the bench to find his bottle and his cigar with the ashtray. "These are mine," he told her as he took them back to the couch and poured a single glass. Mason was very tempted to light the cigar but remembered the social worker's instructions that the sight of fire could throw Hannah into a tizzy. Bringing the glass to his lips, Hannah let her hand fall onto the piano keys making loud clang. Mason didn't let that deter him as he enjoyed the double shot. When it came time for Hannah to retire for the night, she waved him away and did not want him to watch over her as she went through her nightly routine.

Thursday night he took the bottle out again, set it on the table and didn't get up. Hannah sighed disapprovingly and moved back into the corner of the couch. When he poured the liquor into the glass and took a sip, she got up and wandered off to the bedroom where she shut the door tight and didn't come out for the rest of the night.

Friday night, the bottle was gone but the cigars were still there. However, he knew that before he got home. Right around lunchtime, he stopped the day for a little Hannah TV and while Betsey made lunch, he watched her fish the bottle out of its place between the couch and end table. She tucked it behind the teddy bear she was carrying and brought into the bathroom where she closed the door, opened the bottle, and poured it down the toilet. She then tucked the empty bottle beneath the pillows on the bed. When nature gave Betsey a long call, Hannah snuck it outside and buried it in the trashcan behind the house.

Oh, the Nanny Cam was a wonderful invention.

Upon coming home, he looked for it, asked her where it was, and she just sat there giving him the most innocent look he had ever seen as she shook her head to indicate she didn't know where his bottle went.

Mason stood there thinking of what an effective liar she was, especially for a Good Catholic girl, and that he never would have guessed that fact. If he hadn't watched her dump it, he would never know Miss Sweet and Innocent there was lying right to his face. He would have to watch that in the future.

On Saturday morning, Mason bit the bullet and took Hannah shopping. He couldn't stand looking at her in those ragamuffin clothes any longer. They needed to go to the furniture store as well. If Hannah was going to be living with him for at least the next nine months he needed a sofa bed.

Their first stop was Wal-Mart and Hannah didn't appear to enjoy the experience. The mega discount retailer was swamped with people catching up on their Back-to-School shopping. Dazed and confused, she held onto the sleeve of his jacket so tight Mason felt sure the material would rip. She did not like the people being so close to her. When someone crossed the line of Hannah's Comfort Zone, she took a step back to stand or walk directly behind him holding onto the sleeve of his jacket.

The clothes did not seem to hold much interest for her although she did pick up a few shirts and jeans; she just sighed and put them in the cart. Looking at them, Mason couldn't say he blamed her; Wal-Mart may be great for 'living better' and 'saving money' but their clothes lacked any sense of style. He suggested that they go somewhere else for clothes and they left the megastore empty handed.

They drove to the mall in Killingworth, it was a big place and he knew Hannah wasn't apt to like it very much but the variety it offered might be enough to help her get her curiosity going. Thinking back to the girl that he once knew they stopped in front of a store. "How about this one? Think you might find something better in there?"

Hannah looked up at the sign trying to recognize the color or the shape of the letters. She couldn't read it but from the logo, she knew it was a store she liked and remembered from days gone by.

The sign read; American Eagle Outfitters

"Wanna try?" Mason encouraged.

Like Wal-Mart, the store was packed with people, kids and teens were running wild everywhere and Hannah stuck very close to Mason. Unlike Wal-Mart, mingled in with the madness of harried shoppers were interesting things that caught her eye like fluffy sweaters and jeans that looked comfortable.

Mason led her around the store and while she continued to stay close to him within a few minutes, she was taking steps away to look at things. He stood back and observed but didn't make any move to wander away from her. He immediately noticed two things; she did not pick anything overly bright; nothing orange or red or striped. Maybe Steward was right and she wasn't schizophrenic. The second thing was that she was looking inside the clothing for the tags trying to determine if what she picked up would fit her or not. She wasn't doing a good job nearly every item she picked up was several sizes too big for her.

Standing there watching her, Mason silently cursed himself for not paying a tiny bit more attention when they were at Walmart. He'd have to look at the clothes she bought there but he had feeling he'd either be making a return trip to the store or a donation to Goodwill. "Try this one," he grumbled handing her a pink sweater like the one she just draped over her arm but in a smaller size. She looked at the tag then compared it to the tag on the sweater she was carrying. Mason didn't know if she understood the numbers but from there on out Hannah picked up items marked Size 3 instead of Size 13. When she got to five items, she looked up at him with questioning eyes then pointed at the price tags.

"What?" Mason asked. It wasn't noon yet and the people around her were making her anxious, but he knew Hannah could still talk to him. "What is it?" He also knew she was asking him how much money she could spend.

Hannah reached behind him and tugged at the back pocket was where his wallet was stored, "Hey, stop that." He protested lightly, "No butt-grabbing in public." Hannah's eyes blinked and grew wide as though he had insulted her. "What do you want?"

The voice near her feet reared its head: *He's just being mean. He wants to embarrass you in front of all these people. He knows what you're trying to tell him.*

Out of the corner of her eye, Hannah looked around at all the shoppers who weren't paying them any attention.

"Well?"

Hannah looked up at her brother. "Mah-mah," she stuttered.

"Mama? No mama here. Take a breath, don't get frustrated. Try again."

The voice of God that always guided her and looked over her countered the mean voice: *You can do this. You know you can. So does he that's why he's pushing you like this. Don't be angry just try. That's all. Just try.*

"Mah-un-ee."

"Honey?" Mason asked and slightly admonished himself for pushing her when he perfectly understood what she had said.

"Mun-eey." Hannah said in a clearer voice and then pointed to the clothes.

"Oh, money. I see. Yes, I have money. Do you want to know how much you can spend?" Mason took the wallet from his back pocket.

"Yyy, yes."

He produced three one-hundred-dollar bills that he held up and showed to her. "You can spend this on clothes." Hannah reached into the pocket of her raggedy jeans and produced the twenty he'd given her earlier in the week with a grin. "I thought I told you to get a pizza." He put the money in

168

her hand and Hannah continued shopping while he hung back and watched.

Left to her own devices, Mason decided she had a very feminine yet relaxed sense of style that recalled a simpler time, like the 70s. Very retro in her choices but they worked on her. By the time they left American Eagle Outfitters, Hannah had almost a completely new wardrobe and she desperately needed it. Everything she tried on in the dressing room she walked out to show him, do a little spin, and a little prance while she waited for him to say yes or no. Mason didn't say either, all he would say was 'If you want it then it's yours.' Hannah decided on four pairs of jeans, three sweaters, one sweatshirt, and a pretty blouse she found on the Clearance Rack. Purchasing her items, she went back to the dressing room to change into a new pair of bellbottom jeans and fuzzy pink sweater depositing her old clothes in the American Eagle Outfitters bag. She also had $50.00 left in her hand. Exiting the store, she looked up, across the mall saw another familiar sign. She looked up at Mason with a strange expression on her face then pointed across the way. He looked over to where she was pointing.

The sign across the way read; Victoria's Secret.

"Hummmm," he mused. There was no question that she needed new underwear. Did she need new sexy underwear? Was she even associating the two or did she just know there were pretty panties in there? Either way, it didn't matter because she desperately needed new undergarments. Hers were beyond rags. "Ok, but you go in on your own." Lingerie shopping with his challenged sister just felt wrong. Yeah, no matter how you sliced that one it was just wrong. "I'll be right outside." *Yep, right outside watching what catches your eye,* he thought.

Hannah breathed a sigh of relief.

"Didn't want my company anyway?" He asked as though he were insulted, she gave him an apologetic grin. Mason couldn't remember the last time he'd been in Victoria's Secret

169

but he was certain that fifty bucks wasn't going to get her very far in there. "Here," he gave her another fifty. "Go on."

Hesitantly Hannah took the money and went into the store. She kept looking up every few minutes to make sure Mason was still standing outside and she was not disappointed. He stood on the other side of the glass staring at her intently watching her pick up panties and bras until she felt uncomfortable. Hannah turned her back to him so he couldn't see what she was buying. It was only when she paid for her purchases and she came out of the store that she opened the bag to show him what she had; four sets of matching bra and panties all pastels, all solid colors, and all very pretty. If they were on another woman, he would not mind seeing them at all.

"You still need a winter coat," Mason told her, "this way." He made her walk the entire length of the mall on those wobbly legs until they reached The Coat Factory where he handed her a last hundred dollar bill and told her to buy what she wanted so long as it was warm. He reminded her that like the Upper Peninsula, Vermont got very cold in the wintertime. Hannah chose a full-length black trench coat with a zip-out lining. It was exactly one hundred dollars and the label read Anne Klein. Like the other clothes she had chosen it was very stylish.

On their way to the register, they passed a small display of shoes with winter boots on special. "A pair of those too." Mason said as he stopped in front of rack.

Hannah chose a pair of winter boots with no heel and a fake fur lining. They were black suede and matched the new coat. At just thirty bucks, Mason considered them a steal.

Their last stop for the day was Wayside Furniture where Mason, with Hannah's input, picked out a new sofa bed for his living room. She looked all of them over...twice...she sat on all of them...twice...she touched all of their cushions...twice.

170

Just when Mason was starting to think they'd still be there after the store closed, she sat down on one, looked up at him, smiled, and nodded.

It was dark chocolate sectional made of leather than felt like butter. It would be perfect for his living room and they could place it so that it faced the fire and the piano. Not that the fireplace that he loved so much was going to do him a great deal of good this year with Hannah's pyrophobia.

One thing was for sure he couldn't keep sleeping on the couch it was killing his hip and back. No matter how many mornings he woke up achy and told himself he was sleeping in his own bed that night, he just couldn't bring himself to make her give up the bedroom.

This sectional sofa was the first thing that Hannah picked out that Mason would consider expensive. It had a price tag of $3,500. Mason stood in front of where Hannah sat on the couch and he looked around the store taking special note of the other couches she seemed to take a shine to. He wondered what was so special about this one. A few of the others were even more expensive. Why not one of them?

Hannah patted the cushion next to her and waved for his to sit down.

That was when Mason discovered her reasoning. Some of the others may be more expensive but none were more comfortable. "Ahhh," he exhaled and sat all the way back feeling like a babe cradled in its mother's arms. "Oh, yeah, this one, definitely this one, little sister. Good choice."

Hannah smiled proudly but then frowned a little as she hesitantly pointed to the price tag.

"Don't worry about it," Mason chirped, "you're paying for it."

The slight frown turned into a look of shock before that faded and was replaced by, what looked to him to be, exasperation.

"What?" Mason asked as he leaned his whiskery chin on the wolf's head handle of his cane. Her estate would reimburse him for the purchase of the couch and all of the clothes she was taking home with her tonight. It seemed to him Hannah knew that and he wasn't the first one to say so to her. "Too expensive now? We can get a cheaper one." He offered.

Hannah let her hands glide over the soft leather and the smile returned it was brighter this time and she shook her head 'no' before settling back again.

"We'll take this one," he said to the salesman who promised delivery on Monday.

Sunday morning arrived and Mason awoke to a massive Sunday Breakfast eggs, bacon, sausage, English muffins, French toast and coffee. As always, Hannah prayed over her breakfast before she ate. Then she disappeared into the bedroom without doing the dishes which was out of character for her. She was in there so long Mason began growing worried and he limped down the hall to knock on the door, "Hannah, what are you doing in there?"

A few moments later, the door opened and there she stood in her white dress, her hair neatly pulled back into a bun adorned with the silk lily-of-the-valley and her white canvas shoes on her little feet.

Once upon a time, the dress probably fit her frame very nicely but now it was loose and hung like a cheap suit. "Sunday, huh?"

Hannah nodded emphatically.

"You want me to take you to church?"

Hannah gave him another emphatic nod with a bright smile.

"No," he said crossly. "I told you no church. You might not say much but you're not a weak minded fool who can't think for herself...most of the time."

Hannah slammed her foot on the hardwood floor, grabbed him by the upper arm and did a little dance until they exchanged places then she pushed him into the bedroom where she had already laid out his best suit. She pointed to it and then to him and then to the front door.

"No. That's all there is to it. No. I'm not going to go sit, stand, kneel, and pray to a God that *doesn't exist*."

The smile on her face turned into a furrowed brow as she clasped her hands together, put them over her heart, and brought her shoulders in as though someone was hugging her. Then she slowly brought her hands out in front of her and raised them to the sky. "Gah-ah-d."

"You love God?" Mason watched her nod. "Well, He doesn't love you."

The hands raised in praise fell to her sides before she shook an angry finger at him and flicked his lips with it while she gave him the raspberry, "Pffffft." Putting her hands squarely on her hips, she leaned toward him until they were nose to nose and began to stutter as she tried hard to work her voice, "D-d-d-d-OU-ttt-iiing..."

"Thomas," Mason finished. "No dice, little sister, you can be angry with me all you want, it's not happening. Go pray in there in your fancy dress."

Yes, she could pray wherever she was but that wasn't the point. If she missed Sunday Mass, she missed the Eucharist. Hannah held her hands out to him, one on top of the other, brought them into herself and pretended to take something from the palm and lay it on her tongue.

"Communion? You want to take Communion?"

Hannah nodded, hitched her thumb toward the bedroom and shook her head, "N-n-no."

"Nope, no Communion Wafers in there but I'll tell you what. I got some crackers in the kitchen—you bought 'em— and a bottle of wine in the fridge. Want me to bless them for you?"

Hannah slammed her foot on the floor so hard the pain shot up through her rickety legs to her hip as she stammered, "T-urch! T-urch! G-GOOO T-urch! PR-AY!" Hannah reached into the bodice of the dress and pulled out a twenty-dollar bill.

173

The word she was looking for eluded her so she made the motion of putting the money into the collection plate and stammered, "P-p-poor."

"Gimme that!" Mason snatched the bill out of her hand. "If you're just going to piss it away I'll hold on to it."

"AGH!" With great disgust and determination, Hannah plucked the money out of his fingers, "Y-you...stew-pid ah-ld man nah Rick-y." She shook the money in his face before stuffing it back in her bra. "Bah-liii-nd."

Mason's mouth dropped open as he went to let one of his razor-sharp witty remarks fly but no words came. Just a guttural rumbling almost too weak to hear rose in his throat. Words having failed him, Mason turned around and stormed down the hall back to the living room in silence. With every step he took, he felt her disapproving angry little stare boring into his back. When he plopped down on the couch and grabbed the bottle of J&B from its hiding place along with the pills from his pocket Hannah slammed the bedroom door. The only clear thought in Mason's head as the echo resounded in his ears was that he had just blown that big Sunday Dinner.

In the bedroom, Hannah threw herself over the bed and cried while her brother drank in the living room.

Ten minutes later, there was a knock on the front door.

"Oh what the fuck?" Mason bitched to himself. "Go away!" He yelled at the door. "We don't want any!"

Accustomed to the warm welcome Spaulding knocked again as he spoke, "Mace, it's me. Open up."

"I already said I don't want any!"

"You can open up or I can stand here knocking annoying your neighbors."

Knocking down the last of the J&B in the glass Mason huffed so hard his lips rolled knowing that Spaulding was apt to follow through with his threat, "Coming!" Hoisting his lanky frame from the sofa, he limped over to the front door to open it. "What do you want?"

174

"Hi, how are ya?" Spaulding returned in a mockingly easy tone as he grabbed Mason's hand and shook it while patting him on the shoulder with the other to move him aside so that he could enter the small house. "Good to see you too."

Shutting the front door while watching Spaulding make his way into the living room and start taking off his coat Mason chimed, "To what do I owe this pleasure?"

Finishing dispensing with his trench coat Spaulding rubbed his hands together to warm them from the autumn chill, "I was just in the neighborhood and...."

"The whole fucking town is 'the neighborhood', cut to the chase," Mason stumbled back to the couch without his cane.

Clearly Mason was worked up over something the bottle of J&B on the table told Spaulding that much. Perhaps he'd come at a bad time, "You ok? Where's Hannah?"

Mason sat down heavily on the couch, grabbed the bottle and refilled his glass, "Sulking in the bedroom, you still haven't answered me, what do you want?"

"And you're sulking out here." Spaulding sat down on the couch. "What happened?"

Mason sipped off the glass and then reached into the drawer of the end table to pluck a Jamaican cigar from it. Settling back into the well-worn leather, he lit the stogie and took a long inhale before letting it go in little ringlets. "She wants to go to church."

Spaulding's mouth opened and then closed as his brain quickly took over. It was no secret that Mason hated religion and that he was very unbiased in that view as it applied it across the board to every single religion on the planet. The two of them had many spirited debates on the subject over the last two decades with Spaulding still considered himself Catholic even though he had not been inside a church since his cousin got married fifteen years ago. "And," he stopped and cleared his throat, "you don't want to take her?"

"Hell no I don't! If I sat in a church through Sunday Mass I'd be no better than the other hypocrites there."

Spaulding knew better than to argue the merits of religion with his old pal so he decided on a more logical approach, "This is something that's important to Hannah?"

"Catholic Girls," Mason barked and knocked down the last of the glass.

"And you're her Conservator, her Guardian, the one person who's charged with looking out for her well-being..."

"What do you think I'm doing? Whistling 'Dixie'?"

"Just wait and hear me out. You're supposed to take care of her and look out for her making sure she's treated fairly and that her rights aren't violated..."

"What are you getting at?"

Spaulding continued in a cautious tone, "You're interfering with her Constitutional Right to...."

"Freedom of Religion?" Mason laughed. "That's exactly what I'm doing; freeing her from the choking ties of religion."

"No," Spaulding countered unshaken, "you're interfering with her Constitutional Right to *worship*, how very un-American of you, Major Mason."

"Fah—what the fah—...."

Down the hall the bedroom door opened and Hannah emerged wiping her eyes, "T-urch," she huffed at Spaulding as she sniffed back the tears.

Mason wasn't going to like it but Spaulding knew a way out of the situation in which both brother and sister could consider themselves the victor, "How about if I take her?" He didn't wait for Mason to answer as he looked to Hannah, "Would you like that? Would that be ok, if I took you to church?"

Hannah's face came to life as she raised her open hands to the sky and nodded. On unsteady feet, in her pretty white dress with the fake flowers in her hair, she toddled down the hall to the couch as fast as she could, "Puh-ph-lease....Rick-y?"

"Don't I look like the shit-bag if I say no?"

"Yep," Spaulding chirped as he rose to his feet and grabbed his coat, "Come on Hannah, I'll take you to Sunday Mass."

Hannah laughed and tittered like a little girl as she cheered, "YAAAAY!"

Holding his arm out to her Spaulding smiled both happy to take Hannah to church and to stick it to his old buddy, "Shall we go?"

With uncertainty on her face, Hannah stepped forward and took his arm, "Y-y-yes."

Knowing he was trapped between a rock and hard place Mason gave in, "Fine, go to church, conform, be a good little brainwashed do-bee."

Although she knew he was insulting her Hannah didn't care. She bent down to lay a loud smooch on his whiskery cheek, "Th-th-ank yew, Rick-y."

"Whatever," Mason waved a hand in the air as if he didn't care, "I still want my pot roast, my Sunday Dinner, tonight."

With a wide smile, Hannah kissed the top of his head and tousled his hair, "OH-Kay."

"You come right home after church, young lady, you got that?"

"Don't worry, Mr. Mason, I won't keep Hannah any later than that," Spaulding returned and made Hannah cackle with delight.

The upswing to Spaulding taking Hannah to church was that Mason had an hour all to himself in the quiet house. He took out his bottle of J&B, his cigars, and his ever-present amber bottle of Oxies. Putting his feet up on the coffee table he flicked on the TV to watch Sunday College Football where the Wolverines were playing Notre Dame.

II

Saint Anthony's Catholic Church was the only Catholic Church in the tiny town of Willington, VT—or within 20 miles for that matter—and it was less than two miles straight down the hill from Mason's house. A picturesque little fieldstone

177

church set on an acre or two of open land it was quintessential New England. Spaulding and Hannah arrived just after the start of Sunday Mass.

When Scott opened the door for her, she slipped out of the car and toddled along beside him up the steps and through the big dark green double doors. She stopped at the fontanel to make the sign of the cross with holy water before entering the nave and finding the small congregation already engaged in worship.

Scott gave her his arm and she took it as they walked quietly down the main aisle and took a seat nearer the front in an empty oak pew. He felt a little uncomfortable as eyes shifted to them, the newcomers, but Hannah didn't seem to notice. She just picked up a hymnal and laid it on her lap then gave her full attention to the priest at the altar.

When the priest said, "Let us pray",

There wasn't enough room for her to kneel so she just bowed her head and put her hands together.

When the priest said, "Glory to God in the Highest"

Hannah stumbled through the response; "Ah-d peese to His peep-le on Ear-th."

Hannah took a great but simple joy in her worship, she smiled through the entire Mass and when it came time to give praise through song she tapped her foot and hummed along with them.

The Rite of Peace came and Hannah shook hands with everyone around her as she quietly said; "Peese be wit you."

Mass began nearing its end with the Celebration of the Eucharist. As the priest and congregation prayed, Spaulding saw Hannah tear up just a little bit as she stuttered to echo the response with everyone else; "Ohn-ly say the ww-ord and I sh-all bee heal-ed."

In that moment he couldn't help but wonder if she really was waiting for God to heal her of all the wounds He'd seen fit to lay on her.

178

Hannah wasn't shy about getting up and getting in line with the rest of the congregation for Holy Communion. Although the church was far from overflowing on this Sunday morning, Scott thought it best to go with her. They waited in line together with Hannah on his arm waiting patiently.

When her turn came, holding out a communion wafer, the priest looked at her and said; "The Body of Christ."

With her mouth open ready to receive she uttered, "Ah-Men."

The priest hesitated before giving her the wafer, "Sister...?"

"Han-nah."

"Sister Hannah, I'm Father Murphy. It's nice to have you with us today, my child." T

"Th-ank you," she stuttered with a smile.

Father Murphy repeated the phrase, "The Body of Christ,"

"Ah-men," Hannah said again just before he laid the dry cracker on her tongue.

The two turned to go but the priest tapped Spaulding on the shoulder, "My son? I don't recognize your face."

"Scott," the good doctor said suddenly nervous as he cleared his throat, "I'm just accompanying her today Father," Spaulding stuttered.

"Are you Catholic, Scott?"

"Yes, Father, I am."

The priest held up the wafer, "The Body of Christ..."

"Amen," Spaulding replied and took communion for the time in more than a decade.

"I hope to see the two of you again," the priest encouraged as they walked away.

Back in the pew, Hannah was fidgety and Scott snickered, "It always sticks to the roof of your mouth." He leaned in a little as the congregation finished taking Communion, "What do you say we get a cup of coffee after this. It'll drive Mason absolutely crazy if you're twenty minutes late."

179

Hannah covered her mouth as she held back the laugh but her eyes sparkled bright.

Every Sunday after that, Spaulding showed up at Mason's door promptly at 11:45am to take Hannah to mass.

Chapter Eleven

Monday evening Richard Mason came home to a new sofa bed and a new arrangement of his things.

Betsey explained that she thought Hannah was bored and she had tried to stop her but Hannah had arranged everything in the house in color order from darkest to lightest. Where that wasn't possible, she arranged items by size.

She had been very meticulous about it.

Opening the kitchen cabinets, he saw that every plate, cup, saucer, and glass was neatly arranged. All of the silverware was lined up in the drawer. All of his movies were lined up neatly in the bookcase in color order and he found that interesting since, like his books also newly arranged, so many of them had black spines. That did not stop her, she arranged those by the color of the font on the titles, where that wasn't possible—a lot of them used gold or red lettering—she arranged them by size from largest font to smallest. She even did the same with his sheet music.

Hannah was perched on the new sofa under a comfy blanket. To him she looked as proud as she did tired. "Been busy today, I see." He said as he saw Betsey out for the night. Coming back inside he saw the mail sitting on the piano. Among the bills and junk mail was a letter from the Lawrence Law Firm in Victorville. Hannah's first monthly check had arrived. "Looks like your money's here," he said waving the envelope slightly.

She went off to the kitchen and came back with a pen. Up until now he hadn't asked her to write her name or anything else because he didn't think she was capable.

She proved him wrong.

Mason put the check down on the coffee table and Hannah painstakingly printed her name on it before handing it back to him. "Is this what you did at your group home?" He asked. "You signed it over and someone cashed it for you?" That was what he thought and whoever was supposed to cash it and give her the money had been ripping her off or he wouldn't have had to spend $500.00 on new clothes for her.

Swallowing hard Hannah nodded her head.

She didn't look like she wanted to pursue the matter and Mason had a long day at The Mountainside. "What's for dinner?"

At that she perked up and laid out a spaghetti dinner for him.

On Tuesday he came home with the money in ten twenty dollar bills. He meant to give it to her not dangle it in front of her like some carrot before a mule. Before he could hand it to her, Hannah snatched two of the twenties from his hand. To him it looked like Hannah got forty bucks a month and somebody got an extra sixty to put in their pocket. When he stood there holding out the rest waiting for her to take it, she shook her head and made the sign for 'dirty'. "The money's dirty?" Mason asked and looked at it. "Looks fine to me," He kept holding it out to her but she wouldn't take it. Her gaze slowly dropped to the floor, they seemed to linger over his crotch as they went.

Dirty.

Maybe Hannah got a little extra spending money if she was an extra good girl. If she did a small favor for whoever cashed the check? For whoever gave her The Clap.

"You get extra now that you live with me so take it," Mason pushed the money into her hand. "It's yours. No strings attached. Yours. Got it?"

Her eyes widened and her cheeks flushed wildly with color as she gazed down at the $200.00 in her hands.

"Oh, no, I know what you're thinking. Don't you dare put that in the collection plate," he warned sternly.

Hannah clutched the money to her chest and hot-footed it to the bedroom to find a good hiding place.

As the week went on Hannah started to become more active, almost as though she were waking up from a long daze. She seemed to have more energy and that let her show a

182

deeper interest in the piano and making music with him in the evening. She got better at learning songs she didn't know and retaining the information at least for short periods. Still, he had hard time keeping her awake and alert past 9 o'clock or so.

He noticed that, while her hands were still cold, they were no longer taking on that bluish tinge late in the day. Her circulation was getting better, the quality of blood flow improving. With that came a few drawbacks, Hannah began to rub her legs and her temples during the day—which he watched through the Nanny Cam—and in the evenings. The increased blood flow was letting those misfiring pain receptors know that her legs hurt and she was getting headaches.

He noticed her watching the clock at first, waiting until it said it was time for another painkiller, but within a few nights she was asking him for more before the appropriate time. Usually it wasn't by much, only an hour or two and she certainly wasn't downing as many in a day as he was. He had no qualms about granting her requests and giving her more Oxy.

As the week went on, Doctor Richard Mason became very busy at Mountainside. Several nights during the week, he was unable to get home until late in the evening. The home aide agency wasn't thrilled with that and started to get on him about giving them more advanced notice if someone was going to have to stay late with Hannah. They understood his position but he couldn't call them at five o'clock and expect someone would be available until nine or ten that evening.

Friday morning Mason brought Hannah into work with him so that Goodspeed could administer a stress test. The first try was a standard EG on a treadmill. It didn't work very well for Hannah. If the treadmill had been a double-wide she might have done better. The result was uninterpretable so Goodspeed tried her on the bike and she had an easier time peddling that then putting one foot in front of the other in

183

such a confined space. Still, her heart rate didn't climb as swiftly as it should. Considering that, he thought that she still had more water than blood in her veins. Goodspeed administered thallium to boost her heartrate.

At the end of it all, Goodspeed gave him the news that Hannah had myocardial ischemia which meant the oxygen flow to her heart (and probably other areas of her body as a result) was very poor but Goodspeed felt certain that the condition would get better as her circulation and quality of blood in her veins improved. Her INR had been a grand .98 this morning, up three-tenths of a point from nearly two weeks ago.

With a bit more caution, he broached the next part of his report telling Mason that he come across something on the ECG that he couldn't explain.

At one point as she was peddling the bike, Hannah stopped, and Goodspeed said it looked like she had indigestion, she rubbed the area around her heart and the ECG gave a long wavy line, which lasted for nearly as long as she stopped peddling. Goodspeed thought it could be a murmur or an arrhythmia. Those might explain why she had been put on the Vasotec.

Mason didn't react so he went into the rest of it.

Hannah had a splitting headache after the stress test. She grimaced and held her hand to her head as she whimpered and shut her eyes tightly. Hannah was unsteady on her already wobbly feet when Goodspeed had her stand up so he could take her blood pressure, she dropped the hand from her head to her stomach, clutched, turned her head to the side and threw up a small amount of bile. Goodspeed thought that, like the other problems she was currently experiencing, the headaches, which seemed to be coming a little more regularly now, were merely the result of increased blood flow to the brain and they would soon subside. The blood vessels in her brain and other areas of her body were expanding with the increasing flow of blood and therefore causing her pain. The nausea was probably caused by her ulcer.

"That's a few too many 'probablyies'." Mason sat back in his office chair. "Anything conclusive?"

"It's a long process, Mace, be patient," Goodspeed advised.

"Don't talk to me like I'm just a family member," Mason returned heatedly, "I'm not one of them."

Goodspeed stood up leaving his files behind for Mason' perusal. He made it to the door with his mouth clamped shut but just couldn't silently walk through it. He turned around to his boss, "That's exactly what you are right now and what she needs you to be. A family member." He didn't wait for a response before taking his leave.

On Friday night just as Mason was arriving home, his cellphone rang. Fishing it out of his pocket only to see that it was his lawyer calling, he put it through to voice mail before getting out of the car and going into the house.

Hannah was sitting on the couch under a blanket and she was unusually quiet. Before he could ask Betsey if Hannah had a bad day the phone in his pocket buzzed letting him know he had voice mail.

As was his usual custom, he gave the mail on the piano a glance only to see a certified letter sitting on top of the pile.

The house phone began to ring.

Picking up the letter and seeing it was from the Victorville County Court he turned to the ringing phone. *I am so not going to like this,* he thought as he reached for the phone with the caller ID telling him it was the lawyer on the line.

Holding the unopened letter in one hand and the phone in the other, he sat down hard as his lawyer informed him that someone was challenging him for guardianship of Hannah. Franklin MacNeill was bringing a petition before the Court claiming that Doctor Richard Mason was a workaholic who kept strange hours that were unsuited to the stable environment that Hannah needed. It further stated that he

185

was disreputable, often keeping the company of ladies-for-hire and drinking himself into a stupor at Tony's Bar. According to several prior Malpractice Law Suits filed against him, he was; reckless, a suspected drug addict, and he had a volatile temper. If all that wasn't enough, Mason didn't even have a proper place for his sister to live. Therefore, he was unfit to care for her.

Both of them had to be in Victorville next week to answer the charges and prove them untrue.

"Who is this guy?" Mason demanded. "What right does he have to say or do any of this?" Hannah was sitting all curled up in the corner of the couch, he looked to her and asked, "Do you know Frank MacNeill?"

Now that he'd said the name, it did sound familiar. He watched Hannah nod rather emphatically indicating that yes she knew him.

Hadn't his mother said that name when he talked to her last? Hadn't she said that Frank MacNeill was Hannah's boyfriend? The one she was dating when she had the accident?

"When's the last time you saw Frank?" He wasn't sure she could answer the question; Hannah's concept of time wasn't like most other people.

Hannah took two steps back before she shrugged her shoulders giving him that innocent stare.

Something in those brown eyes told him not to believe her. Hannah knew when she had last seen Frank MacNeill. Maybe she couldn't give him a date but he felt certain that if he pressed her she could come up with details about it. "He's just after the money," Mason said hoping not to upset her but wanting to see her reaction. Maybe Frank was the one cashing the monthly check and getting a little bonus on the side. Hannah just stood there looking down at him. Maybe he wasn't.

Londregan answered that charge, "He's not asking for the money, Richard. It doesn't say anything about the Trust or

186

removing you as Trustee. Whoever he is, *Hannah* is what he's after *not* the money that comes with her."

Over the phone, the lawyer explained that he didn't know who Frank MacNeill was but he already had someone working on it and Mason should come by the office Monday afternoon when he expected to have a full dossier.

"How does he know so much about me?" Mason snapped.

"Google's a wonderful tool," Londregan replied as easily as he could, "that and he's probably got his own PI digging around. Is there anything I should know, Mason? Anything more unsavory than usual that he might find?"

"Yeah, I'm a doctor by day and an axe murderer by night," Mason slammed down the phone.

Chapter Twelve

Over the weekend, no matter how Mason, demanded, bitched, whined, moaned, complained, kicked his feet, or threatened her, Hannah emphatically refused to communicate with him regarding Frank MacNeill. At first, she did this by constantly putting her finger her to his lips to shush him. The more she did that telling him it was a secret, the more irritated he became.

Hannah tried to distract her brother from his path several times by sitting at the piano indicating they should play a song rather than argue. Mason didn't budge. Instead, he told her over and over how important it was that she give him some clue as to what Frank MacNeill might be after. He was trying to remove her from her new home. Why would he do that?

Either Hannah didn't know or she'd been sworn to secrecy upon pain of death or burning in hell. Several times, she made a sign that he didn't recognize right off, even though he had been brushing up on his American Sign Language. The reason he didn't recognize it was simple, it was not an official sign.

She stood there staunchly with one finger to her lips blowing air hard enough to fill a hot air balloon and making that loud hiss; *Shhhhh!*

When that didn't shut him up, she stuck out both forefingers and brushed one across the top of the other a few times then tried to shush him again.

Hannah must have done it three or four times before he finally caught on to the sign.

Shame. Shame.

He hadn't seen that particular gesture since he was in junior high school. Mason supposed it was even possible that one had to grow up Catholic to understand it. Whatever it was that Hannah was hiding, it wasn't just a secret but a shameful secret. No matter how many times and in how many ways he told her he didn't care about that, he wouldn't judge her for whatever it was she was hiding and wouldn't think any less of her, Hannah remained tight lipped.

After a while, she stopped making any signs at all and just sat crammed into the corner of the couch clutching her teddy bear. Mason continued his interrogation and by Sunday morning, he had aggravated her so much she threw up twice. By Sunday afternoon, she refused to come out of the bedroom.

On Sunday night, Mason was awoken by a bright light falling across his face. Looking up he saw the door to the front mudroom was open letting in the streetlight. "Hannah?" Sitting up he looked down the hall to see the bedroom door open. Throwing the covers off he grabbed his cane and scrambled to the hall where he found the front door wide open. "Hannah?" He called out in the darkness. Panic started to rise inside him as his eyes scanned the night looking for any sign of her. Did she wander off? If so, where? "Hannah!"

Something across the street moved, and he knew that she was over there, sitting under a tree staring back at him. It was nearly two o'clock in the morning as he stumbled across the wet street to gather her and bring her back into the house. She didn't give him much trouble, didn't try to argue or fight but to say she went willingly might be an overstatement.

Mason put her back to bed and double-bolted the door but a few hours later Hannah woke up screaming in the dark. She didn't seem to know where she was or who he was, she just kept screaming as though someone was burning her. The teddy bear clutched tightly under one arm and the other reaching out for something that wasn't there. It took a shot of Diazepam to calm her down and put her back to sleep.

Monday morning Mason blew off work and went to Londregan's office where he discovered that nearly twenty-five years ago James Rice took out a Permanent Restraining Order on Franklin MacNeill. Claiming that the man was a threat to his daughter and that no matter how many times

189

and in how many ways the man was told to stay away from her he just would not comply. Franklin MacNeill showed up unexpectedly and at odd hours of the night at the group home where Hannah resided. He brought her gifts and, at times, tried to take her off the property.

At first it seemed Hannah welcomed his visits and was often seen being 'inappropriately affectionate' with him. This wasn't something Franklin MacNeill seemed to dissuade but encourage. James Rice became incensed and eight times in four years he had Franklin MacNeill arrested for violating the PRO and once for attempted kidnapping when he was caught trying to get Hannah into his car.

As a result, Frank spent a total of a year in the county lock up for violating the PRO and another nine months in the local minimum-security prison for attempted kidnapping. Still, he would not quit. Each time he got out, within a month or so, he was right back at Hannah's door. The last time he was caught doing so was eighteen years ago, that last visit upset her so much, according to the police report and subsequent DMR report, that Hannah had nightmares for weeks after and had to be heavily sedated.

It seemed to Mason that Hannah's nightmares returned with the man. "If he tormented her then, why is he even being allowed to bring this petition now?" Mason asked as he sat in the lawyer's office.

"Because Judge James Rice is dead. The PRO no longer applies. If you want to enforce it, you'll have to take one out yourself but you'll have to prove he's a danger to her now. Until then, this case will go forward, Richard and there's nothing anyone can do about it."

"He's stalking her," Mason insisted. "What kind of a lunatic stalks a mentally disturbed woman?"

"I wouldn't go into Court and call him a stalker if I were you," the lawyer said staunchly. "From the reports he's become a well-known and well respected member of the Victorville community, he owns a small chain of garages and a

190

horse stable. He has a lovely four-bedroom home on five acres of farmland. He was married for fifteen years and his wife, Connie, recently died of ovarian cancer."

Well, that explained his sudden disappearance from Hannah's life and his subsequence reappearance. "So he thinks he'll replace her with Hannah?" Mason mused aloud. "More likely, Frank thinks that wherever Hannah goes, the money follows." Mason retorted.

"That is one possibility," the Londregan agreed in a leading tone.

"And another possibility would be?"

"That he actually does care for Hannah."

Mason snorted, "Yeah, right. Do you really think some grease monkey with an arrest record is better suited to caring for her than I am?"

Mason stopped and wondered if he was looking at the story of high school sweethearts kept away by Fate and a cruel controlling daddy. Romeo and Juliet kept apart by a mean father. He wondered if Hannah wanted to be with Frank. If that was so, she didn't give any indication. Maybe he should have asked her *that* over the weekend instead of treating her like she was a prisoner in Gitmo.

"No, I don't but contrary to your religiously held belief that everyone is a selfish lying bastard, I'd like to remind you that every now and then people are motivated by good intentions."

"Humm, I hear the road to hell is paved with them." Mason returned quickly.

Shaking his head with a slight sigh Londregan reached into his desk to produce a bottle of Gentleman Jack. He poured two glasses and pushed one toward Mason.

Mason looked down at the glass in front of him and then at his watch to see it was 10:30, "A little early for that, don't you think?"

"Do you?" The lawyer countered.

191

Swallowing hard Mason reached for the glass it took half of it down before settling back in the swanky leather chair.

"Don't get me wrong here, ok?" Londregan began no longer speaking Lawyer to Client but Mano y Mano. "Just between you and me, if you want to fight for Hannah you've got a good case, but if you don't, Richard, if you're looking for a way out of this, then this could be your golden opportunity. I'm sure Hannah doesn't exactly fit into your lifestyle—"

"Oh, yeah, you mean my rockin' swingin' sex life? Yeah, she's really puttin' a crimp in my style." Mason mocked. "I haven't been to bigbustybabes.com in over a week."

"All I'm saying is that if you don't want this responsibility—and why should you?—or if you don't want your own past dragged through the mud and your colorful character called into question in such a public forum yet again..." he suggested letting his voice trail off.

A week and a half ago, Mason might have jumped at the chance but not now, no now he was deeply insulted by the idea that he'd follow in Dear Old Dad's footsteps by passing her off to some complete stranger and washing his hands clean. "I don't believe it," Mason said, "he's just after the money."

"All right," Attorney Londregan agreed," in that case, that's the position you'll take in court. Your only job here is to prove to the Court that you're providing a stable, safe, home for Hannah. That she is being cared for while you're at work and not left to her own devices. You have the law and Rice's last wishes on your side." Then the attorney had the dubious responsibility of informing Doctor Mason that someone from the Department of Developmental Services would be contacting him to do a home study for the State of Michigan. They would want to interview Hannah so they could make an independent report to the Court as to their assessment of her mental condition

"I have a safe place for her to live, she isn't being neglected, in fact, she's getting better. We were able to get rid of several of her medications. She had a stress test on Friday she did all right, not great but all right, especially for a woman who doesn't get any regular exercise."

"The fact that you're giving her such great medical care will definitely look good to the Court. I'll find someone out in Victorville to represent you if it's what you want, but you really might like to take some time to reconsider."

"Could get ugly, huh?"

"Depends on how serious he is and he may be deadly serious about this, Richard." Returning to a more professional tone Londregan refilled the empty glasses and then shuffled through the folder on his desk. "Did you know that Hannah had a baby?"

"How do you know?" Mason asked suddenly taken off guard. Certainly, he hadn't seen Hannah's test results. Then he was pushing a piece of paper in front of him.

"Death records are public knowledge," he said easily.

Death records? Hannah wasn't dead. Obviously, Frank MacNeill wasn't dead either so what was he talking about? Mason looked down at the paper to read the death record for one Richard Morgan MacNeill, son of Johanna Morgan Rice and Franklin Angus MacNeill. Little Richard was born September 5, 1986 died September 20, 1986. The cause of death listed was immolation. She named her son after him and the poor little boy only got to spend fifteen days on planet Earth. "The baby burned to death."

"I know what immolation means," Mason's eyes kept coming back to the year, 1986, fully two years after Hannah's accident. She would have been twenty, a legal adult. Was she already judged incompetent? Why? All of the X-rays and all of the tests and all of the old medical records indicated there was nothing wrong with Hannah's brain after the accident. More than that, if it was true, if she was deemed incompetent by the court then Frank MacNeill was engaging in sexual intercourse with a woman who, whether she wanted to not,

193

couldn't legally consent. That made him a rapist. Was that Hannah's big shameful secret or was it the baby?

Not liking the look on his client's face, Londregan began the unpleasant task of continuing with what his investigator found. "There was a fire," he fished in the folder again and pushed a copy of a newspaper clipping across the desk. "The baby and two young adults died in the fire."

The headline read *St. Anne's Home Burns to the Ground*. The first paragraph informed Mason that St. Anne's wasn't a group home but a home for unwed mothers. That meant in 1986 Hannah was not incompetent. It also informed him that, while the Fire Marshall suspected the ultimate cause of the fire would be a shoddy electrical system they were looking into arson as a possible cause as well. The fire broke out in the nursery claiming the life of a newborn baby boy before it spread down the corridor to claim two more lives, both pregnant teenage girls, and then consuming the rest of the house.

Hannah must have been inconsolable. She lived and little Richard died. Did the fact that she hadn't been able to save her son drive her over the edge? According to the attorney's records, it was shortly after that when Hannah entered her first group home and James Rice tried to ban Frank MacNeill from her life for good.

No matter how you looked at it, surely, the fact that his Good Catholic daughter was pregnant out of wedlock hadn't set well with pillar of the community Judge James Rice. No, not at all. The man broke his daughter's arm for an offense Richard Mason couldn't fathom and he'd bet his last dollar it was James Rice who stomped on Hannah's foot while drunk and yelling about burnt cookies. What did he do when she turned up pregnant without a ring on her finger? He sent her away to a home for unwed mothers Mason almost found that funny. Seemed James Rice was a rare breed, a non-hypocritical Catholic. No abortion for Hannah. No baby either. Undoubtedly, he intended to see to it that his grandchild was

194

given up for adoption whether Hannah agreed or not was irrelevant. After all, Rice was the County Judge.

It's a secret. A shameful secret.

Suddenly it seemed that just about everything about Hannah Rice was a shameful secret.

"Twenty, she was twenty," Mason said to himself. Young but not too young. If MacNeill had been attempting to do the right thing, to stand by her, then what?

"And two days away from a court date which, by all accounts, would have terminated James Rice's guardianship over her. For Hannah's sake, if you think it's appropriate, you might want to work out some type of visitation schedule," he quickly added, "supervised of course I'm not suggesting you leave this man alone with your sister. Perhaps all he really wants is to be sure that she's all right, road to hell or not."

"She was conserved then? In 1986?"

Londregan nodded, "For medical reasons she was conserved shortly after the accident..."

"Like, right after her eighteenth birthday kind of shortly?"

"That's right. It was so that Rice could continue to act on behalf of his adult daughter while she recovered."

"From the accident? The one that left her crippled...physically."

"It's not like you to beat around the bush, Mason," Londregan poured two more short glasses. Sitting back in his quilted leather chair, he took a long sip as he tried to size up his client's frame of mind. Londregan handled two malpractice suits for Mason after the Good Doctor helped build the new cutting-edge clinic. He also helped Mason draw up a new Last Will & Testament (in which Mason left everything to his mother, Claire but in the event of her death it all went to a friend of his named Scott Spaulding), along with a Living Will and Appointment of Health Care Agent (power of which also went to Scott Spaulding). In those sessions Mason was matter-of-fact but now he looked shaken and in need of answers to tough questions. The kind Mason was more used to asking than answering. "But I know what you're asking me and the answer is no, she wasn't mentally feeble after the accident. In fact, she was well on her way to taking back her life when the baby died. From what I can gather that pushed her over the edge."

Pursing his lips as his head bobbed on his shoulders and his throat let out a rumbled Mason looked at the lawyer, "I don't suppose there's anything in there about when she stopped talking."

Londregan looked down at the file in front of him and answered honestly, "I don't know. All of this just came in an hour ago and I didn't have time to thoroughly read all of it." Closing the file, he pushed it across the desk, "I know you Mason, and you're dying to read it. Take it. You paid for it."

After downing the small glass, Mason snatched the file from the lawyer's desk and left the office. He took two more pills on the way to his car before throwing the file onto the passenger seat. It flew opened and the papers scattered. Mason looked at them in disgust. "Judge Rice," he crooned, "you just couldn't give up control of her, could you? I mean, without you, who'd punish her when she burned the fucking cookies?" Jamming the key into the ignition of the old Lincoln, he peeled out of the parking lot and headed for home. Popping open the glove compartment he grabbed a hidden Jamaican and box of wooden matches. He smoked the high-priced cigar to the nub before he reached the driveway under a full head of steam.

Chapter Thirteen

Hearing the car pull in, Hannah realized Ricky was home early. Hoping nothing was wrong and he wasn't about to tell her he'd found another place for her to live she went to the door to greet him hoping he would like the Beef bourguignon she'd been making for him as a peace offering. When the door opened, Ricky pushed her aside without so much as 'hello' then he slammed the door, threw his coat over the couch and limped into the living room. "I'm home, Betsey, you can leave now."

Betsey came out from the kitchen where she'd been checking on Hannah's meal, "Is everything alright, Doctor Mason?"

"Yeah, played hooky today. You can too, go on, go home, I'll pay you for the whole day."

Grateful for half a day off, Betsey grabbed her coat and slid into it with a smile, "See you tomorrow Hannah." She waved to the woman she sat with every day. Hannah didn't smile back and she only twiddled her fingers in the air to wave good-bye.

When Betsey was out the door Mason grabbed the bottle of J&B from the bookcase where he'd hidden it behind the Encyclopedia Medica. Ripping off the cap, he drank straight from the bottle in a long gulp.

Even with the distance between them, Hannah could smell the tobacco on him as the reek of alcohol began to spread out through the air. The look on his face, those stern eyes and that tightly set jaw told her she was in trouble.

Hannah's broken mind recalled younger days. It warped her back in time as surely as any DeLorean equipped with a flux capacitor could. Suddenly she was standing in her own living room back in Victorville and her father's eyes were smoldering as he drank just before he started to yell.

Swiping the back of his hand over his alcohol soaked lips Mason demanded, "Hannah, tell me about Frank! Tell me about the baby about your *son*, Richard."

Hannah put her finger to her lips.

Mason lost his temper as he strode toward her, "Don't you shush me!" Mason reached up and grabbed her wrist pulling her hand away from her mouth. "No, no more secrets. It's time to talk now."

Looking down she heard the voice hiss in her ear; *Talk now? Why talk now? He said never want to talk! NEVER! Or you'll BE IN TROUBLE!!*

Listening to the voice, Hannah gave an absent nod knowing that was right. Her father always said not to say a word about Richard even though his loss was all she could ever think of, the horrible way he died and how desperately she tried to save him as he screamed and cried out for her. Being silent never stopped the scar his death laid upon her heart from aching and oozing putrid green pus.

Never say a word, that's what James Rice said. *Not one word about that filthy little bastard.*

Her eyes drew slowly to the ceiling like a drowning woman trying to find the surface of churning waters.

The voice up there, the one that was always soothing, the one that belongs to God gently reminded her; *He's dead. He can't hurt you anymore or tell you what to do or think or say.*

Yes, that was right. It was. Months ago they told her that her father was dead. Finally. Blessedly. Gone from this Earth and she had silently rejoiced at the news. Yet here he was standing in front of her yelling, his face gnarled and the hand holding the cane flailing in the air, the other clamped around her wrist, smelling of booze and tobacco just like always.

Planting her foot against the bottom of the sofa for extra leverage Hannah gave it all she had as she tried to pull her wrist out of his grasp. Yet, it did no good. He was a lot stronger than she remembered in later years.

198

"Stop it! Right now!" He spat sharply. Hannah stopped squirming so suddenly he thought she would topple over backwards but instead of falling back, she came forward swiftly and planted the palm of her free hand over his mouth.

"Shhh!" She demanded. "Shhh!!" Hannah applied more pressure as she came in closer, those dark eyes alive with fear and anger. "SHHH!!!" With her hand clamped over his mouth and pinching his nose shut, Hannah pressed up against him to use the momentum to spin him around and deposit Mason on the couch with a heavy thump. Hannah didn't let go. She followed him down landed on his lap pinning him to the cushions with her knee between his stomach and an even tenderer region.

Struggling for breath Mason watched Hannah's eyes shut tight and her cheeks puff out until they went from alabaster to bright crimson. He thought she would hyperventilate then pass out.   Still holding the hand over his mouth Hannah opened her eyes and took a breath attempting to compose herself. She came in close one more time, eye to eye, she raised the finger she had been using to shush him and shook it at him. "No," she said in a very clear and lucid voice though it didn't quite sound like her own. That finger made a swift slicing motion in the air. "Ceee-ret. No. No."

Ripping her hand away from his mouth and nose, he took in a big gulp of air as he stared into those wild eyes. Mason did not know what she was thinking but the look in her eyes said; *we don't talk about this buddy and if you keep it up there's apt to be some serious bodily injury incurred.*

When the knee in his gut began to pull back Mason pushed forward and she stumbled away from him but the determination didn't leave her face. "It's not a secret anymore because I know about it. I know about you and Frank,--"

Hannah's mouth dropped open, her eyes grew wide as she clasped her hands over her ears and shook her head violently from side to side. Yet nothing could block out the booming voice resonating in her head.

199

Shut up! Why can't you just shut up, Hannah! Just be a good gurl! Be quiet! Don't talk about it! Just LET IT GO! It NEVER HAPPENED! Do you hear me, gurl? It NEVER HAPPEENED! SO JUST....

Mason pulled her hands away from her ears. "I know about the baby and the fire..."

Scooping up the magazines on the coffee table, she hurled them at him. "SHUT UP!" Hannah bellowed her face bright red once more. The well-set jaw and staunchly determined chin began to quiver. The hands that had been gripping, shaking and shushing now shook as they went first to her belly and then came up together as though she were cradling a baby. "Secret."

"Secrets kill people. Lies kill people. Ask me, I know, I see it every day."

Hannah began to rock side to side on her feet as she looked down at the non-existent baby in her arms and she began to cry. "My--mah--my bab-ee. Gone." She held her hands over her ears again and closed her eyes tightly as though she could block the sounds in her head. The sounds and the images came anyway and her eyes could not closely tightly enough to keep the tears from falling. The memories in her mind so long buried and denied flood through her like a hurricane. It brought her crashing to her aching knees and left her wailing in agony.

Fire. So hot. Smoke. Smoke so thick it choked me! It burned my eyes and my lungs. Couldn't breathe. Richard, he screamed! Oh he screamed! Can't reach him. They won't LET ME GO! They're pushing ME OUTSIDE and he's in THERE! He's SCREAMING! He's BURNING! BURNING, BURNING, BURNING, he's BURNING ALIVE!

Cheeks wet and eyes red Hannah raised her head and held her arms up to her brother, "Bab-ee. Mah-ne! Mah bab-ee."

Mason didn't hesitate to comply as he sank to the floor beside her and took her in his arms, "You don't have to keep

200

the secret anymore. You don't have to feel ashamed any more. It's not your fault. I'm so sorry you lost him, little sister, so sorry."

A primal and undeniable cry arose from her languid vocal cords. It was so loud and deep that it shook the windows in their panes and vibrated right through him. At first, he thought it was the sound of thunder or maybe a large truck suddenly applying its brakes. Then it sounded like it was coming from somewhere deep under the floor at his feet.

It was none of those things. It was Hannah, in his arms she was screaming. Before the thought that she was injured could complete itself in his mind he knew it to be the sound of aguish long buried in Hannah's soul, of grief long denied coming to the surface to make itself known to the world. Hers was a type of pain he did not know how to heal.

All he could do was hold her shaking body a little closer and kiss the top of her head. "It's ok, Hannah, it's all right now." What he really wanted to tell her was that he loved her but those words never came easily to him. Something was stinging his eyes. He realized he was weeping with her and for her.

Hannah wailed a good ten minutes or more and he let her. Mason didn't even think about stopping her. Some things you just could not hold back forever or they really would kill you. She cried so hard that she grew weak. Half-hour later she was on the couch under a blanket with a cup of Valium laced tea that he made for her. Her head was spinning and her chest hurt. It was hard enough to tell Up from Down most days but right now it was damn near impossible as the cup rattled on the saucer in her hand.

Mason sat down on the couch next to her. It was getting late, she was exhausted physically and emotionally, it wasn't fair to keep doing this to her but now that the secret was out, it wasn't a secret anymore, maybe he could get some more information out of her before the tea put her out for the night. "When did you see Frank last?"

Hannah's head was foggy and she was so very tired all she could see is her father sitting there. The tone of his voice frightens her more than when his voice is raised. *Why are you being so nice? Why do you care? You just want to get him into trouble.*

The way she was staring right at him that sent chills through his lanky frame. "Who am I?" Mason asked calmly and reached for the teacup that was starting to titter in her hands. "Hannah, who am I?" He put the cup down on the table.

Her upper lip curls as she scoots further back into the corner of the couch; *What a stupid question. How retarded do you think I am now, father? How incapable? How incompetent? How shameful? How embarrassing? All this time you've told me to shut up, be quiet, behave like it never was, but it DID! Now you want to be nice to me?*

While she was looking dead at him, Mason knew she wasn't seeing him but someone else. "It's Richard, Hannah, Richard Mason, Ricky, your brother." Her hand went to the locket around her neck. "Do you remember when I fell out of the tree and you caught me?" He reached out and put his fingertips over hers. "Richard Mason, remember?"

The face in front of her didn't so much fade away as the years seemed to melt away from it making him grow younger before her eyes. Hannah nodded.

With her eyes starting to focus again and her heart slowing she looks at him and thinks; *Yes, of course it's Ricky, of course. That's why he's not angry and telling me how much I'm going to suffer and burn. It's Ricky who else would it be? I'm here in Ricky's house.*

"Can you answer me? When was the last time you saw Frank?" He put the teacup to her lips and made her take another sip. "Hannah?"

Time was a difficult concept and she was tired. Hannah could monitor the time of day by the hands on the clock but to ask what happened in the past and expect her to remember at most times was insurmountable. The days ran together so did the months and the years. Hannah tried very hard to remember the last time she had seen Frank; it was at the old group home, she was sure of that. Then again maybe not. Pink was coming to her mind, pink walls and pink floor. None of the rooms in the old home had been pink. There was something else, something...what? Something.

Sitting next him Hannah absently started sniffing the air. "What do you smell?"

Something familiar and good. Something hot and crunchy. Something that you eat with ketchup.

It was a diner. They had French fries, a heaping basket of fries sat on the table between them.

How long ago?

Yesterday? Last month? Last year? She could not remember but she did remember it was good. Being out of the home was good. The French fries were good.

Something in those concentrating distant sorrow-filled eyes sparkled. "Do you want to see him? If it's what you want then I'll let you."

Hannah held her hand in the air with the palm down and wiggled it from side to side; maybe.

"Drink your tea." Mason wasn't sure if that was good or bad. "Do you want to go live with him?"

No distant stare, no thinking, Hannah signed 'no' as well as shaking her head then she began to rub her temple with one hand, she let out a little moan as the teacup tittered again. He took it away for the last time that night noting she drank the entire cup. "Did you have sex with him the last time you saw him?"

Did she? They went to the diner. They had French fries. They held hands across the table. They went to the park and sat beneath the tree.

Hannah shook her head but without much heart. Truth was, she did not know the answer to his question, and she was too tired to go looking for it.

It was not long after that she crashed for the night. Even with the bit of Valium he slipped into her tea, Mason expected to wake up to the sounds of Hannah crying out as she was caught in the grip of nightmare or to find the front door open but she stayed in the room the whole night. Mason knew that because he got up several times to check on her but each time he found her looking very comfortable in his bed holding onto the white teddy bear and snoozing away.

Morning came and he woke to another scrumptious breakfast courtesy of Hannah, he sat there in his boxers and undershirt, still unshowered and unshaven while she poured coffee into his cup. "Good morning, Hannah." She usually answered with a grunt, a stutter, or other vocalization. Not today.

"Good morning, Ricky."

At first, he was sure must her clear voice must be in his own head until he realized that the fork was falling from his hand, it hit the plate making a little ting sound as it went from plate to table to floor maple syrup whirling in the air as it fell

Chapter Fourteen

Doctor Richard Mason did not believe in miracles or overnight recovery. Even though Hannah continued to speak to him, to answer questions as best she could and make her own opinions known he took her in to the hospital with him. Hannah was not thrilled with the idea in the least. She had been poked and prodded enough over the last few weeks.

Having just come back from the extended magnet donuts they called an MRI machine, she was sitting in a hospital Johnny in Steward's office she swung her legs, banging her feet against the examining table. Doctor Steward kept telling Doctor Mason that this was good news; there was nothing wrong with her and no physical explanation for Hannah's sudden newfound speaking ability. That did not please Doctor Mason; it was unsatisfactory to use his words. Doctor Steward wanted to know why Doctor Mason couldn't just be happy with it. Take it for what it was and stop looking a gift horse in the mouth—so to speak.

"You sit there, we'll be right back." Mason told her and she let out a very deep sigh. "Stop swinging your legs."

Hannah looked down wondering if she was doing that again and found that she was then watched them walk out of the room shutting the door behind them.

"You know," Steward began, "most people would see spontaneous recovery as a good thing, leave it to you to think it's a sign that she's dying."

Mason wanted nothing more than to believe that but he couldn't. "People don't go from," he grabbed Steward by the upper arm and led him further away from the door trying to keep his voice low so Hannah didn't hear him, "babbling stuttering idiots to loquacious orators overnight. Something's going on and I wanna know what it is."

"I don't know what to tell you," Steward said, "her MRI is exactly the same as it was last time. Have a look for yourself."

205

"Love to, now get the Court to let me," Mason hissed through tight teeth. "I'm just sitting in here, remember? Just another family member waiting on the Great Doctor to tell me what's going on."

"Fine, I'll leave them in your office and you can 'find' them, ok? In the meantime, nothing's changed." That was not good enough for Mason. "Go over the events of last night again." He sighed and shook his head. Steward listened as Mason told him, again, of last night.

"She was irately st-st-st-stuttering away at me," he mocked,

"That's not nice, she's your sister." Steward admonished. Hannah had not been very talkative with him. She answered 'yes' or 'no' with relative ease but if he asked her a complex question she looked to Mason for the answer. That only pissed Mason off. They knew she could talk and now she was refusing to do just that. Undoubtedly, Hannah had her reasons and Steward thought he knew what they were. "Show the woman a little respect."

"Show me a reason why her brain is suddenly all lit up and functioning again."

"It's not, I told you..."

"Yeah, yeah, yeah, she's exactly the same," Mason interrupted. "That's bull. There's something there...find it."

"Are you talking as a doctor or a family member?"

"Both. Just find it."

"What happened after that?"

"After her blood chilling wailing was over, she calmed down, I gave her some Valium to take the edge off, she went to bed, she got up, and now I can't shut her up."

Standing there listening to Mason explain the night before, Steward knew that he was going to be lambasted for this but thought it was his duty as Hannah's official attending physician that he explore all angles. "Have you stopped to think that what Hannah had is a spontaneous breakthrough? I mean, I don't know, who would ever think of *you* as therapeutic but still..." Yes, this was not going over well at all he could see in Mason's glaring eyes but he was almost finished with his thought so continued. "Maybe Hannah's speech problems are mental and not as physical as we first thought? By making her face this terrible shameful secret of hers, you opened up the doors in her mind. If it's been a secret so long maybe the only way she could keep it was to stop talking not just about that but about *everything*."

"You saw her in there, she hardly spoke to you. I know she can do it, you should have heard her in the car."

If left uninterrupted, Hannah would just talk, she talked about the apple tree, and cookies, and thanked him over and over and over again for letting her stay with him until he just wanted to tell her to shut up. Told him that she had missed him and was happy he was back in her life.

However, when it came to answering a question, such as, 'how do you feel?' or 'are you dizzy?', Hannah's response time was as slow as it ever was and she seemed to look off to the horizon for the answer before plucking it from thin air and giving it the simplest of voice. A voice which was shaky, a little stuttering, but clear nonetheless.

She volunteered nothing more about Frank MacNeill or the baby.

"Yeah, I did hear her in there and you know why she gave me such short answers? It's because she trusts you," Steward asserted, "Me? Why should she trust me? I'm just another doctor in a long line of doctors who have poked at her, prodded her, and given her drugs she didn't need. You? You're her brother, her *big brother*, you may not feel like it, but that's the way she sees you." He ventured a few more steps closer even though he knew he was risking his boss' ire. This was important and he needed Mason to get it, or at least try to, "She loves you, she wants you to love her, she wants to trust you but most of all she *wants to talk to you*."

Mason opened his mouth and popped an Oxy, before he could start bitching Steward spoke again.

"She's probably never going to be a great orator but take her home, talk to her, be patient with her and let her talk to you. Listen. Let her lead you. Other than that, you know the drill keep an eye on her, start a journal and note anything that seems different about her over the next few days. But for right now just leave it alone. Everything else is normal, her blood pressure is coming up and that's good, her pulse is strong, lungs clear, eyes bright..."

"Yeah, she's got a nice shiny coat, must be all that Dog Chow I keep feeding her."

"Must be," Steward agreed.

"Some doctor you are, I'm looking for answers you give me dog food commercials and psycho-babble bullsh—"

Steward interrupted. "It's a beautiful day, take her to the park, go for a walk with your sister." Mason looked down at the cane and then up at Steward with tightly pursed lips. "Hey, look at this way; you and Hannah are almost even in that department. But she is one up on you." Steward walked off to poke his head into the exam room. "Go on and get dressed, Hannah, everything's fine. Mason's is going to take you for a walk in the park." Behind him, he heard Mason groan, Hannah heard it to, and the corners of her mouth turned upward in a sly grin. Typical little sister, Steward thought. "I'll see you next week, ok?"

"O-K." When he shut the door, Hannah slid off the table and back into her new clothes. She liked her new clothes, they fit properly, and they didn't smell bad or make her skin itch. They weren't ripped and faded. They were pretty, colorful, and comfortable. She told herself that, yes, perhaps it was silly and even tittered on the Sin of Pride but they made her feel good.

"I guess we're going for a walk." Mason said after he knocked on the door before opening it.

Hannah looked out the window at the warm shining sun. "Bike?"

"Bike?" Mason mused. There weren't many good riding days left in the season and soon he would have to put the motorcycle up for the winter. "Hot dogs?" He suggested.

Long ago and far away in the town of Victorville on summer Saturday nights those with cars and motorcycles would caravan out into the sticks to party around bonfires but first they would stop at Bobby's Shack for pounds and pounds of hot dogs to bring with them. He'd been to his share of those teenage tribal gatherings and as he remembered it, so had Hannah—was she with Frank? He couldn't remember, but he did remember that Frank MacNeill had a motorcycle, an old beat up Honda 550 that he rode everywhere.

"That...sssounds...good."

After a quick trip home for warmer clothes, helmets, and, of course, the motorcycle, Mason took Hannah for a ride around the knothole town and ended up taking Steward's advice when they pulled into Woodfield Reservation, a 107-acre municipal park not too far from the Willington town line.

Taking the turn off Old Great Road, he parked the bike in the gravel parking lot. This wasn't a manicured park but a hiking park filled with mature forestland, wildflowers, streams and several interesting rock formations. He did not intend to take her on a vigorous walk, neither of them was up to hiking, but he thought she would enjoy the scenery just the same since so much of it resembled the open spaces in Victorville.

In the parking lot stood the Munchie Wagon, a Fair Weather operation if there ever was one. In the summer, he appeared seeming out of nowhere that the guy who manned the vending cart was up to his eyeballs in people clamoring for summer's delights. Come the first week of November he was gone on the chilling wind and he wouldn't return until the second week of spring. Nice work if you could get it, Mason thought, the guy was probably set for the entire year and he worked only five months. No lives to save. No worried family members to deal with. No late nights—park closed at sunset.

209

Just hot dogs, sodas, chips, and ice cream galore. The Simple Life.

Helping her off the bike, they walked over to the Munchie Wagon and, although she was nervous, Hannah asked the vendor for a hot dog with mustard and relish.

Sitting at a nearby table beneath the noonday sun they ate their hot dogs, drank their sodas while looking at the wildlife and trees around them. "Pretty," Hannah said finishing her hot dog in no more than three bites.

That was usual for her, Mason noticed that most of the time she pushed the food around on her plate without eating much of it at all or she could take up to 45 minutes to eat her dinner. "Want another one?"

Hannah wiped her lips with the paper napkin in a very lady-like fashion. "No...th-thank...you." She smiled and then looked back at the park around her. It was mid-September and the air was getting crisp. The turning leaves were starting to curl just the smallest bit. When she was younger, she loved fall best of all but now September was nothing more than a bittersweet reminder of the life and family she could have had. Maybe soon, with a little luck and a little work, it could make her happy again reminding her of the new family she'd finally found with her brother.

"Ice cream?" Mason offered. To him she looked like she was still hungry. They wandered back to the Munchie Wagon, ordered two small ice cream cones, and began taking a leisurely stroll along the nearest path. Hannah held onto his arm with one hand while she toddled along beside him. "Anything you want to talk about?" He coached. "Since you seem to be doing so well at it today I just thought..."

Hannah leaned her head against his shoulder and sighed before she stopped and looked up at him. It took concentration and it took focus but she found the words she was looking for and pushed them through her lips. "Ah-re you mad?" She moved the hand with the ice cream cone back and forth between them.

"About what? Having you here? No." That was truer than true. In a very short space of time he'd grown not only accustomed to having her around but to enjoying her company and anticipating seeing her smile when he walked through the door after a long day's work.

She took a breath and searched for the words once more. "No. Ah-re you ann-gree?" Hannah moved the hand back and forth again. "Aa-about us?" The hand with the cone went to the locket around her neck.

Are you angry that you're my brother?

That's what she was asking him.

Are you pissed off that you were given away? A bit peeved about having been lied to for so long?

"Not with you." Mason told her. "Nah, I like...I like that you're my sister," he confessed, "you're kinda cool." Taking a lick off the ice cream, he playfully bumped into her and she smiled before she bumped back. "How long have you known?"

Hannah tilted her head to the sky and thought of the words. She knew what they were but they slipped out of her grasp so easily it was hard to keep hold of them until she could get them through her lips. "Mah Burth-day. You...'member...the lay-ke?" She said absently and stroked the gold locket. "Mom told me."

That's a hell of an inappropriate birthday present for a ten year-old girl, Mason thought but before he could say anything Hannah spoke again.

"See-cret...no more." Hannah smiled wide and stood on her tiptoes to give him cheek an icy peck.

Richard Mason couldn't help but smile or feel bewildered when he the color rush into his cheeks. "No more secrets ever." Mason told her. "Since we were kids, huh? Why didn't you tell me?" He tossed his head and rolled his eyes. "Never mind, I know, it was a secret. You're very good at keeping secrets, aren't you?"

211

Hannah held her fingertips to her lip and twisted them to the side then tossed them back over her shoulder; tick a lock and throw away the key.

"You should always keep the key," Mason advised in what suddenly realized was a very big-brotherly tone, "never know when you might need it."

Perhaps that was good advice and from now on, she should keep the key whenever there was a secret. Hannah started walking again, the ice cream in her hand nearly down to the waffle cone.

The path grew steep from here; he had taken a stroll down it once or twice but didn't know how well Hannah would do with it. "Maybe we should head back to the bike."

Hannah looked up ahead and saw a sloping hill; she wanted to know what was on the other side. She looked back at him and concentrated very hard. "Poh-key."

"Pokey?" Mason said with an unbelieving shake of his head. "Did you just call me 'pokey'?"

"Poh-key," she said again with a big smile and pointed to his cane then to the crest of the hill in an unmistakable gesture of; I'll race ya.

"I'll beat you up that hill," he challenged glancing down at her legs.

Without warning, Hannah pushed the rest of the ice cream cone into his mouth covering his lower face with chocolate. She tittered like a fairy and took off.

Did she just do that? He tossed the cone out of his mouth as he drew his sleeve over his face. Looking down he saw melting ice cream. *Yes, she did just do that. Little sisters. What a pain.* "I'll get you! I'm not that pokey!"

Toddling up the hill as fast she could go, Hannah turned around and shouted, "Fas-ter 'an you! Poh-key!"

She was. Little feet planting down on the ground side to side she went right up the hill and beat him by a good minute. Hannah stood there waiting for him with her hands on her hips as she tapped her foot.

When he got to the top and joined her by saying, "You think you're pretty cute, don'cha?"

Hannah laughed again, looped her arm through his then she turned away so she could see what was on the other side.

Chapter Fifteen

The week went by Hannah and stayed the same. She was very active in the mornings up until early afternoon but as the day wore on, she grew listless and tired just as she had done before. More often than not Mason would catch her rubbing the side of her head as though it ached or suddenly putting her hand over her chest, right over her heart.

He'd ask her what was wrong she'd grimace while pointing to her chest.

He would ask her to describe the pain; did it burn? Ache? Throb? Stab? Shoot?

Hannah said no to all of those things and could not find the word to describe it for him, not properly anyway. "Bloop," was what she would say to him.

Bloop.

That was not a medical term Doctor Mason was familiar with and certainly not one of the 12 adjectives normally used to describe pain. He couldn't figure it out. Whatever it was, it didn't seem to affect her for longer than thirty seconds at a time. That did not mean he liked it.

The day the caseworker from the DMR came and inspected his house, Doctor Richard Mason was not allowed to be present, as the people from DMR did not want him influencing Hannah. Mason didn't like the idea of leaving her alone with them and, when they called, told them that Betsey, Hannah's home aide would be present. They didn't seem to have a problem with that so long as Betsey stayed in the background.

Although she was very nervous, Hannah was very clearly able to tell the woman that she did not want to go and live with Frank MacNeill but to stay here with her brother who was taking very good care of her. Hannah made sure to get those last words out of her mouth even though she didn't really want to talk to the DMR person. In her vast experience, people from the DMR always said they wanted to help and

214

some of them even pretended to be helpful but all they really wanted to do was lock up people like her.

They only dropped by every now and then to make sure she was still breathing, other than that, they did not give a damn. Most of the time she didn't even bother to acknowledge their presence in the room any longer, let alone to speak to any of them no matter how nice and kind they may have seemed at first.

Today was different. Today was important. Hannah had an extra long, extra hot shower, brushed her teeth until they were shiny, and did the same with her hair. She dressed in her prettiest fuzzy pink sweater and her favorite new bellbottom blue jeans.

The DMR worker, a portly woman in her early thirties who wore her black hair so severely pulled back from her face she looked like some old western school marm, showed up and promptly dismissed Doctor Mason from his own home telling him he should return in an hour. Then she proceeded to give her simple tests to judge her competency; did she know her name? The date? The President of the United States?

The DMR woman gave Hannah a game of 'Perfection', set it in front of her, pointed out all of the shapes and that they were to go into the little boxes before the timer was up or all of the pieces would pop out of the game.

God's voice whispered in her ear: *This is important. You have to do this. Now focus.*

Hannah did not work very well under pressure; it just made everything so much weightier. The constant little grinding noise of the timer did not help. Still, she tried her hardest and was able to get three-quarters of the little shapes into their proper holes before the time was up and they all spilled onto the table. Hannah was very disappointed with herself for not finishing the task in the allotted time and hoped this wouldn't affect her chance to stay here. The worker showed her flashcards of shapes and pictures and asked her to tell them what they were. She got them all right

215

but was maddeningly slow as she fought to find and give voice to the proper words. The DMR worker asked her several questions.

The worker wanted to know if she missed her old group home.

No, she did not.

Did she miss the people there?

No, she did not.

Was it too quiet here?

No, it was not.

Too loud?

No, it was not.

Was she bored?

Sometimes.

What did she do when she got bored?

She played the piano.

The worker wanted to know if she liked it here.

Yes, she did.

The worker wanted to know if she thought it was a good place.

Yes, she did.

On and on it went until Hannah's head started spinning and splitting.

The worker wanted to know where she slept.

Hannah showed her the bedroom, hoping that the nosey woman firing off so many questions would be satisfied that Ricky had been good enough to give up his own bedroom for her.

The bedroom was still very masculine and to the worker it appeared as though Hannah and her brother were sharing it. "Does he sleep in the bed with you?" She asked in a sharp accusatory tone.

Staring at the woman and not liking the expression on her face or the tone of her voice Hannah thinks: *Well, yes, sometimes he's nice enough to do that. If I've had a nightmare*

216

or something. Yet, she felt that if she tried to explain that to the pushy woman she'd only end up making things worse.

"No," Hannah said and pointed back to the living room and to the couch where they had been sitting.

"He sleeps on the couch?" The worker asked still in that sharp tone.

To Hannah it seemed the woman didn't believe her.

"Y-yes." Hannah's feet started circling each other and she felt flushed. That's when God spoke to her again in His kind and gentle voice.

Think, Hannah, think. You can do it. Nice and slow. Don't be scared.

"Ricky...sleeps..." She made a pulling motion with her arms to indicate that the sofa pulled out into a bed. "Bed."

"I see," the woman said with a disapproving frown.

The woman still had questions.

The worker wanted to know if she had enough to eat.

Was someone caring for her every day or was Betsey just here for appearances?

The worker wanted to know if Ricky was mean to her, if he resented having her around.

Did he leave her alone at night?

On the weekends?

Bring strange women into the home?

Strange men?

The worker noted her notes and asked; "Has he touched you inappropriately? Are you overly affectionate with him, Hannah?"

Hannah's mouth dropped open. "B-b-b-br-other," she stammered and pointed to herself. "Mah-ine."

"Yes, I know he's your brother but you do live in very close quarters." The worker stated flatly as she glanced down at the notes from the previous social worked; Hannah is inappropriately affectionate.

Close quarters? Hannah thought as her eyes wandered around what she considered a spacious house. She wondered

217

why none of the other social workers cares about 'close quarters' at her group homes where so many shared a bedroom all crammed together in a four bedroom house. "R-room," Hannah said and gestured to her surroundings. "Lots."

That left the social worker unfazed, "Have you ever seen him do drugs?"

Hannah had to stop and think of how to answer once more. By now, her head felt as though there were an alien inside ready to bust out at any second. The top of her skull would just blow completely off and some strange looking thing would jump onto the woman's face just like in the old movie. The thought made Hannah snicker.

"This is very serious, Hannah," the woman said in a cold voice, "now answer me."

Ricky did take a lot pills, too many for her own personal liking, but they were the same pills she had been taking for years and, like her, he had a good reason. Not to mention the fact that he was a DOCTOR. He must know what he was doing...or so she thought, "Me...too." She said.

"Doctor Mason makes you do drugs with him?" The DMR worker asked clearly shocked and displeased.

That wasn't quite what Hannah meant but, "Yes."

At that point, the DMR worker began firing questions at her so rapidly that Hannah shrank in her chair.

"You're confusing her," Betsey said from behind them.

"You're not supposed to interfere," she barked at the aide.

"And you're supposed to help not hinder." Betsey McCormick might be fresh out of nursing school but she was no dummy and . Hannah was one of the best clients she'd ever had, the girl never gave her a single lick of trouble, Betsey was not inclined to sit back and hold her tongue. "Let me try. Hannah?" Hannah looked up at her. "Have you seen Doctor Mason smoke marijuana? Do you know what it is?"

"I know," she mumbled, they smoked a lot of pot in the group home, everyone did. Red used to call it Quiet Time

218

Therapy. She sort of missed getting stoned but not the 'therapy' that ensued.

"Does he?"

"No pot."

"Did you ever see Doctor Mason put a needle in his arm?" Hannah's eyes grew wide. "No." She said strongly.

"Put white lines of powder up his nose?"

"No." Stronger still.

"Does he drink a lot?"

"No." That was the only answer Hannah felt might be a lie but she wasn't sure. Ricky did drink but it wasn't near as much as their father imbibed on a nightly basis. Their father could drink a whole quart of J&B in one evening and Ricky drank less than half of that...most nights.

"Then what sorts of drugs do you do with him, Hannah?" The DMR worker asked clearly annoyed. "Are you lying?"

"No!" Hannah looked up at Betsey for assistance but she couldn't give her any. "P-pills," Hannah said finally, "take the pills."

"What pills?"

"This is going to go on forever," Betsey said calmly, "you know what pills she's talking about and so do I. You're only upsetting her and pardon me but I thought that was one thing that was not in your job description."

"Well, we'll find out what pills she's on about when Doctor Mason's drug test comes back," the rude woman looked down at Hannah, suddenly reached out and plucked several strands of hair from her head.

"OW!"

"Hey!" Betsey cried from her place in the kitchen.

"Your drug test too, Hannah." The DMR worker said snidely. "We'll know exactly what you've been up to when we test this." The woman stuffed the strands of graying hair s into a plastic bag.

Hannah's face fell as her mind began racing: *Drug test? Then they will know I've been smoking pot! I didn't mean to,*

219

Red gave it to us, he said it would help us. I know it was wrong but it was...so very nice and I did like it but.... If they find it then they'll think that Ricky....

Hannah snatched the bag with the strands of her hair out of the mean woman's hands. "Nope." Hannah stated flatly and then sat on the bag. "Nunya."

The woman tried, very rudely, to push Hannah aside so that she could retrieve the bag as she huffed, "Nunya? What's nunya?"

Behind them door opened and in walked Mason. "Nunya business," he said evenly but was alarmed when Hannah rushed to his side. "What's going on here?"

"We're not finished." The DMR worker informed him in a cold tone.

"You said an hour, I gave you," Mason looked down at his watch, "an hour and three minutes, you're done."

"Give me the bag, Hannah." She ordered and held out her chubby hand.

Mason looked down at the item being requested and Hannah looked up at him with guilty eyes. "Drug testing her too?" Mason asked. "Give me," Hannah reluctantly gave him the plastic bag and watched as he handed it over to the social worker. "It's yours, but, just so you know, whatever you find past, oh the last three weeks or so, doesn't have anything to do with me. Other than that, we're done." Mason opened the door and pointed through it.

Standing slightly behind her brother, Hannah balled a fist and strike it sideways in the air to indicate victory as she thought: *Ha! Told you! You witch! Get on your broom and fly out of here!*

Two days later the DMR worker submitted a report which while criticizing Doctor Richard Mason's behavior, saying he was curt, gruff, and almost downright rude, but, in the end, supported Hannah staying in his home. It noted that, although the only drugs in his system were those he was prescribed....

"Pot?" Mason asked her as he sat in his living room reading the report and drug test results. "You smoke pot?"

Hannah shrugged her shoulders and gave him half a grin. "Sorry." That didn't take the scowl off his face. Unknown to her, the scowl wasn't directed at her but at Doctor Steward who Doctor Mason figured must have known this little gem of information but had, for unfathomable reasons, chosen not to share it with him. Maybe Steward didn't think it was a big deal. Mason disagreed if that was the case. "R-Red gave it to us. Ther-a-py. 'Lax."

Marijuana was legal in the State of Michigan but, looking down at the paper again the percentage number next to the drug in question he only had one conclusion; she'd been smoking for decades. When it wasn't legal either recreationally or medicinally. Therefore, he was left to wonder what kind of therapy was she talking about. Then it hit me.

'Lax

"Oh? *Re*lax? Yeah, got'cha."

He smirked as he thought; *Yeah, get 'em all stoned, toss 'em a bag of Doritos, turn on the TV and everybody's happy, right?*

Another thought came to his mind. "Who's Red?" Mason asked remembering that Red was the guy who liked coffee and got his meals served first.

"Bed." Hannah huffed and rolled her eyes knowing that wasn't the right word—well, it was sort of the right word but not really— and so she tried again. "Bah-ss."

"Boss? You mean the group home manager?" Mason asked and she nodded. "Nice guy."

Hannah stuck out her tongue and blew a raspberry in the air. "Jer-k."

"Yeah," Mason agreed and put the paper aside. "Jerk."

Suddenly Hannah toddled off toward the kitchen, when she returned she had one hand behind her back and she stood there gazing him with sparkling eyes.

"What have you got?"

221

Hannah licked her bottom lip and thought for a minute until she picked the right word from the air. "Sur-prise." From behind her back, she produced a brand new bottle of J&B with a big red ribbon around the neck and presented it to him. "For you."

"For me?" He took the bottle. "Where did you get this?"

Hannah shuffled her feet and gave a half grin that looked very guilty. "Sorry." Earlier that day she and Betsey had gone for a walk since the weather was still nice. When they rounded the corner on the path home, they passed a liquor store. Hannah still had $180.00 of the money Ricky had given her and she went into the store, by process of elimination, found the right bottle, and paid for it herself. Betsey didn't seem to be sure if that was a good idea or not but she kept saying Hannah was an adult and could do what she wanted. It had been a very long time since anyone had said anything like that to her and Hannah was very pleased.

"Thank you," Mason said and put the bottle down on the table without opening it. To his surprise, Hannah opened it for him and then poured him a small glass. Then she stood up straight and smiled at him as she waited for him to take a drink. Mason understood that Hannah was not just trying to make him happy and to please him; she was showing him that she trusted him. She trusted him not to get drunk and fly off the handle because the cookies got burned or she couldn't stay on her bike as she was learning to ride a two-wheeler.

Mason complied and took a small sip then Hannah sat down at the piano. Glass in hand, Mason settled back on the couch and waited for her to reach over to the bookcase and turn on the radio or CD player.

Hannah put her fingers on the keys and began to play. It was less than twenty seconds before he recognized the tune; *Someone to Watch Over Me.* She played the whole song right through with much emphasis and feeling. When she was done, Hannah smiled and blushed when her brother clapped and told her what a good job she'd done. "I...learned it...for you."

Doctor Richard Mason with his massive ego and rough-around-the-edge demeanor was stunned and almost humbled by his sister in that moment, he didn't know what to say to her other than, "That was beautiful," he clapped for her again. His heart felt light when she smiled and her whole face came to life. "Nice job, little sister, very nice."

"Yah," Hannah brought her shoulders in tight and did a little dance on the piano bench. "Love...you...Ric-ky."

Again, he was humbled and stunned. Mason was not one for saying 'I love you' even when he felt it the deepest as he did right now. Taking down the last of the shot, he took the easy road out by changing the subject, "Are you ready for our trip tomorrow?" Pushing himself off the couch with the aid of his cane, he crossed over the room to sit on the piano bench next to her.

Hannah nodded, "Yes."

"Are you ready to see Frank?" Mason inquired.

Mason took the attorney's advice and by the end of the week got Hannah to agree to talk to Frank before the hearing. Hannah seemed hesitant at first but, so long as he kept telling her it was all right with him, she warmed up to the idea. Mason's lawyer talked to MacNeill's lawyer and they agreed that Hannah would meet with Frank MacNeill for an hour before the hearing and the Court Officer would supervise the visit. At MacNeill's insistence, Doctor Mason would have to wait out in the hall as MacNeill felt Mason's presence would influence Hannah. That did not sit very well with Mason, he wanted his own chance to speak with Frank MacNeill outside the courtroom, and find out what was really going on. Hannah had yet to talk to him about Frank or the baby. He tried to bring it up several times but she just got a wistful look on her face, her eyes welled immediately as she tried to hold back the tears and, instead, she would lightly shake her head. The sorrow in her eyes damn near broke his heart so he broke his

223

Cardinal Rule and gave up on asking. Steward might be right; Hannah might want to talk to her big brother, but not about this...not yet anyway. Maybe she was saving it for Frank.

Hannah rubbed her thigh and her feet started to twirl in opposing circles. Pointing to herself with a half closed fist she shrugged her shoulders and frowned knowing that she was a little better but she was still crippled. She was still an embarrassment. Still, she wanted to see Frank again even if it was just for a short visit. "I...guess." She stammered as she held her hand out to him. "Hurts," she winced and rubbed her head.

Mason looked up at the clock to note there were still two hours left before she was supposed to take her bedtime Oxy. "They're not for headaches," Mason reminded her.

Sitting there staring at him she thinks: *Fine, I can play too.*

Hannah moved her hand from her temple to her knee and rubbed. "Hurts," she said again. "Ow."

"That's better," Mason fished in his pocket, produced the amber bottle, and put an Oxy in her hand. "It hurts more now, doesn't it?"

Hannah did not know if her head hurt any more or less than it did yesterday, she didn't realize he was speaking about the frequency with which the headaches were coming and not the level of discomfort. If she had, then she might have been able to relay to him that, yes, the headaches were coming more often than before. "Maybe." She agreed as she got up and toddled off to the kitchen for a glass of water. Hannah never took her pills dry and often marveled at her older brother who swallowed the nasty things with such ease. If she tried that, they got stuck in her throat and melted there leaving a bitter taste behind for the rest of the day.

"You have an appointment with Doctor Steward the day after tomorrow; we're going to find out what's causing your headaches." *And I'm going to find out why he didn't tell me that you're a pothead.* "Wanna play me another song?" He asked as she resumed her seat next to him.

224

Hannah nodded. "You too."

"Ok," Mason agreed. They started in on a tune they had been working on throughout the week; *Heart & Soul.*

Chapter Sixteen

Bright and early the next morning, they departed from Rutland Airport for a two and half hour flight to Victorville, Michigan. Other than their familial relationship and their mangled lower appendages, Richard Mason and Hannah Rice had one more thing in common; a desire never to return to Victorville. Yet, here they were. Landing at the most ungodly hour of 7:30 am—after having gotten up at 3am—they stumbled through the airport bleary eyed. After standing in line at the car rental place, they drove to the nearest diner.

Walking into the small but clean diner, Mason noticed its pink walls and matching tiled floor. So did Hannah.

Looking around her face lit up as she thought: *This is it, yes; this is where I saw Frank last. We sat at that table over there by the window.*

Hannah sniffed the air.

"Smells good?" Mason asked. "What do you want? Pancakes?"

She wasn't looking for breakfast but for the scent of French fries. It was still too early in the day for the cholesterol-laden treat.

When she didn't answer him, he took her hand and led her to a booth on the far wall. "You ok?" To him she looked pale.

Hannah shook her head. "Feel...funny." She rubbed her head again and grimaced deeply as the other hand went to her heart.

"Sit down. Funny, how?" Instinctively he grabbed her wrist to take her pulse and found it a bit thready. The pale skin turned ghostly white and she looked as though she might vomit. "Hannah?"

"Bloop," she replied in a deep groan. Soon the little blooping feeling, which was getting to be a very large blooping feeling that seemed to make it difficult for her heart to pump

226

for just one painful second, subsided and her heart beat normally. "I..d-don't..like..that."

"Neither do I," Mason agreed, "how's your head?"

How was her head? It was not as clear today as it had been over the last few days that was for sure. Today of all days! She had to see Frank and she had to go into the court and tell the judge she wanted to stay with Ricky. What would happen if the words failed? If she couldn't find them? Couldn't tell them she did not want to leave? Would they take her away? Would they make her go back to living in some nasty group home?

"Hannah?!" Her chest was heaving up and down at a very rapid rate. "Stop, you're going to hyper-ventilate. Breathe slowly, breathe deeply." Maybe the flight had been too much. Even though it was only 5am when the plane departed the flight was still full and noisy. Hannah was not accustomed to being around quite so many people in a confined space. "How's your head?"

Hannah searched for the word and found one almost like it but not quite, she was very disappointed when it slipped through her lips. "Fa-fa-fa-ur-y."

The first thing Mason noticed was the stutter. Mason didn't like hearing the stutter; it was far too early in the morning for her to start tripping over her own tongue. Hannah had done very well the last few days and he had enjoyed it just as Steward said to but maybe Steward was wrong. He usually was. The second thing he noticed was she had said the wrong word. "Furry? Your head feels furry?"

Hannah shook her throbbing head and then stopped as the movement only made it worse. She winced in pain.

God spoke to her: *No, not furry. Try again. Look at him, he's very concerned. Try again.*

"F-u-zzzzz-y."

"Fuzzy," Mason said and stood up with a sigh. "Does it hurt?" Hannah nodded. The waitress was coming over with glasses of water and menus. "Here, take this, but this is the last one before we go in." He put an Oxy on the table in front of her and popped two into his own mouth.

Hannah didn't think about it, she grabbed for the pill and swallowed it dry just like her big brother. As the pill kicked in and their breakfast cooked, her eyes wandered back to the empty table by the window. "Frank." She said absently and pointed.

Mason turned around to see who walked in but there was no one there. "You see him? Where is he?" He half expected her to tell him that Frank MacNeill was standing right behind him but she didn't.

"S-s-sit...s-s-s-at...th-ere."

"How long ago?"

Hannah shook her head very lightly to indicate that she didn't know.

Mason didn't press her but he did keep an eye on her as they ate. Hannah seemed to level off through breakfast, the stutter became less noticeable, and her color came back. She seemed more alert as they headed for the courthouse.

II

Clutching a bouquet of flowers, Frank MacNeill nervously paced the hallway outside the courtroom. His heart and mind raced as he thought of what he was going to say to Hannah. It had been so long since the last time he saw her and the time before that was decades. Would she remember him? Would she smile and toddle to him with her arms open? Would she be angry that he'd let so much come between them?

The second he heard Judge James Rice III went on to his final hellish reward, Frank started investigating his options for taking care of Hannah. He was bowled over when he discovered Rick Mason was awarded her care and even more dumbstruck to find that Rick was her brother. All of those years he spent jealous of Rick Mason because he was sure Hannah was secretly in love with him even though she heatedly protested otherwise were for naught. Frank felt sure that Hannah knew Rick was her brother but it was a secret and

228

secrets in the Rice household had to be kept upon pain of death.

Then Mason's Response to his Petition came Frank was dumbstruck once more. Rick Mason wanted to keep Hannah and according to the DMR Report Hannah wanted to stay with him. The DMR Report went on to suggest that Hannah not be removed from the care of her brother. As always, trying to make a life with Hannah was an uphill battle.

Behind him the heavy doors opened, he turned around, at the bottom of the stairs he saw her toddling through the door on Richard Mason's arm. Frank's heart skipped a beat at the sight of her and he smiled nervously.

It had been more than three decades since Richard Mason laid eyes on Frank MacNeill but he still knew the man when he saw him. Even though Frank was over fifty he hadn't changed much over the years except for a few gray hairs and lines around his eyes. His dark sandy hair was graying nicely at the temples setting off his dark brown eyes. He was wearing well-fitting blue jeans, light blue dress shirt, and tan jacket. Not a bad looking guy at all, it was easy to see how he had attracted Hannah so long ago. From the way the man was looking at her, it was also easy to see that he thought Hannah was a very welcome sight for his sore eyes.

"Hi, pretty lady." Frank said from the top of the stairs. There she was, after all these years, she looked...great. She looked alert and healthy. In fact, she looked better than he'd seen in a very long time. Her cheeks were pink and her eyes were bright. "Do you remember me?"

The last time she'd seen him he looked different there was no gray in his hair and he didn't have those deep creases around his eyes. Looking up and clutching Mason's arm Hannah cleared her throat, "H-h-hell-o...Frank."

Just when he thought nothing about this situation could surprise him she spoke to him. She spoke! At the sound of her

229

voice, Frank rushed down the stairs toward her, "Say it again. Say my name again."

Frank's blitz down the steps startled Hannah who took a step back to hide behind her brother.

Feeling her tremble behind him Mason held his cane out at the running man to keep him at a distance, "Slow down you're frightening her," Mason advised.

Stopping three steps short of the last stair Frank hoped Rick was wrong. "Frightened? No, she's not afraid of me, are you, Hannah? You know I would never hurt you. Not ever." Judging from the way she was peeking out at him from behind Mason's arm maybe she was afraid. Slowly taking the last steps to the landing he held out the bouquet, "I got these for you. I know how much you love flowers."

Hannah looked up at her brother before reaching out for the lovely bouquet Frank was offering. "Thank you," she stammered as she took them from his hand and then inhaled deeply of their scent. Gingerly her fingers skipped across the tops naming off each flower in her head; *red roses, pretty daisies, white baby's breath, purple hyssop, and green fern leaf.* "Pretty."

The situation defused Mason lowered the hand already held up to stop him and turned to shake Frank's hand, "Frank."

Frank took it, "Rick, been a long time."

"Not long enough," Mason grumbled, "no personal offense I just hate this place."

Frank wasn't sure if Rick was talking about the courthouse or Victorville. "Shall we?"

Mason led Hannah up the stairs very slowly, she might toddle fast from side to side, but steps were definitely another story for her. With Frank on her right and him on her left, Hannah leaned heavily upon him with each right step she made which didn't do him and his bum hip much good. "Jesus!"

At his side, Hannah cleared her throat and gave him a sour glance.

Mason ignored his bit of blasphemy, "Hasn't anyone in this place heard of the Americans With Disabilities Act? I'm pretty sure this courthouse is in violation."

At the top of the stairs, they found the Court Officer and an empty room waiting for Frank and Hannah. Mason wanted to tell her that he would be right outside the door if she needed him but that was not true and he refused to lie to her. "I have something I have to go do," he said, "I'll be back before the hearing starts. If Frank gives you any trouble, that guy," he pointed to the big black man in the blue uniform, "will take care of it. Understand?" Hannah nodded. "I won't be long."

Hannah wanted to ask him where he was going and what he was going to do but from the tone of his voice, Ricky did not want to share that information. Therefore, she didn't pry. Instead, she went off into the big room with its heavy mahogany paneling to visit with Frank MacNeill.

"I want to talk to you afterwards, no matter how it goes." Mason said to Frank.

"Yea, me too." Frank agreed and watched the other man turn away. "Rick?"

Mason turned back to face him.

"Thank you for letting me see her."

"Don't thank me, it's what she wanted." Mason turned around again and made his way down the stairs out the doors of the courthouse.

III

Ten minutes later Richard Mason was standing on the porch of a red farmhouse with a white door trying to get up the courage to knock upon it. Taking in a deep breath and telling himself to behave, he used the handle of the cane to rap on the faded paint. Inside he heard shuffling sounds before the door opened.

"Richard! Oh my God! Richard!" Claire stumbled onto the porch and wrapped her arms around her only son. "I've been calling and calling you. I was so worried."

Mason blushed a little and felt guilty for not returning her many phone calls over the last few weeks. He just didn't know what to say to her but he did know what whatever they said to each other he didn't want it to be over the phone. "Hi, Mom," Mason hugged her tight. When she stepped away from him, she looked pale and haggard as though she hadn't been sleeping well. That was probably his fault. As she kissed his whiskery cheek, he caught the faintest whiff of Bailey's Irish Crème on her breath. It was after 9 o'clock on a weekday morning and she was standing there in her nightgown and housecoat. That was very unusual normally the first thing Claire Mason did every morning, after making her bed, was to get dressed for the day. She hadn't even combed her hair and his mother was normally very meticulous about her appearance. "You ok?"

"Sure," she tried to smile but it came off wanting. "It's so good to see you!" Even though the sight of him suddenly standing on her from porch alarmed her as it told her that something must be terribly wrong she was still very happy he was here. "Where's Hannah? Did you leave her home?"

"She's at the courthouse with Frank MacNeill," he admitted, "I can't stay long the hearing's in just under an hour."

"Hearing? Frank? What..."

"Mind if I come in?"

"This is your home, you're always welcome here." Claire put her arm around his waist as they walked through the big front door. Closing the door behind them, she added. "I think he really loves her."

Richard Mason had been starting to get that impression as well. "That doesn't mean he's the best thing for her."

"No, it doesn't." Claire quietly agreed. "I have fresh coffee, do you want some?"

Drinking coffee and making small talk before getting down to business was not Mason's strongest suit. He agreed to the coffee as he took a seat on the couch in the living room. Surrounded by things that readily reminded him of his childhood from family photographs to the handprint he made in Kindergarten and the academic awards he'd won proudly perched in her antique display case. Mason felt oddly nostalgic as he stumbled through a conversation on how Hannah was doing and how he was doing with her. Claire was genuinely pleased when her son told her about Hannah's little breakthrough and the fact that she was talking again. "I didn't come here to talk about Hannah, Mom."

"I know you didn't." Claire raised the steaming cup of Colombian coffee with its healthy shot of Bailey's to her thinning lips. Sitting in the winged chair across from her son, Claire Mason steeled herself against his next words. Claire wondered how she would find the right words to tell him the truth. A truth Richard probably already knew being in the inquisitive skeptic that he was and knowing her son the way she did Claire had no doubt Richard had already done a DNA test. Yet he was here because he didn't want to face the truth and needed his mother to confirm for him. "You look so much like him," she mused, "it's uncanny, you must confuse Hannah sometimes, her mind is so fragile, she must think you're him."

That was not what Mason wanted to hear and it made him angry, "If you say I'm *like* him I don't know what I'll do. I might be an egotistical loud-mouthed prick but I would never, ever, break my daughter's arm or her fingers or her toes because she burned some goddamn cookies. I wouldn't shut her away in one lousy group home after another like some...some...some...embarrassing retard."

"That's terrible! Don't call her an embarrassing retard," Claire admonished. "He always called her that and I hated him for it. Hannah was a lovely girl and he could never see that. I know you don't want to hear this but, yes, in your own inimitable way, you are a lot like him." James was loud and

233

brash, if ever a man thought his shit didn't stink it was Jimmy Rice. "Thankfully, you're more like your mother." She said quietly.

"That your way of complimenting yourself on doing such a good job keeping this from me?"

"No," she said in the same quiet even tone. "I'm complimenting Adelaide." Richard stopped pacing the room and stood perfectly still. Claire had his undivided attention. "After I married your fath—" Richard's eyes narrowed on her and she corrected herself, "After I married Edwin Mason we soon discovered we couldn't have children. Adelaide and Jimmy were dating, she got pregnant, her parents sent her to St. Anne's so no one would find out. No one would know their shame."

"Their shame? You mean me? Thanks. St. Anne's," Mason whispered, "it burned down, you know? With my nephew in it."

Claire's eyes misted and she found it hard to speak past the lump in her throat, "I know," she confessed quietly, "I love you, Richard and your father loved you too. I know you don't believe that. I know you think he was abusive and that he was too strict. He was a military man. I also know you don't believe that's any excuse. You could be right."

"Say it!" Mason was tired of beating around the bush, "Just spit it out."

The words were on the tip of her tongue but they seemed to weight a ton and Claire had to force them out through her lips. Across the room Richard's lip twitched and the hand holding the cane began to shake. "Who would have ever thought they would have gotten married a year later? Adelaide's parents hated him they forbid the marriage they wanted her to forget the baby, forget you, and move on with her life. Jimmy won in the end and he whisked Addie away the day she turned twenty-one and married her." Gathering her strength she looked her son in the eye as the words finally

234

slipped through her lips. "You're the biological son of James Rice and Adelaide Morgan."

"I *am* adopted."

"Yes." She admitted. There it was out. It was over. In that fact, there was a certain amount of relief but the storm had yet to pass. "Your fath—Edwin—insisted that we never tell you. He didn't want you to feel different or unloved."

"There's a joke and half," Mason steamed. "That man never once told me he loved me."

"He loved you but, like you, showing emotion was hard for him." Claire said wistfully. "Then Hannah came along and, well, Edwin and I weren't going to have any children, it was good for you to have a sister..."

"Even if no one told me she was my sister? What sense does that make?"

"She loved you so much, both of them did, Adelaide and Hannah." Claire shook her head as memories of happier days came back to her. Claire began to cry. "She loved you; she didn't want to give you up. Her parents insisted back then she had no say in it. Everything was up to them. Addie must have told them we were having a hard time conceiving because they came to us." Wiping the tears from her cheeks, she forged ahead. "It seemed the perfect solution when Martha Morgan contacted us asking if we wanted Adelaide's baby when it was born. She wasn't supposed to know and we went to such great lengths to hide the truth from her..."

Indeed they had. No one knew Richard was adopted not even her own family. As far as everyone knew, Claire became pregnant and gave birth to Richard while Edwin was stationed in Japan.

"We adopted you just after you were born just two days after. That's how long it took us to get here from Osaka. You're my son, you'll always be my son and like it or not I'll always be your mother."

"So...so...you brought me back here for a few weeks out of every year to what? Visit my parents or torture my birth

235

mother?" Mason shot as he reached into his pocket and took out his favorite amber bottle. Popping the cap to the look of disapproval on her face, he swallowed two dry before putting the bottle back.

"That's not fair! Addie was my friend, we went to school together, she was like a little sister to me. I wanted her to know you and be some part of your life and to watch you grow knowing you were loved beyond measure."

"That's why she killed herself?" Mason asked his words cutting through the air like a sword.

"I don't know. Maybe," Claire admitted. "You look so damn much like him! How could she not guess the truth? One day when you were nine, she came right out and asked me if you were the boy she'd given up. She was so upset she could hardly talk straight." Aging eyes full of dew took him in lovingly before she confessed, "I couldn't lie to her. I tried but I just couldn't and it's so damn obvious that you're his son." Swallowing hard to keep down her shame she shook her white head sadly, "That was, well that was when the light in her eyes started to die."

"Is that why you started sending me to her for piano lessons? You were hoping to ease her pain and your guilt?" Secrets kill people. He believed that with all his heart. It looked like he was right. Secrets really were venomous things. "It didn't work, did it? It only made things worse for her until she ended up inhaling carbon monoxide in the garage. But, before that, at some point she told Rice about me and then she told Hannah. That's how I got her."

"It would appear so or he guessed it on his own, he was wicked but he wasn't stupid." Claire drank the last of her coffee and refilled the cup wishing she could pour a stiff shot of Bailey's into it. "Can you ever forgive me?"

"For what? Stealing your friend's baby and calling him your own? For lying to him all of his life and for not telling him he has a sister?"

236

"Richard, don't say that, I didn't steal you, I didn't!" Claire stumbled to her feet and held her arms out to him.

"Ummm...no," he said with a single shake of his head as he turned toward the door, "I gotta be in court now. Bye, mom." Without thinking or looking back, he let himself out of the house.

"Richard, please!" Claire called after him from the front door. "Please! I love you, you're my son, you always have been..."

"Not always," he called back as he opened the door of the rental car then slammed it shut.

"You always will be," Claire whispered knowing he could not hear her. She walked back into the house to cry and drink Bailey's straight from the bottle.

Half way down the road, Richard Mason pulled off to the side to cry and pop two more Oxies.

Chapter Seventeen

The room was big, too big, and it was bright, too bright. Sunlight streaming in through the huge arched windows flooded the room and bounced off the highly polished wood paneling as well as the complimenting desk and chairs. No matter where she looked, a glare hurt her eyes. Hannah's head hurt but she knew her brother was not around and, even if he were, he wouldn't give her another pill until after they all heard what the judge had to say.

"You seem well," Frank said and reached for her hands across the table. Hannah pulled them away.

"No physical contact," the Court Officer informed them in a dry tone.

"Yes, right," Frank agreed and pulled his hands away. "It's good to see you, Hannah. I missed you. Are you all right? Is Rick being good to you?"

Hannah nodded but that made the pain in her head even worse, now it didn't just throb but felt as though someone were slowly trying to drive an ice pick out through the top of her skull. "It's...good." She mumbled. "Better."

"Yeah, well, anything's better than that group home," Frank said snidely, "I'm amazed it took them so long to close it down. Are you happy? I can't believe you're talking to me, Rick must be doing something right, huh?" He couldn't remember the last time he heard her voice, he thought he would never hear it again. "Living up to his reputation, is he?"

That reputation was not the greatest in the world. Medically speaking, Doctor Richard Mason was the man to go to if you were ill and no one knew why. He was an excellent physician who, by all accounts, had the worst bedside manner in the history of medicine. Some people might call him a maverick and applaud him for all of the lives he'd saved over the years. Others would call him reckless for the outrageous chances he took with said lives. To Frank's way of thinking, the last thing Hannah needed was another bullying male pushing her around telling her what to do. Maybe Richard Mason could help her it was obvious that he'd already made big strides but that didn't mean he was best for her.

Hannah sat there with the sun in her eyes trying to think but the words were getting furrier on her. "Wh-y?" she mumbled.

"Why? Why what?" Frank asked.

Her lips trembled slightly, "Here."

"Why did I bring you here? To court?" Frank asked and watched her nod knowing that she knew where she was and why she was here and even that was a big improvement since most of the time it was hard to tell if Hannah knew what planet she was on. "I tried to call him at the hospital...several times." Frank told her. "He never called me back."

That was true. Over the course of the last few weeks, Frank left more than 3 dozen messages for Rick and not one of them had been returned. What Frank didn't know was that Mason didn't really believe in checking his messages. Add to that the number of time Mason's mother called over the same time span and it summed up to a little pile of messages carefully taken by Mary that he just dumped into the wastebasket without looking at them.

"I didn't know what else to do. I just wanted to see you and make sure that you're all right." He leaned forward to be closer to her but kept his hands to himself. "The Protective Order is over with, Han, I can see you now and no one is going to come and arrest me. They're not going to drag me away again. Do you understand? I don't have to sneak around to see you anymore."

She had begun to understand that, now that her father was dead, seeing Frank was something that could be allowed. No one would be in trouble or be thrown in jail. Before it was awful, Frank would come to see her and the police would come, they would throw him around and take him away in

239

handcuffs. The last time they took him away, the day he tried to take her for a ride in the car, she didn't see him again for what seemed like forever. Then her father yelled at her, he put her into the last group home so that Frank could not find her.

Father wanted to know when she was ever going to learn, stop being so goddamn stupid! He would have Frank thrown in jail for the rest of his miserable life!

Under the table, Hannah began to twirl her feet but it didn't do much good through the shoes. It always worked best to bring her comfort if she was barefoot, so she kicked off the shoes. Seeing Frank again was making her nervous but it was nice just the same. He was still handsome, and still had those incredible deep brown eyes. Those lips still looked soft and inviting. "So?" She asked wanting to get to the point and hoping she'd be able to understand it.

"So...I'd like to see you," Frank told her, "I want to take care of you. I have a beautiful house, Han, you'd love it. There are horses and a big barn. The house is huge you'd have your own room. I think you would be happier with me. Don't you think so? Don't you want to come back home where all of your friends are?"

Hannah snorted something that was more of a grunt than a laugh and it made that ice pick in her head come alive once more.

Friends? What friends? Who came to visit her over the years? To the best of her faulty recollection, it had been Frank and Claire Mason. Once in a great while her father stopped by but not often. And, maybe, just maybe, there had been a pretty blonde lady who came a few times. She was nice and brought her gifts but that could just be a delusion.

"Rick-y...home." Hannah asserted. "You...why?"

"Don't you know I love you? I've always loved you, Hannah." Frank wanted nothing more than to reach out and scoop her up his arms but the Court Officer would not like that. "My pretty lady," He smiled for her. She did not smile

240

back. He was pushing too far too fast and it was all so long ago and so very far away. Why did it seem like just yesterday they were making love under the apple tree and making plans for their future? Maybe Hannah didn't love him anymore; she certainly didn't look as though she trusted him. "If you don't want to come live with me then I guess I'll just have to understand that. But I wanted to ask you myself and not hear it from some social worker or lawyer."

Hannah didn't trust her own judgment but if someone forced her to give an opinion on the subject right now, she'd say Frank was telling the truth. However, that didn't change how she felt. "I stay with Rick-y," she said in a slow deliberate voice, "it's good. Hap-py...fam-ily. You vis-it me may-be."

"Time's up," The Court Officer said from behind them. "Let's go."

Hannah didn't have anything else to say as she toddled out into the hall where the light was not as bright and was instantly thankful for it. Looking around she didn't see Ricky anywhere and was instantly alarmed by his absence.

"Come on, Miss Rice, Court's being called into session, your lawyer is already in there." The Court Officer said in that dry authoritative voice.

The Courtroom was big, it was huge, massive, and on the far wall sat a very intimidating Bench. Walking behind Frank but not taking his arm Hannah wandered inside passing rows and rows of hardwood chairs that looked very uncomfortable.

Where's Ricky? He said he would be here. Where is he?

The Court Officer led Hannah to the table on the right side of the room and to two men standing there who introduced themselves as Richard's lawyers. She saw Mr. Lawrence sitting in a chair and was told he was there to sit-in for the interest of the Trust. "Where's Doctor Mason?" The attorney who called himself Bruce Chamberlain asked as he motioned for Hannah to sit down.

At the front of the room the Bailiff stood before the intimidating bench, "O, ye, o ye, Court is now in session," he pronounced, "the Honorable Judge Elroy Granger presiding."

Everyone stood up as the judge entered the room and took his seat. "Court is now in session," he declared with a hefty bang of the gavel, "please be seated."

Everyone sat down before Attorney Chamberlain rose again. "Begging the Court's pardon, Your Honor?"

"What is it?"

"We require a brief delay; it seems the Respondent isn't here yet." He said apologetically.

"Yes, I am." Mason grumbled from the back of the room. "Parking around here's a nightmare don't you people know what Handicapped Parking is? And those stairs, what's with them?"

Hannah felt very relieved as she watched him come down the aisle. Then the relief went away as he got closer and she began to worry.

"Doctor Mason," the judge said in an admonishing tone.

Mason took the cue, "Sorry, Your Honor." He stood next to Hannah. She was staring up at him with wide eyes. "Stop that," he whispered out of the corner of his mouth then felt her hand on his chin.

"Look...at me." Hannah said softly and brought his chin down. "Oh," she sighed, "why sad? Wh-at...hap-pen-ed?"

"Are we ready to proceed?" The Judge asked in that same tone of admonishment.

"We'll talk about it later." Mason assured her and couldn't have been happier when she looped her arm through his to stand and face the Judge.

"Yes, Your Honor, we are ready to proceed." Attorney Chamberlain said.

There was a murmuring mumble on the other side of the room before Frank's attorney stood up. "Your Honor, if it please the Court, at the time the Petitioner, Frank MacNeill, would like to withdraw his Petition to have Doctor Mason

242

removed. The Petitioner would like to capitulate to the fact that Doctor Mason seems to be the most capable and appropriate Guardian for Miss Rice. We apologize for wasting the Court's time."

"What did you do?" Mason whispered to Hannah still from the corner of his mouth. From inside same corner he pushed his tongue into his cheek and raised his eyebrows at her.

It was a nasty gesture and Hannah knew what it meant. "N-no," she said uneasily.

"I don't suppose there's any objection on the other side?" The Judge inquired.

"No, Your Honor."

"In that case," he banged the gavel, "case dismissed. Go on your way."

"That's it?" Mason asked. "We flew two hours, on a plane, I was drug tested, had the DMR crawling up my as—"

Hannah clamped a hand over his mouth and shook her head.

"Heed your sister's advice, Doctor Mason." The Judge advised. "You won, be happy."

That was good news but, still, in light of earlier events it was difficult to be happy about it but Mason didn't want to push his luck either. "Thank you, Your Honor," Mason took Hannah's hand away from his mouth.

Walking back up the center aisle Frank asked if he could buy them lunch. They had a lot to talk about and maybe it was best if they did it outside of a courtroom. "Well, we do have, oh," he looked down at his watch, "five hours before our flight home." A little lunch, a beer or three, might be good.

Hannah and Mason followed Frank in their rental car to the Dew Drop Inn. Driving down Black Rock Road, Hannah huddled close to the door as though she were trying to pass through it. When they reached the ditch where her Chevette came to rest so many years ago she hugged herself as she rocked in the seat.

Halfway to the Dew Drop they drove past the cemetery. Hannah put her hands on the glass and rested her head between them. Her parents were in there, she was sure of that. She was wondering where Richard, her son, was buried. If he'd been buried at all and her father didn't just toss his grandson's remains out with the week's trash. As far as Hannah knew there'd been no funeral for her precious baby boy, at least none she'd ever attended. She turned back to her brother once the graveyard was out of sight wanting to say something about the baby, wanting to ask him to pull in there so could see the grave and lay upon it the flowers Frank gave her but Ricky has a strange look on his face. "What's wrong?" She asked trying to keep her voice steady as visions of the accident, the fire, ran amok through her head and the echoes of her son's anguished cried rang in her head. "Where...did...you go?"

"To see my mother," Mason answered through gritted teeth as he drove with his eyes fixed on the bumpy dirt road ahead.

"She...made you...sad?"

No, she pissed me off and then she made me sad, he thought but didn't say. "I don't want to talk about it, ok?"

If there was one thing Hannah understood it was the desire not to talk about bad things. She reached over and wrapped her hand around his shoulder. When they came to a stop sign in the middle of nowhere she grabbed him by the jaw and turned his face to hers. "Look me."

His eyes were still filled with sadness.

Hannah didn't know what weighed so heavily upon her brother's heart all she knew was she wanted to make it better for him in the way that so very few people had ever made things better for her. "O-K, ev-ree-ting, O-K." She nodded seriously even though her heart hurt and her eyes welled with tears. "O-K. Sorry...you hurt." The hand holding his jaw traced soft fingertips along the outline of his whiskery face, while the other covered his heart. "I love you."

244

Little sisters. What a pain.

II

In the car in front of them, Frank MacNeill was driving down the road with butterflies in his stomach. He had done the right thing in dropping the case, Hannah was happy and she looked fantastic. Richard was taking care of her and if he, Frank, really loved her then he reasoned that he would just have to live with the fact that she was so far away.

It figured, after all these years, he finally got the open opportunity to just walk up and say 'hello' to her whenever he wanted and now she was a few hundred miles out of his reach. He fought Judge James Rice tooth and nail for years, but Rice was her father and he had all of that money.

And power.

What did Frank have? An old Honda motorcycle? Big deal. After Frank's last arrest for attempted kidnapping and his stint in Green River Prison, he got smarter about it. He couldn't beat Rice legally and above board, but if he was slick, he could still see Hannah. He could still keep an eye on her and make sure that she was all right. While he was in prison, Rice moved her to another group home and it took Frank a year to find her again.

Fresh out of prison, down on his luck, no money in his pocket, no one wanted to hire him. Not because of his records or because he didn't have any marketable skills. They didn't want to hire him because they didn't want to be seen as crossing Judge Rice.

Frank looked for a job for months until Old Man Traynor took a chance and hired Frank as a grease monkey in his garage. Traynor knew he was a skilled mechanic and a hard worker who would working in his own father's garage if he hadn't died eighteen months ago.

Frank worked for Traynor for five years before the old man died. Traynor never got married, never had any kids and all of his siblings were dead. Traynor didn't even leave a will. What he did leave were a lot of bills and a big mess. Frank volunteered to straighten out of the mess for the Probate Court, if in return, instead of an executor's fee, he could have the garage and all its contents.

The court agreed to Frank's proposal, Frank tied up all of the loose ends concerning Old Man Traynor's estate and hung a new shiny sign over the doors; Frank's Garage. That was ten years ago and now Frank MacNeill was the proud owner & operator of 7 Frank's Garages spread out over the Upper Peninsula, the latest one opening just last month and specializing in the repair and restoration of farm equipment.

Originally, he meant to turn the first garage into a business so profitable he'd have enough money to fight Rice in court. Life had other plans for him.

Along the way to his goal, he met Connie Johnson, a sweet, pretty, towheaded thing with big blue eyes. He was smitten with her right away and the feeling was mutual. Frank felt like shit, he felt like he was cheating on Hannah even though he wasn't. He told Connie almost everything about Hannah. He even brought Connie to the group home to visit with her. Connie understood and she loved him anyway. She even went to visit Hannah on her own and brought small things for her, things that he couldn't bring her like a CD player and a music box. Hannah loved music.

A life with Hannah was yesterday's dream but a life with Connie was dancing in the palm of his hand. They were married just over a year after they met. It wasn't the same intense love affair he'd had with Hannah but it was good not to be alone, to have someone to come home to, someone who was happy to see you, someone to talk to and hold in the dark of the night. Was it such a huge crime simply to not want to be alone anymore?

Then, a strange thing happened and Frank thought it was fate. Almost five years ago, he opened his fourth garage near a local strip mall out on I-64. It was the jewel in his crown then and it still was. It was where Frank ran the entire outfit along with personally servicing vehicles. People paid a pretty penny to have him work on their cars restoring them or overhauling them. A few weeks after that garage opened, he was standing in the bay when a green mini-van pulled into the parking lot of the strip mall. Not an uncommon occurrence. He stood there talking on the phone about a GTO he was restoring when he saw her. Hannah. She climbed out of the mini-van and turned to help those behind her. She held a hand to shade her eyes against the sun as she looked toward the garage. Frank dropped the phone. She looked like shit, dressed in raggedy clothes and too skinny but his eyes still lit up at the sight of her. He dashed across the highway to talk to her, just for a minute, just to say 'hello'. Hannah gazed at him as though she had never seen him before.

Red Martin came out from around the mini-van and told him to get away from her. He knew there was PRO on Frank and he was not going to get away with anything on Red's watch. Red had always been a bully, the only thing he'd ever really been good at was left tackle on the football team.

Once a month that green mini-van pulled up to the strip mall and all the residents of Hannah's group home climbed out, including Hannah. Frank watched from across the street.

Other than a bully and good football player Red Martin was a conniving greedy little man. Every now and then Frank would slip him a hundred bucks for a few moments alone with Hannah.

That lasted for a few years until Connie got sick and the doctors said there wasn't anything they could do—where was the Great Doctor Richard Mason then?? Not that he could have saved her from the breast cancer that took her life but it might have been nice if he'd been able to try.

A week or so after her funeral, lonely, sad, and lost, Frank found himself on the doorstep of Hannah's group home, giving Red money so that he could take her out for the day. They went to the diner in town and split a basket of fries, Hannah always loved them. He held her hands across the table and told her that Connie wouldn't be visiting her

247

anymore, that she passed away. Hannah didn't say anything she just blankly stared at him. He took her for a walk in the park and they sat down under the tree. For reasons he still didn't understand, she kissed him. Long, slow and deep just like she had so many years ago when they were young and all that life had to offer them was still ahead. No one was around. The park was empty. He was lonely, grief-stricken. Hannah didn't seem to mind when he kissed back. It was wrong, he knew it then just as he knew it now, but he just couldn't help himself. Frank made love to her under the tree in the warm afternoon sun.

Had that really been nearly five years ago?

Frank chased those memories away as he pulled into the parking lot of the Dew Drop Inn. Now that he'd been able to see her, Frank felt a little better about the situation. Rick was good for Hannah and she was happy with him. If she stayed with him and continued to improve then maybe one day the Court would restore her to capacity. Then she could make her own decisions and she might even decide she wanted him.

Inside the Dew Drop, the place hadn't changed any. It was still standing on heavy wood paneled walls that looked as though they hadn't seen a new coat of varnish in a hundred years. The pool tables were still off in the left hand corner, the dartboard in the right. The bar still dominated the room with its twelve feet of bottles and glasses on either side of the huge mirror. It still smelled of bar food, stale beer, cheap perfume, and desperation.

It was getting on lunchtime and the place was filling up, the Dew Drop was known for its good food, without it, the place would have closed ages ago because the whisky was always a bit watery. The three of them found a table near the middle of the room by the bar. Mason sat with his back to the bar, Frank sat next to him on the left and Hannah to the left of him so that she was facing Mason and the bar behind him.

The jukebox was blaring *Swingtown* as the waitress came over with menus. "Rick?" She said looking down at him. "Rick Mason, is that you?"

"Yeah, it's me." He said looking up at her and not recognizing the face at first but then he thought the woman could be...

"It's me, Betty Andrews," she said, "my lord it's been a long time. Are you in town long? Maybe we can get together later and..."

Betty Andrews better known as Back Seat Betty, Mason remembered that she'd seen the back seat of his Camaro once or twice on a hot summer night. Betty had big dreams of being an actress, she was going to go to Hollywood and be a star. Here she was, 30 years older, stuck in the same small town with a shitty job. "Just for the day," Mason said wanting the woman to take his order and walk away.

"Oh, that's too bad," Betty mused and then looked at the company Rick was keeping. Unfortunately, for Betty who was quietly reminiscing about younger days, there was another familiar face at her table. "Frank? Frank MacNeill? Do you still have that bike? I'd love to go for a ride." As her eyes swept the table, she thought of how odd it was to have two old and long-since-seen lovers sitting at the same table. Then she took in the woman sitting with them and gasped, "Hannah? Hannah Rice?" No one had seen Hannah since her father sent her off a group home saying she was a danger to herself and those around her. Story was she went completely mad and ended up at Central Michigan State Psychiatric Hospital sitting in a corner in a straightjacket drooling on herself. "I don't believe it. What are the three of you doing here?"

"Nunya," Mason said curtly, "can we just get some drinks?"

Hannah snickered. She too recognized Betty and remembered how she'd once stolen Frank away. Now she was plump and wrinkled. Her boobs hung almost to her waist and she had three fat moles on her once pretty face.

"Hump, sure," Betty said returning to Waitress Mode and taking the pencil from behind her ear. "What can I get you?"

"I'll have a scotch, double, neat." Mason said.

"Sam Adams," Frank said.

Hannah's turn but she didn't answer, she just sat there looking up at Betty whose eyes were darting from Ricky to Frank and back again. She didn't like the tension in the air. She didn't like Betty.

Betty tapped the end of her pencil endlessly against the pad in her hand as she waited for Hannah to answer. "Hannah, dear, what do you want?" She shouldn't be short with the woman obviously she wasn't walking around with all of her marbles.

Without looking at Betty, Hannah pointed to a sign over the bar. Budweiser.

Mason's eyes followed to where she was pointing and was shocked, not to mention a little disgusted, "A beer? You want a beer?"

Frank turned in his chair to read the sign and then turned back to Rick, "Is there a reason she can't have one?"

Mason thought it over. It wasn't the best idea but it wasn't the worst and she was well over 21, "What the hell? We're celebrating, right? Bring the lady a Bud." He stopped and looked to Hannah, "But just one, with the meds you're on..."

Hannah snorted and rolled her eyes as she gave her brother an accusatory stare that froze the rest of the words in his throat.

Yea, right," Mason said and forced a smile as he turned back to Becky, "We'll order food when you come back with the drinks." Mason told her in a dismissive tone.

She walked away giving both men a snotty look as she went.

Before the drinks arrived, Frank explained how he'd tried to get a hold of Richard and the man never answered him. He was sorry he dragged them both all the way out here but he just had to be sure that Hannah was all right. After the drinks arrived and Richard was halfway through his, Frank ventured that Hannah said she might like him to come visit with her from time to time.

"Is that true?" Mason asked his sister.

The beer was bitter but it was cold and her throat was dry licking the foam off her lips she turned to her brother, "Yes."

"Ok," Mason agreed and finished the drink in his glass as he signaled for a refill though he didn't really want to see Betty. What he really wanted was to get on a plane and get the fuck out of here. Undoubtedly, considering the distance between them, Frank's visit would take place over the weekends. "Once a month maybe you can come to Vermont," Mason ventured. "There's a hotel not far from my—our— house. You can stay there for the weekend."

"Really?" Frank said in a bright voice. He was so used to being told 'no, forget about it buddy, you're screwed,' where Hannah was concerned he couldn't believe his ears.

"I didn't say you were going to take her anywhere so don't get too excited." Mason advised.

In the car, Mason had done a dastardly thing. He felt so guilty about it and that just added to his bad mood. After Hannah told him that she loved him, he told her he was sad— not because of any conversation he had with his mother—but because he didn't know what was going on with her and Frank. The lie worked like a charm

Hannah told him everything because she thought it would make him feel better.

She talked of police who broke down doors and hauled Frank away even though he hadn't done anything wrong. She talked about a pretty blonde woman who came and brought her gifts that she said were from Frank. She talked about secret meetings in parks and movie theatres and that he was always close by at the garage. She saw him when they went shopping. Sometimes Red would take her to him and leave her with him for a while though she didn't seem to like those times. She cringed when she tried to articulate it and then sighed. In the end, Hannah didn't seem afraid of Frank but she didn't really know what to make of him either. Neither did Mason.

Betty returned with Mason's second scotch and took their order while he used the contents of the glass to wash down another pill. He knew that he shouldn't take any more of these and he certainly shouldn't be drinking while taking them. He had to drive after all he couldn't let Hannah behind the wheel. The two men ordered and then came Hannah's turn again. Mason knew she couldn't read the menu but that didn't stop her from ordering French fries. Then she seemed to get stuck. Before he could say anything, Frank spoke up.

Reaching across the table for Hannah's hand he didn't look at Betty as he gave her Hannah's order, "She'll get a burger with that, please, medium rare. Tomato and lettuce, no cheese."

Hannah nodded happily in agreement. Her glass was empty she held it up to Betty for a new one.

Betty looked to the two men as she took the glass.

It went against his better judgment but he didn't want to seem like a hypocrite, "Just one more," Mason warned astonished to see she'd finished the first one at all let alone so quickly.

When Betty went away again Hannah looked over at Mason, "Ba-bath-room."

Frank got up, pulled out her chair for her and helped her to her feet. Hannah toddled off toward the rear of the bar for the ladies room. "Got something to say, Rick?"

"Yeah, what the hell is your game?" Mason asked straight out. "Keep your hands to yourself."

"She doesn't mind."

"That's not the point. Look, Frankie, if it's her money you're after..."

Frank laughed. "I don't need her money. In fact, Rick, for all of your brains and lifesaving ability, I probably pull down

252

more in six months than you do in a year. So, no, it's not about money."

"So what is it? You want to ride in on a white horse, sweep her off her feet and ride off into the sunset?" The glass empty he signaled for his third.

"Don't you think you should slow down?" Frank asked.

"I know my limits," Mason assured him, "and hers. She isn't ready to be whatever the hell it is you want her to be. She's not ready for a romantic relationship. She doesn't even understand what it means. I don't know what you're trying to pull but I'm watching you, if you hurt her, I swear..." Mason leaned in, "I'm a doctor you know, I can kill you and not leave any evidence behind."

Frank sat back in his chair and held his hands out. "Wow," he said softly, "you really do give a shit about her, don't you? I'm amazed. I figured she'd be too much of a burden for someone like you. An embarrassment to someone of your stature."

"Don't worry about my stature you just keep your dick in your pants."

"Excuse me?"

"Don't bullshit me, I know it was you. Who else would it be?"

"Who did....."

Mason tossed his head around and looked for Hannah but she had yet to come out of the ladies room. "The last time you visited with her in some clandestine little place you left her with more than your love and affection, you gave her The Clap. So keep your dick in your pants." He hissed.

That was impossible. "I've never, listen to me closely here Rick," Frank advised as he leaned in to the conversation, "I have never had an STD. Ever. If you found that Hannah did, it didn't come from me and, just so we're clear, the last time I let my dick out of my pants with her was about five years ago."

"Well, if it wasn't you then who?"

Time was up, Hannah was coming toward them again.

"Smile, Rick." Frank said with a grin. "Don't want to upset her."

As they waited for their food to arrive, they made small talk and watched the lunch crowd roll in. The door behind Mason opened and closed frequently letting in and then shutting out the sunshine.

Betty came back with their plates.

Mason didn't touch his third drink but Hannah drank the second Bud and ate the fries. Out of the corner of her eye, she saw the door open again, a familiar figure walked through but he was in silhouette with the strong midday sun behind him. The door closed, he sidled up to the bar and squeezed in between the patrons and she saw him clear as day in the mirror behind the bar.

Mason turned to follow her gaze.

"What?" Frank asked as he did the same. "Jesus, Red." He mumbled. "Looks like it's High School Reunion Day."

Mason stared at the man who had his back to him then glanced beyond him to his reflection in the mirror. Red...*Martin?* Something in the mirror caught the man's stare or maybe he just felt the weight of the eyes on him. He turned around and saw Hannah. His eyes locked to hers and she looked down at the table as her glass plopped onto it. It rocked from the force before it teetered over and rolled off the table to the floor where it shattered.

Under the table, Hannah's feet began with twirl as she thought; *Please Dear God don't let him come over here. Don't let me see me. Don't come over here. You didn't see me. I didn't see you. Don't come over here. Go away. Just turn around and go away. Dear God, please!*

Her desperate plea to God went unanswered. She did not have to look up to know he was coming in her direction she knew the sound of his footsteps all too well for that.

"Frank MacNeill, ain't there a PRO out on you, boy?" Red asked in his deep gravelly voice as he approached the table. "Oughtta have you arrested." Then he turned his attention away from Frank. "Hey, Hannah, how you doin', girl? Been a while a long while. Did'ya miss me?"

Hannah did not look up at him; she just stared at the table and started to tremble.

Mason looked from her to Red who was looking at Hannah like she was a juicy steak and he hadn't eaten in weeks. The pig was even licking his lips.

"Girl never was right. I said, HELLO HANNAH." Red waved a hand in front of her face.

Hannah didn't as much as blink.

Feeling the tension mounting Mason shifted his feet under the table only to find a puddle on the floor. At first he thought it was the contents of the broken glass but quickly remembered it had been empty. With a bit of dread because he already knew what he was going to find, Mason glanced down to see that Hannah wet herself, urine was dripping off the rim of her chair. Below that, her feet were endlessly twirling around each other.

"Whatever, Banana" Red sneered, "I gotta use the little boy's room anyway."

"Yeah, why don't you go do that," Mason said gruffly, "we're trying to have lunch here."

Red wandered away from the table and Mason watched him go into the bathroom before he excused himself from the table.

In the bathroom, he found Red standing at the urinal trying to pee. "Come on, man, damn that hurts."

"Problems?" Mason asked trying to keep his voice in check. "Red Martin, isn't it? You used to play football for St. Mark's. Left tackle, right?"

"Yeah. Who are you?"

"Yeah, that's right, I was just a summer kid, you probably wouldn't remember me. Richard Mason." He pointed down at

255

the man's exposed faulty penis riddled with suspicious sores. "Doctor Richard Mason. Problems peeing, Red?"

They all knew about the Infamous Doctor Richard Mason. Victorville's favorite Home Town Boy. Even though the guy didn't live here and wanted nothing to do with the place. Every time his name made a medical journal or police report it was the talk of the little town. "I remember you, man. "What he didn't understand was why Mason was here and with Frank MacNeill and Banana of all people. It didn't matter, he was here now and Red was always up for a little free medical advice. "For the last few months, it hurts like a bitch when I try to pee."

"The Clap'll do that to you." Mason stated flatly and took a moment to enjoy the way the smug look on Red's face fell away to shock.

With a little help from the scotch and the Oxy, before he knew it the rage of the day overtook him. Mason grabbed the cane in both hands, placing one just below the curve of the handle and the other near the rubber tip. He put everything he had into the swing. The silver wolf's head handle connected with Red's jaw and the big man went down hard. "You pig! You fucking pig!"

Suddenly down on his knees on the filthy bathroom floor and seeing stars Red groaned, "What the fuck, man? What'd I do to you?"

"Not me, Hannah." Mason just couldn't help it. Red was on his knees with his jeans around his ankles as she threw up his arms to cover his face from another blow of the cane. That left Red's cruddy sore encrusted cock dangling in the breeze and winking at him.

Before suffering his hip injury, Mason was a good golfer and those days crashed in on him as his angry blue eyes focused on that nasty pus-weeping thing between Red's legs. Mason held his cane like a driver and swung for three hundred yards. This time the hard mahogany connected with Red's disease infested worm and two hairy friends. The ex-jock to

256

screamed in agony as he curled up on his side and held onto his wounded member.

Mason became aware of his surroundings and stopped for a moment. The music was loud out there in the bar and the lunch crowd was whooping it up. No one heard him.

"You were supposed to look out for her, supposed to protect her! Instead you turned her into your little house slave, made her into your own personal little sex slave when it came to getting her monthly check. What kind of man are you? You coerce a woman who doesn't even know what's going on into having sex with you? She doesn't know enough to fight back!"

Red Martin made the mistake of his life but he had always been a wise ass so why should he be untrue to his nature now? Swiping a hand across his aching jaw he looked down to see his hand covered with blood. "She fought back," he said snidely, "believe me, she's a feisty little spitfire, that's the way I like 'em."

Nearly all control lost, all ration and reason flown out the open bathroom window, Mason turned the cane around and planted the crook firmly against Red's throat. It wasn't long before Red's face matched his nickname. "I should kill you. I'd be doing the world a favor." Mason mused as he applied more pressure.

Then he saw Hannah's face dancing behind his eyes and, heard her voice echo in his head. She was telling him that she loved him. What would she do if he were in jail? Where would she go? Who would take care of her?

"You're not worth it," he growled, "but she is. So I'll make a deal with you, you don't tell anyone about our little conversation and I won't have you arrested for raping her."

"Rape? It wasn't rape, man, I swear." Red croaked as his face went from crimson to dark blue.

"You're a fucking liar!" Mason took the cane off Red's throat only to bash him in the head with it one last time knocking him out cold. Leaving the wretched man on the grimy bathroom floor Mason hurried out of there.

"Geez, that took you long enough." Frank complained as Mason came back to the table.

"Come on, Hannah, we're leaving." Mason told her.

"She seems really upset about something..."

"I know!" Mason growled yanking his coat off the back of the chair he'd been sitting on. He put it around her shoulders. "Put your arms through, it's ok." He whispered in her ear. "I took care of him he's never going to come near you again."

Hannah whimpered loudly as she looked up at her brother with heavy eyes full of gratitude.

"What are big brothers for, huh?" Her arms through the sleeves he coaxed her to her feet and drew the coat closed. "There, it's ok. No one will know. Let's go."

Hannah held the coat tightly closed as they hurried out of the bar so no one would see the mess she had made when her bladder unexpectedly let go.

"Do you want to tell me what's going on?" Frank demanded once they were outside.

"Not really." Mason answered, "Maybe another time."

"It's hours before your flight, where are you going? What's wrong?" Frank grabbed his arm to wheel him around, "Damn it, Rick! What the hell happened in the bathroom?"

"Nunya," Mason snapped. Right now, he was ready to drive all the way back to Vermont if he had to. "Home, call my lawyer, he'll give you my home number. We'll make arrangements for you to see Hannah." Jumping in behind the wheel Mason peeled out of the parking lot of the Dew Drop Inn in a cloud of dust leaving Frank standing there alone.

They spent several boring hours in the airport where Mason bought Hannah a new pair of blue jeans and pair of underwear for the flight home. He stood outside the airport ladies room while she changed. She didn't say anything to him, she looked so far away, those deep brown eyes stared out at him from some lonely place that he'd never visit and never wanted to see.

An hour into the flight Hannah began to complain that her head hurt. He gave her an Oxy but it didn't seem to help. She held her hands to her head and wept.

"Hurts...puh-lease...Reek-y ...hurts. Ow. Ow. Ow."

The seatbelt light came on and he had to strap her in as she'd started to fidget and found it hard to sit still. He heard the landing gear lock into place, saw the runway right below them and thought that he would take her to The Mountainside as soon as they departed but his thought was a little too late. "Just sit still, we'll be home soon. I know it's been a hard day."

Hannah winced and tried to nod but the motion made her eyeball feel as though it were going to explode. She nestled down in the seat and closed her eyes.

A little over halfway through the flight they hit a harsh patch of turbulence. Mason turned his head to look at her wanting to point out some interesting designs in a farmer's field below hoping it would take her mind off the bumpy ride. Hannah was staring back at him with those blank eyes. The left side of her face froze in the grip of a spasm so deep that her cheek curled up all the way to her lower lid making her look like Popeye. "Hannah!" In front of everyone on the plane, Mason ripped open her blouse to lay his ear to her heart making everyone around him gasp and mumble. Her heart was still beating but she wasn't breathing. He reached down for the lever even though the seatbelt light was lit up and reclined her all the way back into the lap of the person behind him who cried out at the inconvenience of having her head in his lap. "Shut up!" Mason snapped before the passenger could speak. Ripping off his own seatbelt he prepared to do CPR, moving in to put his lips over hers he saw a terrible sight. "No! No! Hannah! Hannah!" Blood was streaming from her eyes, ears and nose.

"Sir, the seatbelt light is..."

259

"Shut up you stupid bitch!" he spat, "can't you see she's in trouble? I need a medical helicopter to meet us on the field as soon as we land! Don't just stand there! Get the med kit! Go! Tell the pilot!" The flight attendant scrambled off toward the cockpit.

"Stay with me, Hannah." Mason begged and began to breathe for her. "Come on, baby sister, don't you leave me."

Chapter Eighteen

The time between getting Hannah off the plane, into the Life Star helicopter that met them on the tarmac, and then, finally through the emergency doors of The Mountainside were utter chaos. Everything was a blur.

The whirring blades.

The bright flashing lights.

The EMTs pushing him out of the way so they could do their job...

HIS job! T

The only thing he did remember, or thought he remembered anyway, was screaming at them to hurry up!

An aneurysm, Hannah had an aneurysm in her brain and they missed it

(Steward missed it)

Nope, he didn't need anyone to tell him what was going on. Hindsight was always 20/20.

From her medical records, they knew Hannah had a blood clot in her arm several years ago. She had been put on blood thinners for it and she had been pronounced healthy. Part of the clot broke off and no one noticed. The blood thinners didn't work on it because of the birth control pills she was taking. Therefore, instead of dissolving, it made a nice home somewhere in that misfiring brain of hers. It was probably very small, just enough to make her seem even more distant and confused than she really was. Just enough to hinder her ability to speak.

Enter Doctors Mason and Steward who took her off the blood thinners. Her blood thickened. At first that was good, it was why she was talkative in the morning. She lay down all night, instead of being on her feet, the brain got a better supply of thickening blood flow, and in the morning...voila...she spoke. She was more alert, the day went on, the blood drained away, it couldn't get to the brain as

261

easily and she wound down.   Hannah did not have some spontaneous breakthrough that night.

No, she raised her blood pressure so high and so fast that the clot actually shifted to a different position. In that position, the blood flow passed by just a bit easier making her lucid and talkative for a few days. Everyone thought she was getting better but she was really getting worse. She tried to tell them that, to tell them about her headaches, and all of them missed it!

She stayed off the blood thinners, the blood thickened, and as it passed by the clot, some stayed behind and the clot got bigger. The headaches got worse until the blood could not get past it any longer and began to pool. Then it was only a matter of time until it ruptured. The flight pressure served to hurry that along for her. Now all of that too thin, too weak, blood in her veins was spilling into her brain, out of her eyes, her nose, and her ears.   How long did she have before she bled to death internally? Minutes? Seconds?

The helicopter landed on the helipad atop The Mountainside, the sliding door opened, the EMT pulled the gurney to the asphalt, and Hannah's heart stopped beating.

Mason yanked down the side rail and climbed onto the gurney mindless of the pain in his leg. "MOVE!" He shouted at the EMTs and started chest compressions.   One, two, three. "Come on, Hannah, we're here! Don't you quit on me now!"

Four, five, six

The EMTs rushed the gurney inside the ER where Steward, Wylds, and Goodspeed were already waiting for them.   "In here! In here!" Steward shouted directing them through the crowd of Friday night drunks and minor accident victims.

Seven, eight, nine,

"Come on, Hannah!" Mason demanded.

"Get him off of there," Goodspeed directed.

"No!" He growled.

262

"Get down!" Wylds ordered.

Ten, eleven, twelve.

The gurney safely in the room, the EMTs turned their attention to the frantic doctor and pulled Mason away from her as he screamed out, "Hannah!"

"I've got a heartbeat." Wylds announced. "She's back."

Relief was short but incredibly sweet as it washed over Mason. Then he was rushed out of the room just like any other dreaded family member and the doors between him and Hannah closed. An orderly appeared at his side and ushered him down to the Family Waiting Room.

A few moments later, Sinclair came into the room with a clipboard in her hands.

"Let me outta here!" He sneered at her.

"No," she said lightly, "You have to let them do their job now, Mace."

"What good am I in here?" Mason railed. "It's an aneurysm! She needs to be rushed up to OR and..."

"OR's standing by," Steward said as he ducked into the Family Room to the site of his frantic boss, "We know what it is."

"NOW you know? NOW?! You're FIRED!" Mason shouted at him.

"Go on," Sinclair said to Steward, "Go take care of Hannah, I've got him."

"We're doing everything we can, Mason...."

"Don't give me that bullshit!" Mason shouted back at him. "Just go save my sister!"

Steward fled out the door.

Feeling helpless, Mason nearly fell to the leather couch behind him.

"I'm not going to lie to you and treat you like any other family member," Sinclair began gently, "It's bad, Mason. Really bad, we tried to get a hold of you an hour ago to tell you not to get on the flight. The good news we have everything ready

263

for her, the best neuro-team is upstairs right now, all prepped and ready."

"Why now? Why does everyone suddenly know now when it's too late?"

"It's not too late." She held the clipboard out to him. "Sign."

"For what? What are you going to do?"

"Surgical clipping," Sinclair said knowing how Mason was going to react. "It's the only way. I know what you're going to say and endovascular coiling just isn't an option, Mason. Believe me, I wish it were."

"You want me to let you cut off the top of her *skull*? With her INR levels? She'll bleed to death before they finish sawing through!"

He was absolutely brilliant and absolutely right, there was every chance the procedure would kill Hannah but if they did nothing she would be just as dead. This was her only shot and was deep down inside of him, Sinclair knew Mason was very aware of that fact. "If it were anyone else, any other patient, you'd be screaming your head off for them to consent." Sinclair pushed the clipboard at him. "Sign."

No choice. Mason grabbed the pen and scribbled his name on the consent form. "You better be right about this."

"I am and so is Steward." Sinclair reached out to touch Mason's arm.

"Steward's fired," Mason snarled. "He missed this; she wouldn't be in there if he'd been smarter!"

She wouldn't be in there if I had been smarter either.

"Steward came in and he looked over Hannah's MRIs late this afternoon," she began, "you were still insisting he find out why she didn't or wouldn't talk very much and her headaches were bothering him so he wanted another look. That's when he found it," she stopped knowing how lame the excuse was, the mistake of a first year medical student. "He missed it earlier because he was looking on the wrong side of her brain."

264

"Wh-what?"

The image of the x-ray of Hannah's broken left hand danced in his head. St. Mark's, run by the finest old-fashioned nuns one could find. The kind of nuns who took a special sadistic delight in slapping left-handed students with wooden rulers and berating them until they learned to write with their right hands.

When he examined her, Steward asked her to draw him a picture to determine which side of the brain he should look on, Hannah drew with her right hand. From Mason's experience, Hannah cooked with her left; she flipped pancakes with her left hand, pulled cookies out of the oven, and even presented him with a bottle of J&B with her left hand.

"He came in, he found it, we tried to get in touch with you right away, and we've been trying for hours to get a hold of you, to tell you that Hannah shouldn't fly and to get her to the nearest hospital." Sinclair insisted. "We even tried calling the court house but you were already gone."

Mason pulled the cellphone from his pocket and turned it on to see he had 17 messages and the phone was still in Flight Mode. "Turned it off for the flight," Mason admitted. "Don't you have paperwork to file?"

"Yeah," that was his way of saying 'get out of here I want to be alone'. "One last thing."

"Oh?"

"You can't go in the gallery," Sinclair told him, "in-house seems to feel that, since you're a possible beneficiary and her guardian that you might..."

"Try to tell the neuro-team what to do?" Mason asked incredulously. "So you just want me to sit here? Just SIT here? Like any other *family member*?"

"It's all you can do right now." Sinclair padded his weary shoulder and then walked away.

Sitting there alone in the quiet of the Family Room he looked down at the phone again, "I'm an idiot," he grumbled, "I'm a moron." He stuffed the phone back into his pocket only to take out that most favored little amber bottle of his. Mason put the bottle away without opening it. There was still one puzzle left to figure out. He couldn't do it if he was flying on his favorite pain killer no matter how much he'd like to do just that right now.

He couldn't just sit here doing nothing.

Mason made his way up to his office to wait and think. Spaulding was waiting for him. "How are you doing?"

"My sister's having the top of her head cut off because I'm an idiot, how do you think I'm doing?"

"About average," Spaulding replied in a weak attempt to lighten the mood. "You couldn't have seen this coming..."

"Of course I could have...*I should* have! I'm Richard-fucking-Mason, remember? I cure everybody no matter what's wrong with them. Everybody except my own sister who just happens to love me and to depend on me. Not her. No. I can't save her."

"It's not your fault." Spaulding asserted quietly.

"I was too busy being her brother to be her doctor."

"Being her doctor wasn't your place," Spaulding reminded him.

"No, it was Steward's." Mason spat.

That was an issue for another time after this particular storm passed. "You're really good at the big brother thing." Spaulding said. "I watched you with her."

"I suck at that too," Mason admitted in a guilty tone. All he could see was Hannah in the car at the stop sign that concerned loving look on her face as she told him everything would be all right, his heart would stop hurting, and, if nothing else, she loved him. She was there for him. "I couldn't tell my own sister that I love her, what the hell's wrong with me?" He shook his head. "I wanted to, I really did. The words were right on the tip of my tongue, all I had to do was...say them. That's it. It would have been easy, but no, I couldn't do it."

"She knows." Spaulding wasn't exactly sure what Mason was talking about or what happened while they were in Victorville. That didn't matter.

It had been years upon years since Spaulding was witness to the great loner, Richard Mason letting someone into his life. Hannah just wormed her way right into his heart; he probably never even knew what hit him. She didn't want anything from him. Didn't demand that Mason stop working such long hours or be nicer or go to parties and mingle. Didn't want his money—what there was of it—didn't want his medical expertise (necessarily).

No, Hannah just wanted to play piano with him, go for walks and rides on his bike, and have quiet dinners at home. Overall, if she wasn't his sister, and her mental faculties were a little better, she would be the perfect woman for him. That was rather perverted in its own way. Then again, what woman in her right mind would put up with Mason in a romantic relationship? No, only a little sister could put up with him that much. "You'll tell her when she wakes up."

"If she wakes up," Mason corrected.

Spaulding wanted to tell him that she would but, like Mason, he didn't like to lie. "She's your sister that means she's as stubborn as you are."

An hour went by and then two. Sinclair and Spaulding came in and out of his office with cups of coffee and cold drinks. They didn't stay long, just long enough to make sure he was still alive, fairly sane, and not strung out. He told himself that, no matter what the outcome of this was, he would have to start being nicer to his patient's family members. And his own. That included his mother whom he'd treated so shittily earlier in the day. T

All of that had to wait. He had to wait.

Wait.

Wait.

The slow moving hands of the clock were sheer utter fucking hell! The weight of the silence around him was merciless.

Nothing to do but sit and wait and worry, sit and wait and worry, sit…wait… …worry, sit…

The more time that went by the more he tried to tell himself that it was good. It was good because no one had come in to tell him she was dead. Then again, maybe they were still having a hard time finding someone to volunteer for that particular job.

Sitting on the floor twirling his cane with one hand trying to think of anything but the sight of Hannah, her pretty graying hair shaved off and lying on the floor. The top of her skull in a bowl by the operating table, tubes and wires sticking in and out of her while the neuro-team probed deep into her brain. He held a hand to his heart, just where Hannah's had been earlier today and felt the weight of his own sorrow. "I failed you, I'm sorry, Hannah. I failed." Below his hand, the stress caused his heart to skip a beat.

Bloop.

"Bloop," he said aloud. "Bloop, what the hell is that? Bloop, bloop, bloop,"

Spaulding walked in and found Mason huddled in the corner mumbling and, for a moment, thought the man had finally lost his mind. "Mason?" He asked hesitantly.

"Bloooop," The movement of his lips caught his eye. "Bloooop," he pursed his lips out as far as they would go as he spoke.

"Mason?" Spaulding asked again with more concern and put the coffee down on the desk. "Mason?" Immediately he thought, *Oh great! He took something!*

Mason looked up at him with a raised eye brown, lift his hand with the fingers held tightly together and said the word again. This time as he said 'bloop', he opened and closed the fingers.

"What is it? What have you got?"

268

"It's not what I've got; it's what Hannah's got." He pushed himself with the aid of his cane.

"Which is?" Spaulding prodded.

"A traveler. Come on, let's go."

Hannah didn't have just one clot, she had at least two. One lodged in her brain but the other liked to travel. It hadn't gotten stuck anywhere yet because it was what was what causing her chest pain and the 'bloop' she tried to tell him about. What she felt was the clot traveling through the aorta where it squeezed through, in and out of the heart, she felt the valve open, the clot wiggled through, and then the valve closed.

Bloop.

Mason didn't think there was any time for so-call Clot Busters. No this one had to be found and quick. Finding it before it actually stopped her heart was going to be a bitch.

Spaulding followed Mason out of his office and down to the OR gallery where the security guard refused to let Mason pass. "Get out of my way!" Mason railed and shook his cane at the man. "Move before I just walk into the OR instead!"

"I'm sorry, Doctor Mason, Doctor Sinclair said under no cir—"

"I'll do it," Spaulding said. "Get out of the way."

Sinclair didn't say anything about Dr. Spaulding not being in the gallery and the security guard let him pass. Wylds and Goodspeed were observing the surgery. "What is it?" Wylds asked.

Spaulding ignored her and pressed the intercom. "She's got another clot." He said and Steward looked up. "It's in embolus, we don't know where it is but it affects her heart, you have to find it ..."

Too late.

Out in the hall, with the door part way open and listening to Spaulding tell the doctor inside what was going on, Mason heard the monitors go off. Everything in there was beeping and buzzing.

Hannah was dying.

"If you don't get out of my way I swear to God I'm gonna brain you." Mason threatened the guard still blocking his path. All he could do was stand there listening to what was happening.

"Patient's in cardiac arrest," the surgical nurse announced grabbing the paddles.

With an urgency he'd never quite known before Mason shouted, "No! Don't! You'll kill her for sure!"

"I'm not a heart surgeon." Steward asserted through the intercom.

"Goodspeed!" Mason shouted as loudly as he could. "Go get it!"

A junior on the surgical staff, Goodspeed was the best cardiac surgeon they had. Before Mason could finish giving the order, Goodspeed was already out the door and on his way into the OR, no time to scrub, no time to stop. Just get in there and get it.

As Goodspeed ran out of the gallery, Mason shoved the security guard and dashed inside. Mason thought he'd throw up as he watched Goodspeed split Hannah's chest open with the rib spreaders so that he could get to her heart.

No time to be nice about it.

Through the intercom, the sound of her ribs being broken echoed in the gallery. Breastplate out, heart exposed, team scrambling to keep up with the watery blood pouring out of her.

The top of her skull still sitting in a bowl by her exposed brain.

"Get him out of here," Sinclair whispered to Spaulding.

Mason didn't think he could take much more of it anyway. With Spaulding at his side, he went stumbling through the door, one hand in his pocket holding on to that precious amber bottle and the other gripping the cane.

Through the intercom he heard Goodspeed shout; "I got it! Got it!"

That was good.

The monitors were still going off.

The strength went out of his legs; Mason slide down the wall to the floor. He sat there sweating and panting, caught in the clutches of a panic attack, as the world, the far too quiet world, spun around him. The silence was deafening, he put his hands to ears to shut it out. His stomach wretched and he was sure he was going to throw up after that he would probably just fall over and pass out in it.

"Mason! Mason!"

Spaulding was in his face, he was holding him up, bringing him back to a more comfortable sitting position against the wall. Everything was still spinning.

Glazed watery blue eyes turned upward and Mason slurred, "I need her."

"I know," Spaulding agreed in the same whisper. "They got her heart going. Can you hear me? They're...putting her back together...now. She'll be out of surgery soon." He shook Mason a little. "You hear me? She's not out of the woods yet but this part's over. You called it. You saved her life." Indeed he had, if Mason had not rushed down to tell them about the traveler, the neuro-team would have used the paddles on her, pushed the clot further into her heart stopping it for good. "You did it. Looks you're pretty good at the big brother thing and the doctor thing after all."

II

After five hours in the recovery room, Hannah was stable enough to move down to the Wellness Center's small ICU department. Only Medical Personnel were allowed in there, no family members, so Mason thought it was a good thing he owned a third of this place or he'd be sitting out there going out of his brilliant mind like any terrified big brother.

He sat at Hannah's bedside holding her still hand. She was hooked up to monitors and had a steady IV dripping into her arm. He couldn't stop looking at the heavy bandage around her newly stapled head and seeing the new zipper scar on her

271

chest in his mind. Mason was so engrossed in his thoughts that he didn't notice the door open.

"Richard?"

The sound of her voice shot right through the haze in his head. "Mom?" He looked at Hannah lying on the bed so still, so quiet, before he turned around to face his mother.

"I know you probably don't want to see me but when Scott called I couldn't...I couldn't..." Claire rushed but the warm weight of his arms enfolding her stopped her mid-sentence. She held on to him tightly. "It's ok, Richard," she whispered, "everything's going to be all right, she's going to be fine, we're going to be fine."

"You better be right," he mumbled.

"I am, you'll see." She assured him. "I love you. It'll be all right."

He blew it with Hannah but it was not going to blow this time. "I love you too, mom. I'm sorry, I'm such an ass, I'm sorry. All that shit I said...I'm so sorry."

Claire began to cry. If there was one thing her son never did it was apologize. "I know," she sobbed, "me too."

Chapter Nineteen

Three agonizing days went by as Hannah lay unconscious in the ICU.

The first two days Hannah lay in a coma and scored a grand total of 3 on the Glasgow Coma Scale...didn't get any lower than that.

Sure didn't. S

he didn't open her eyes for anything, didn't respond to pain in any manner and she had to be turned every four hours to prevent bedsores from developing. All Mason could do was sit there feeling sick to his stomach. The only things he had to hold on to were the fact that she was holding her own and her little gold locket. They took it off her for surgery and he found it in a bag of her things yesterday. It brought Hannah comfort; maybe it would do the same for him. Mason put it around his neck and there it stayed close to his heart.

The nurses came in and out, they turned her, changed the catheter bag, the bandages on her head and the IV, they checked on him and then a few hours later they were back to do it again.

Claire stayed with him almost the whole time while Frank paced the hall outside. She went back to his house at night to fix dinner and bring it to him and then she returned again to sleep. In the morning, she came back with breakfast and her knitting bag. She sat and knitted mostly in silence as Mason stared at Hannah as though he were willing her to wake up.

Claire took pity on Frank and, while she didn't let him stay at the house, she did take coffee with him several times. It seemed unfair not to let Frank into Hannah's room just to sit but Mason insisted it was medical staff and family only. When Frank complained to the Chief of Staff, Evelyn Sinclair, the woman backed up Mason and told Frank he could stay in the facility as long as he liked if he didn't become a distraction but he couldn't go into Hannah's room.

This morning, along with her knitting bag, she had a tray of hot coffee, a bag of donuts, and two bacon egg and cheese sandwiches. In the orange light of the dawning new day, her son looked as though he were eighty years old. "You should go home and get some rest," Claire settled the coffee on the small table between two comfortable chairs at the foot of the bed. "You could at least get a shower. Stretch your legs, except to pee, you haven't moved from that spot in two days."

Mason didn't look up at her as he sat beside Hannah's bed, "She's pretty." He mumbled. "How come I never noticed that before? Look at her, she's so...pretty." He reached out and touched her sleeping cheek and watching the EEG monitor.

Claire sat down next to him. "Yes, she is. Very pretty. How's she doing today?"

"Same as yesterday," he looked up at her. "She dreams, you know? I watch her. Sometimes she smiles, sometimes she cries and sometimes..." the breath hitched in chest, "...sometimes she whimpers." He knew she wasn't in any physical pain, as a doctor he knew that but as a brother, well that was just a whole other ballgame. As a brother, he tried very hard not to think of what she looked like beneath those blankets and bandages. "You think she needs more meds?"

In all of his life, she had never seen him so distraught or helpless. It was not a pleasant sight and it did not bring a warm feeling to her heart. Yet, in some strange way, it was good to see. It meant Richard didn't lack empathy after all. She hadn't raised a brilliant psychopath who made a hobby out of saving people's lives. Sometimes, over the years, she had wondered about that. She reached over and put her hand over his, "I bet, when she's smiling she's dreaming about you."

Mason looked back down at his comatose sister. More likely, she was dreaming about Frank or cookies than him, but it was a nice thought just the same. What did he ever give her to smile about? "How could I miss it?"

"Because you weren't thinking of her as your sister then," Claire gently explained. "She was just...Hannah...a woman you got stuck with. She isn't that anymore, is she?"

Mason turned his head to look at her, "No."

"I know what you're thinking and it's not that you screwed up."

"You do? I didn't know you were psychic." He sounded a little more like the old Mason but there wasn't much heart in the comeback. "Dazzle me."

"Ok. You're wondering who she's going to be when she wakes up." She ventured from the look in those heavy blue eyes she knew she was right. "If she'll be...normal again. Or the same. Or worse." She put her arm around his shoulders. "You want her to be normal, you want her to wake up and start talking like there's no tomorrow but you're afraid if that happens, then she won't need you anymore. She'll go away."

Mason turned his face away as those eyes grew heavier and he swiped a hand across his face so she wouldn't see him cry.

"That makes you feel guilty because you don't want to lose her but you don't want to admit that either." She patted his hand hoping he'd turn back to her but he didn't so she went on, "But listen to me, no matter what, if she's better, worse or the same, little sisters always need their big brothers. Always." Claire leaned over to lay a kiss on her son's whiskery cheek and wipe away the tears falling from his blue eyes. Knowing he wasn't going to say anything more, she picked up her knitting and went back to making a lavender stocking cap for Hannah's newly baldhead.

On the third day, as Mason sat by her bedside, Hannah had her very first official visitor. He looked up to see Frank MacNeill standing in the doorway. "How is she?" Frank mumbled looking down at the frail unconscious woman.

"What are you doing in here?"

Claire pushed past Frank to step into the room, "I said he could come in for *five* minutes."

275

Frank waited to see if Mason was going to put up a fuss but to him Rick Mason looked far too tired for anything like that. "Why don't you go get a cup of coffee or something with your mom? I'll sit with her." Frank offered sincerely.

Everyone was always trying to get Mason to leave her side, get coffee, get some rest, and take a damn shower. Even though everyone from Wylds to Spaulding offered to sit with her in his stead and to call him stat if anything happened, Mason didn't take them up on their offers. Frank was different. Frank wasn't here for him he was here for Hannah. "Sure." He stood up on stiff legs. "You just remember that's glass, they can all see you."

"Big brother to end, huh?" Frank said with a grin. "I like it. Don't worry, she's safe with me."

"That's what they said about Red." Mason pushed past Frank. On the other side of the door, he turned around to see Frank sitting down in the chair he'd been occupying for three days. He pulled it up next to her and took her hand; he started to talk to her.

The next day the ritual resumed but now there were more people in attendance. Frank hung back and let Mason sit by her bed. News was good today, better than yesterday anyway. When Goodspeed and Wylds came in to check on her, Hannah did respond to painful stimuli. She moved her foot away from the needle and her arms too. When she woke up the chances that she would be paralyzed from people poking around in her brain were slim. Steward had yet to show his face around here even though he was still officially Hannah's attending physician.

A few hours later, the EEG indicated that she was struggling to wake up. She smiled in her sleep, and then suddenly tears rolled silently down her cheeks. Mason wiped them away with a tissue. When she started to whimper he just wanted to hold her close but he knew he couldn't move her. "Smile, Hannah," he croaked in a sad whisper and slipped his hands over hers, "smile, come towards my voice. I'm waiting

276

for you." He looked around to see that not only were his mother and Frank in the room but the nurses must have alerted the others as well; Sinclair, Spaulding, Wylds, Goodspeed and stuffed behind them all stood Steward. "We're all waiting for you. So smile, come towards my voice, little sister."

Hannah drew in a deep breath and her eyes fluttered open. The world was fuzzy at first nothing but light and shadow. Then Ricky's face came into focus.

"Can you hear me?"

She nodded and it hurt her head. "Ooo."

"Don't move, don't sit up and don't move your head." He advised. "Do you know who I am?"

Yes, she did, she knew who he was. "Ricky." She whispered in a hoarse voice. "I knew you'd rescue me."

"Oh, baby sister," He felt like he could dance on the clouds as he leaned in and said, "I still owed you for the tree."

The End
Lisa Beth Darling
2014
The Sister Christian Series Continues with:
Sins of the Father
Mysterious Ways
Prodigal Son
Please visit www.lisabethdarling.com

About the Author

In the 4th grade I discovered that I **was** a writer when we were given our first creative writing assignment. We were to write stories about a baby bird's flight and read them to the class. I put pencil to paper and was instantly whisked away by a force I couldn't explain. I knew that I was meant to do this very thing, this very simple act of putting pencil to paper and letting my mind free. Everyone read their happy stories to the class. I got up and told of how the baby bird flew too high, hit a plane, crashed to the ground and died. I told of how the mama bird and daddy bird cried of how even God was upset sending the rains pouring from the sky. The class was speechless when I finished they were all just staring at me. The teacher kept me after class told me my story was very good but it was different from the others. She asked me if I'd ever heard of Icarus and did I base my story on him. But, I had yet to encounter Greek Mythology or hear a whisper of Icarus. As she let me leave class, she again told me how good the story was but suggested I might want to write something happier next time. I asked her why and she had no answer. To this day, I'm glad that I never took her advice.

Made in the USA
Middletown, DE
25 May 2021